MW00763002

DISLOCATION

DISLOCATION

Stories

Margaret Meyers

Harold & Ilsa,
Thought I'd send along
my new story collection
with my best wishes!

Margo Meyers

ENTASIS PRESS
WASHINGTON, D.C.

Published by

ENTASIS PRESS

WASHINGTON, D.C.

2014

ISBN 978-0-9850997-2-5

Library of Congress Control Number: 2013954634

"Eau de Paradis" first appeared in *Grace and Gravity*, Paycock Press, 2004.
"Peaceable Kingdom" first appeared in *The Iconoclast*, *#108*, 2012.
"Dislocation" first appeared in *The Antigonish Review*, vol. 42, #168, 2012.

Cover art: J. Y. Delva, oil on wood box, 1978.

For Bruce, Janet, and Ed with love and gratitude.

My warmest thanks to friends and fellow writers Michelle Brafman and Louise Branson, who read portions of the manuscript and offered helpful criticism and unstinting support.
                                        Margaret Meyers

Contents

DISLOCATION

THE THIEF

THE CONGREGATION IS ATTENTIVE, the church so crowded that people are jamming the entrance and children are sitting on the wide, mud-brick window sills. The atmosphere is one of anticipation, of ever-increasing excitement, even though the air itself feels used up, depleted. I take a sip of water from the glass on the pulpit and loosen my Sunday tie just a little. I suspect this is what it's like to be inside an old-fashioned pressure cooker, and I just hope nobody faints. I also hope that if one of the children should die falling out of a window, no one will expect me to raise him or her from the dead. I am not up to miracles in the grand New Testament style — although you could say that the size of today's congregation is fairly miraculous.

I suppose I ought to see this great crowd as the high point of my Congo ministry so far, and I should be thrilled, ecstatic (the Lord at work, etc.), but I'm completely unnerved. I recognize a number of the men at the back, and the day before yesterday they were all in the Bosojala jail. The one face I am looking for, the one face from that jail I'd be genuinely reassured to see, is nowhere in sight.

And so I wonder and worry as I deliver a sermon more notable for its sensational text than for the brilliancy of my exegesis. The Book of Genesis text is about Tamar, who had the kind of sexual misfortunes that somehow come to all women named Tamar in the Old Testament. (She lost two husbands — brothers, actually — one of them the famous seed-spiller Onan, and then she wound up pregnant by her father-in-law, Judah.) This is not the sermon text that I would have chosen, but some denominational bigwig with too much time on his hands has put together a Calendar of Daily Texts, and I always feel obliged to use the one assigned to a given Sunday whether I like it or not. It's a slippery slope, picking and choosing, and I don't want to side with those who won't preach on a certain text simply because they're uncomfortable with it. As it is, too many people arbitrarily reject any text they find too personally challenging — Jesus' admonition to forgive someone seventy times seven, say, or His telling the rich young ruler to give all his riches to the poor. And too many other people waste their time hunting madly for a text to support some speculative eschatological craziness they've taken a fancy to, like the Pre-Millennial, Post-Tribulational Second Coming of Christ. I think you're best off just taking the text you're given and looking for something of merit in it, however small. But I've got to admit that today I'm at a complete loss for even that small merit. I'm just too tired. Last night I lay awake until dawn, listening to the shrill ascending scream of a tree hyrax somewhere out in the humid Congo darkness. Beneath the light quilt I was fully clothed, a heavy metal flashlight in my hand and hostility in my heart as I waited for the intruder who never arrived.

❧

Just one week ago last night, my biggest problem was my usual Saturday night problem for the last three years: my fear of making an egregious language error in my Sunday morning sermon at the Boboto Mission Church. I had yet to recover from the one I'd made nearly a year ago when I somehow idiotically said *molimo masapo* instead of *molimo mosanto*, and thus preached an entire sermon on Spirit Urine instead of the Holy Spirit. The congregation members had laughed themselves silly. I was inclined to resent this until I realized that, due to Congo's many years of war and then the fallout of war, they'd had very little to laugh at for some time, and I ought not to begrudge them the opportunity. They still made jokes about my mistake — "Hey, *Pasteur* Alain, are you filled with the *molimo masapo* today?" — which I always tried to take in good part, but I was anxious not to do anything like it again. My Saturday nights were spent checking and rechecking my Lingala against my *British Baptist Missionary Society Grammar and Dictionary*. And this in itself, I should add, was always an interesting language experience: since I'm not British, words like "vex" and "lodgings" tended to amuse me; since I'm not Baptist, words like "exhort," "falsehood," and "apostate" seemed old-fashioned and heavyhanded. But the BBMS G&D, said to be called the BBMS G&T by foreign service cocktail-party types, was the best I could find, the world not being exactly awash in Lingala grammar books and dictionaries for English speakers. So, of necessity, I worked with it.

By ten o'clock I'd finished revising my sermon on my computer. (There's no electricity in this old mission house some three hundred kilometers from Gemena, the Ubangi District's "big city," but I'd managed to rig up a solar panel to charge my computer and cellphone.) I'd also locked the doors, closed the curtains, and put on my "pajamas," which were actually a threadbare pair of University of Michigan basketball shorts. Now I was ready to relax. Opening the door of my kerosene fridge, I debated the merits of my beer choices. I had my Congolese Primus, rumored to contain formaldehyde as a preservative, and I had two Kenyan Tuskers. (You couldn't get Tusker in western Congo; I'd been given these by a Kenyan traveller who was grateful for dinner and a bed for the night.) Deciding to save the Tuskers a bit longer and thus prolong the anticipation, I popped the cap on a Primus, blew out the lamps, and climbed into bed with my formaldehyde-flavored beer. I drank that beer with such guilt you'd have thought I was having illicit sex — but there's a reason. The Protestants in the Ubangi area of Congo were evangelized for more than eighty years by fundamentalist American teetotalers, and now they believe that drinking a beer once a week and visiting a prostitute once a week are evils of equal weight. My ministry would be over, and I do mean over, if my congregation members ever found out. So I realize I was taking a risk — but the fact is, the risk seemed small. People know not to drop by on Saturday nights. They know the *missionaire* is preparing his sermon, and in a language which he knows as yet imperfectly. What they don't know is that I need that one beer on that one night because otherwise I'd be too keyed up to sleep, and then only God knows what linguistic idiocies might come out of my mouth.

Although the night was blessedly cool from another day of rainy-season weather, the mosquitos were ferocious. They were noisy too, droning away like a fleet of bombers. Since a number of people in the nearby villages were suffering from dengue fever as well as malaria, I decided to play it safe and light one of my precious mosquito coils. Then I sat up in bed in the darkness, smelling that foul chemical stench of burning mosquito coil and singing along with a Lokua Kanza CD on my computer. (Lokua Kanza sings mostly in Lingala so I consider him a valuable part of my language training.) After each phrase, I'd take a big swallow of beer: *yojali - aaay* (gulp) *fololo na motema na ngai* (gulp). Rather sweet lyrics, really — you are the flower of my heart — and I wished Karen were stationed here instead of about one thousand miles south in Congo, in Brazzaville. (Karen is a thirty-something single Mennonite missionary nurse from Goshen, Indiana, and I met her at an inter-denominational conference a few months ago; we talk by cellphone, but that's the only way we can communicate since I have no access to the internet and the postal system is hopeless.) Anyway, thinking about Karen's big brown eyes, throaty laugh, and exceptionally long, shapely legs while drinking Primus made me feel horny, and while I did know perfectly well that sexual desire is a gift from God and nothing to be ashamed of, masturbating sometimes made me feel even lonelier than I did before. Besides, I wasn't sure it was fair to treat Karen like my own little sexual toy, even if she didn't know about it. I decided I'd just polish off the rest of that Primus and go to sleep. The Primus defeated me — it was a large bottle — and finally, half-asleep, I set it down on the floor unfinished.

It was the faint metallic sound of a screen being slit that awakened me. I lay very still, listening. After a moment I heard the soft crunch of footsteps on the woven elephant-grass mat in the living room, and I quickly weighed my options: I could pretend to be asleep and simply let the thief take what he liked, or I could confront him. My body must have already chosen confrontation because all at once I realized that my hand had curled around the neck of my Primus bottle and I was swinging my legs out of bed. The darkness had weight, substance, as moonless Congo darkness does, but at last I made out his faint silhouette, then brought the bottle down on his head. He collapsed with a grunt onto the mat and I set about lighting a lamp so I'd have something to do with this sudden surge of aggressive energy besides beat him up unnecessarily.

I'd lit several lamps, taken a leak, and put on a pair of khaki trousers by the time my thief came around. I was almost relieved to see his eyelids tremble, then open, but I didn't let on. Primus bottle in hand, I stood over him menacingly, just in case he tried something.

"Ah, *Monsieur le Missionaire*," he said tentatively.

"Ah, *Monsieur le Moyibi*," I replied with some sarcasm.

"Thief is a harsh word, monsieur," he said.

"I think it is *le mot juste*." I snapped. "That is my transistor radio you have in that bag there. And that's my thermos too. And my jean jacket."

He seemed disinclined to argue with me. After a moment he sat up and felt the back of his head with cautious fingers. "You are stronger than I expected, *monsieur* — my congratulations! But there's no blood, no open wound. I'm happy to tell you that I think I'll be okay."

I'd been on the verge of telling my thief to take his sorry self off and we'd forget about this, but his tone aggravated me. He actually sounded reassuring, kindly, as if he thought I might be feeling remorse about having given him a goose egg when he was the one who'd ruined my living room window screen and tried to rob me.

"Good. Then you're fit for the drive to Bosojala," I said. "The *commandant* can make room for you in his jail."

My thief didn't seem terribly enthusiastic but neither did he resist when I dragged him to his feet and marched him outside to the pickup. As I bundled him into the passenger side of the cab, I warned him that if he tried to escape I'd hit him again. He said he had no intention of trying to escape, I could trust him, and so I climbed in and threw the vehicle into gear. We covered the twelve kilometers to Bosojala in record time despite the darkness, the potholes, and a great deal of rainy season mud. Although I'd never had reason to visit the jail before, I knew where it was, and as I pulled up to the building I shouted out for assistance. After a moment a guard came around the far side of the jail, a lantern in one hand and a short homemade spear in the other. His uniform was downright bizarre — a Cubs baseball cap, a camouflage jacket with epaulettes, light blue sweatpants, and red plastic thongs — but I was much too annoyed to find it amusing. As he approached us, his swinging lantern casting wild and fiery shadows, my thief turned to me and said, "I must tell you that I never thought a *missionaire protestant* would have a Primus bottle around to use as a weapon. Especially a Primus bottle that wasn't quite empty."

Although I'd prepared with care, my sermon delivery that Sunday was quite a bit less than magnificent. I'd slept badly, and my head ached as if I'd been the one brained by a Primus bottle. News about the break-in had already gotten around the neighboring villages, and several members of the Boboto Mission congregation spoke to me about it. One of the older ladies commented that this thief must be from some distant ethnic group, maybe even from some other country altogether. "Probably he's from the Central African Republic. Certainly he's not a Ngbaka. Not a Ngombe or a Mongwandi either."

"Especially not if he's so short," added a young woman with

an old-woman stoop due to the sleeping child tied to her back with a length of cloth. "I heard he was very short, so I expect he's from the north, the far north, where even the trees are short. A Togbo."

"*Likambo na mokili,*" said an elderly man with a disapproving click of his tongue against his brown and crumbling teeth. "Troubles of the world, that's what's behind it. And I can tell you this for certain: evil times make for evil people."

I went home with my head still throbbing, but a few aspirin and a nap got me back to normal. I spent the afternoon mending the living room window screen with a needle and a couple yards of my carefully hoarded American dental floss. Around four o'clock several boys from Mbala, a village just one kilometer down the road, came by to see if I wanted to play a little soccer. We kicked the ball around the overgrown Mbala Elementary School playground until it got dark. Then they all walked me home and sat on the living room floor listening to Lokua Kanza while I cooked up a huge pot of rice and sardines. By six-thirty they'd polished off the rice and sardines, given their opinion of Lokua Kanza ("He's okay, *Pasteur Alain*, but mellow, more for older people like you"), and then I was on my own again. I organized my weekly calendar, which included sermon and Bible Study prep, visitation of the ill and elderly, literacy classes in both Lingala and French, and pondered the possibility of teaching basic mechanics and carpentry to any of the boys who might be interested. Some village kid without much opportunity might have a better life just because he knew how to change a fan belt or pound a cheap Zambian nail without bending it — especially now, with public primary and secondary education in our area an ongoing casualty of what many called the First African World War. (Very few schools, I had learned, could keep their doors open when the central government was too weak and disorganized to ensure that teachers got paid. Especially schools in small, obscure villages.) By eight I was hungry again, so I made another batch of rice and fried a few plantains. By nine o'clock I was asleep — and then by eleven I was startled wide awake, this time by the squeaking of the refrigerator door. I padded to the kitchen in my bare feet and discovered my thief standing in front of the fridge eating leftover rice with his fingers.

"So you're back," I said, folding my arms and leaning against the termite-infested doorframe. "You escaped."

"No, *Monsieur le Missionaire*. I did not escape."

"Oh, so you are a dream," I replied. "I'm still asleep and you aren't really here in my kitchen at all."

My thief laughed as he put the last of the rice into his mouth. He chewed, swallowed, and then motioned to the little plate of leftover plantains on the top shelf of the fridge. The blackened slabs of plantain didn't look terribly appetizing, but then cooking was never my strong suit. Back in the States I'd tended to live on fast food and frozen pizzas, both when I was in divinity school and during my ten years as a youth pastor.

"You know, these *makembas* would taste a lot better if you heated them up," he said.

The nerve of the man, the utterly outrageous and completely brazen nerve! Such audacity didn't seem possible — and maybe it wasn't. Maybe I really was dreaming after all... But no. I just couldn't doubt the solid reality of the thick, blunt fingernails on that extended hand. I couldn't doubt the material existence of those plantains lying in a congealed orange puddle of palm oil either.

"Perhaps you would be so very kind, so extremely *gentil*, as to give me one good reason why I ought to heat that up for you?" I asked with cold *politesse*.

Even in the semi-darkness of a kitchen lit by one flashlight and one tiny bulb at the back of the fridge, I couldn't fail to see my thief's wide-eyed astonishment.

"But that is *très simple*! You made no provision for my food at the jail," he told me. "So I'm hungry. And so they let me out."

My idea of the order of the world seemed to tilt a bit as I gaped at him. Then I said, "You can eat those plantains cold if you really want them. But you'd better hurry up about it. Because when you've finished, I'm taking you straight back to the jail."

He shrugged. "All right. *Eh dit*, listen, would you mind if I brought along this half-loaf of bread you've got in here?"

"I'm surprised you asked," I said grimly. "But okay. Go ahead."

And of course it turned out that my thief was telling the truth. The *commandant* informed me that he had no food budget at the Bosojala jail, and even if he did, he wouldn't think of buying food for criminals. Times were hard, even with the war technically over. If he started giving food away, everyone would want to be a jailed criminal, and then where would he be? His tone made it clear that only a fool needed to have this explained to him.

"So you really let everybody out just to get food?"

He shrugged impatiently, as if to say, *oh you naive and well-fed Americans who think food is a simple matter of little importance.* "Well, not quite everybody. Surely you've noticed the women stirring pots over cooking fires here in the late afternoon. They are the family members of those who've committed very serious crimes."

"I consider robbery a very serious crime," I told him.

"Fine," the *commandant* said with a scornful lifting of one eyebrow. "Then you better make sure he has family members to provide him with food, or tomorrow we'll let him out again."

The *commandant* sat down at his desk and began to look through a stack of papers. Realizing that I was dismissed, I went off to talk to my thief, and naturally it transpired that he had no relatives near by. I asked where he came from, and he said that I wouldn't know his *mboka*. "It's very small," he told me. "And *mosika mpenza*, very far away. It takes days to get there. Especially with the roads the way they are."

Maybe he really was a Togbo from the north. Or maybe he was just lying. Fed up with the whole situation, I turned on my heel and stomped out to my pickup. Unfortunately my exit lost some of its dignity because I plunged right into a deep mud-puddle, soaking my sneakers and the bottom six inches of my trousers. This, too, I blamed upon my thief, and I roared home like the righteous Jehu, son of Nimshi, who, as the Second Book of Kings has it, "driveth furiously."

I mended the fresh slit in my window screen on Monday afternoon, and on Monday night I slept well. On Tuesday afternoon Ajouda Michel came by to discuss re-opening the Mbala Elementary School, which had been closed now for more than a decade. Although his manner was modest in the extreme, Ajouda Michel was a local personage, a highly-regarded man of education and experience. Until the late 1990s, Ajouda Michel had been assistant head bookkeeper for a large cacao plantation run by the EU. Then came the war and the wheels of commerce quit turning. Although there were rumors that the cacao plantation might re-open, so far nothing had happened. Now, like many rural Congolese husbands, Ajouda Michel depended on his wife's small patch of manioc and field corn for a subsistence living. And he worried about his children's future, especially his boys.

"The violence in eastern Congo is a terrible and ongoing tragedy, we all know this, but things are fairly quiet here. We should be thinking ahead. We just can't have our children not attending school year after year because the government can't or won't finance it," Ajouda Michel said.

The anger and frustration in his voice surprised me, given his trademark calm. I murmured something inane but sympathetic. Who wouldn't be angry about lost educational opportunity? Who wouldn't feel frustrated when the United Nations had just declared your country the least developed in the world?

"Someday all of Congo will be stable again, I just have to believe this," Ajouda Michel went on. "Someday we'll have functional communication and transportation systems again. Business will improve and young people will have opportunity. And when that day comes, our children need to be ready. I'm willing to teach math for free. Would you be willing to teach something too?"

I was already holding adult literacy classes at my house, but I liked teaching. Making time to do more of it wouldn't be a sacrifice. Besides, Ajouda Michel's plan was much better than my notion of teaching the boys a little basic mechanics and carpentry; reopening the school would mean education for girls as well as boys. After he assured me that the whole village supported the project and welcomed my help, I agreed to teach reading and writing in both French and English. "What are you thinking about the sciences?" I asked. "Have you found anyone who could teach a few basics?"

"I'm still working on that," Ajouda Michel said. "Probably it will have to be me. Windo could have done it, of course. He's a nurse, you know. Used to run the dispensary back before the war. Used to be a deacon too. But then he turned to Primus, which was *nsoni mingi*, great scandal! Now he's a drunk and can't possibly be trusted with our children. It's most unfortunate."

I agreed that it was most unfortunate, then offered to finance chalk, pens, and paper. Ajouda Michel accepted my offer, and said he'd recruit a few villagers to replace the threadbare thatch on the school roof. After that we drank tea the Congolese way — strong, with lots of sweetened condensed milk — and we discussed politics, shaking our heads over last year's flawed and violent elections and the continued conflict in the east. Ajouda Michel thought Europe and America should cut off all aid to both Rwanda and Uganda if they didn't quit trying to annex mineral-rich east Congo by actively training and arming rebel factions. "Not that Rwandans and Ugandans are responsible for all of the brutality and bloodshed, I won't pretend that, but it would help a lot. And I would put real money on it," he added grimly, "if I had any."

Just as it was getting dark and Ajouda Michel had announced his departure, a huge rainstorm blew in from the west. He had no umbrella, and I didn't like to think of him trudging home through the rain and mud, so I volunteered to drive him. Slightly exhilirated by all our educational hopes and plans, I was whistling when I pulled back into my yard and parked the truck under the still-dripping breadfruit tree. It was well after dark, and I was momentarily puzzled to see the glow of lamplight beneath my front door. Then I knew, and I unlocked the door and entered my house with a sense of resignation.

"*Mbote, Monsieur le Moyibi,*" I said.

He got up from the small table which doubled as my desk and hurried forward, hand outstretched. "*Ah, mbote, Monsieur le Missionaire,* " he replied. "I knew you wouldn't be long. I've made some rice with sardines. I'll share."

I plunked my jean jacket, the one he'd tried to steal, down on a chair and sighed.

"I dislike being called *Monsieur the Missionaire*," I said. "You might as well call me Allan."

"*Alain,*" he said. "A good name. And I am Alphonse. Listen, I used to work for some missionaries up at Badja Baya, and I'm a good cook. Do you need a cook? A *boi moke*?"

It had been a mistake to let my guard down, to relax. I'd managed to live in Congo for three years without employing the Congolese as servants, and I planned to keep on doing so. Previous generations of missionaries may have found it necessary to employ cooks, gardeners, nannies, and night watchmen, but perpetuating neo-colonial stereotypes was not part of my missionary enterprise. As far as I knew, Jesus hadn't employed a fleet of servants — and if there was one thing I really hated, it was old fashioned terminology like *boi moke* (small servant boy), especially when it was applied to grown men. I couldn't believe that Alphonse could use the term without irony, and probably he didn't.

"No, I do not want a cook or a *boi moke*," I told him flatly. "And if I did, I wouldn't hire one who'd already proven his dishonesty."

Alphonse didn't reply, just slapped a plate of food in front of me. We ate in a stiff silence broken only by the occasional loud crunch of grit meeting molar. (Apparently Alphonse had not seen fit to wash the rice before cooking it.) Alphonse chewed with gusto, eyeing his plate protectively, as if someone might snatch it away from him. My heart softened slightly; he really was hungry, that I could not doubt, and the surface of his fingernails had the corrugated roughness that indicates malnutrition. But then I thought of all the other people in Congo who rarely had the right food or a full belly. What would happen if every one of them behaved like him? Why should he be in effect rewarded for disrespecting other people's property? I didn't feed everyone else — I couldn't — so why should I feed him? It was one thing to turn the other cheek; it was quite another to encourage someone in his criminal behavior.

"When you are done… "

"Yes, yes, I know. You'll take me back to the jail," Alphonse said.

I tried to soften the blow a little.

"You may have two tins of sardines and a half-kilo of rice, if you like," I said. "That should keep you fed for several days."

He didn't speak for a long moment. When he raised his eyes from his plate, the naked malice in them shocked me.

"And that should keep you free of me for several days," he said. "Now, about those Primus and Tusker beers, I noticed they're still in your fridge. I also noticed that you have more Primus hidden in the storeroom off your kitchen. Doesn't it worry you that people trained by generations of *missionaires* to despise alcohol would be very upset to learn that their current *missionaire* is a *molangi*, a drunkard?"

Wednesday and Thursday I spent suffering from worst-case-scenario dread: the Boboto Mission Church elders would demand my resignation, my denominational Board of Missions would recall me for disrespecting cultural values, and Karen, about whom I was having quite a few serious, long-term thoughts, would dump me by cellphone. Every so often I'd try to calm down and think through the situation in a logical, reasonable way.

1) One beer a week is not the last word in moral turpitude, nor does it make me a *molangi*.

2) Surely even those indoctrinated by several generations of

American Protestant Fundamentalist teetotalers have to understand this.

3) Besides, nobody is going to listen to what a thief says about the man he attempted to rob.

But I bogged down on number three every time, because I knew perfectly well that everyone in the Bosojala jail would listen. Furthermore, I was certain a good many of them would take great delight in believing that I was a drunkard. After all, what is more entertaining than the so-called righteous and/or the rich brought low? I myself had thoroughly enjoyed the famous disgrace of televangelists Jim and Tammy Faye Bakker. I'd even dressed up as Tammy Faye for a divinity school Halloween party some years ago, wearing false eyelashes and a Pepto-Bismol pink bridesmaid dress I'd borrowed from my sister Barbara, who was tall and built on generous lines. I'd won Best Costume, partly because it was a little transgressive, but mostly because everyone else disdained the greedy, weepy, ranting Bakkers as much as I did. Oh yes, there was no question about it: this man, *Monsieur le Moyibi Alphonse*, could seriously jeopardize my work.

And the fact is, I loved my work. I loved it chiefly because of the people I'd met here. I admired the gutsy village women who gardened, hauled water, pounded manioc, cared for children, and somehow, God knows how or why, retained a sense of humor. And I felt a keen sympathy for the village men, many of whom were struggling for new roles now that the forest was hunted out for the most part, and commerce at a standstill. Barred from opportunity by non-existent infrastructure and poverty, these men and women still managed to get up in the morning and move through their day. Quite a few of them also managed to care for at least one family member suffering from AIDS, and many others reared orphaned nieces, nephews, and grandchildren. Anxiety, anger, and sorrow abounded, I realized that, but so did hope. So did a certain generosity, a *largesse* of the heart. Sometimes, in the throes of three-in-the-morning angst, I'd wonder if God really thought I had anything to offer them besides my literacy classes and a few school supplies. They probably didn't need my sermons, Bible studies, and pastoral visits. They already knew how to live their particular lives, it seemed to me, and my presence here was pure self-indulgence.

That was another of my three-in-the-morning worries: my reasons for being here in the first place. Unlike most of my divinity school friends, I hadn't experienced The Call. I hadn't heard the Voice of God telling me to become a pastor and then a missionary. I went to divinity school because I grew up in a church with a large, fun youth group run by a minister who enjoyed playing football and telling jokes as well as lively theological argument, and who made ministry seem a perfectly normal thing for an ordinary guy to do. And I came to Congo because I grew up reading all that African explorer stuff by Richard Burton, Mungo Park, and David Livingstone. A big-city boy who never liked the big city, I used to dream of trekking across endless savanna, paddling a pirogue through the whitewater of untamed rivers, hacking my way through lush, almost impenetrable forest. The Ubangi District of Congo still offered slightly modified versions of all of these, and in my adulthood my own dreams had modified somewhat; hacking up endangered forest now seemed an ecologically disastrous thing to do, for starters, nor did I wish for an entourage of African porters to do all the work while I strutted around like some colonial jerk. I considered myself lucky to have found a way of combining my divinity school training and my African dreams, but I couldn't pretend that it had been a deeply spiritual process. And though a lot of my friends back in the States gave me an embarrassing amount of credit for spiritual depth and courage just because they had no desire to live in such a troubled country, I considered Congo's context of urgency an important part of the experience. I actually looked forward to turning on my radio to find out what on earth was happening now: Would the UN be willing to provide more peacekeeping troops? Could the Congolese army pull itself together for maybe five whole minutes? Were those new rumors of a coup against President Kabila true? I even got a guilty thrill out of the occasional drone of military planes overhead. I couldn't imagine admitting this out loud, not even to Karen, but I had the embarrassing suspicion that I was a Missionary Cowboy in the same way that some disaster relief workers who enjoy a danger posting are known as Relief Cowboys. Not that my posting offered significant danger; in recent years western Congo was fairly secure. But I did know that the part of me that would have enjoyed being a lion tamer or a Green Beret if I hadn't been theologically inclined was very glad to be in Congo just now. And while I worried about my reasons for being here, while I didn't give myself credit for any purity of motive, especially at three in the morning, I did not want to be forced out. I did not want to leave in disgrace just because my ministry, such as it was, had been sabotaged by a thief and a blackmailer.

By Thursday evening my worst-case-scenario dread had tied my stomach into such knots that I couldn't eat any dinner. I half-expected my thief to make an appearance that night. I was grateful when he didn't, but knew I lived on borrowed time. Shortly after dawn on Friday morning I sharpened my machete with vicious enthusiasm and walked down to the overgrown playground by Mbala Elementary School. Cutting the grass would be a start at making the place look like an institution of learning again. Cutting the grass would also take the edge off my frustration and anxiety, or so I hoped — and so it did. The rhythmic whack-whack was extremely satisfying: Whack-whack, take-that, Al-phonse, you-rat! (Stronger language was a great temptation, but I resisted.) It was one of those hazy, scorching days that serves as notice that dry season is just around the corner, and every fifteen minutes I had to break for a drink of water. By eight o'clock, though, the job was done, the felled grasses already paling and drying where they lay. Ajouda Michel came by just as I was wiping off my machete blade. He seemed a bit startled that I had cut the grass, but congratulated me on the fine job I'd done. "It's very even," he said. "If you won't take offense, I have to tell you that I'm surprised. In my experience *mindele* generally aren't very good with machetes. It's all about getting into the right rhythm, and rhythm has never seemed to agree with *mind-ele*, especially Protestant missionary ones."

"I got a church elder to teach me the week I arrived," I told him. "I wanted to be able to take care of my own yard."

He laughed gently behind his hand in that way I'd come to think of as distinctly Congolese, and said he supposed he ought to have known that. "We have a saying, 'There are those who use the old paths through the elephant grass, and there are those who carve out new ones.' "

I liked the idea of being a carver of new paths, but I didn't thank him. His remark seemed more descriptive than actually complimentary, and I didn't want to sound smug or presumptuous. During one of our long conversations at that conference several months ago, Karen, who was a forthright woman, had made a comment that still stuck in my craw: "Sometimes you seem a little too sure that you're a new kind of missionary — the cool kind, the kind with all the right social values and lifestyle. And I have to say I'm not at all convinced that smugness or arrogance in a missionary is anything new."

Ajouda Michel told me that he'd arranged for the roof re-thatching to begin tomorrow, and we parted ways. I walked back to the house and poured myself another glass of water. Glass in hand, I went out on the porch and settled into the ancient *goi-goi* chair to eat breakfast. The *goi-goi* chair, an antelope-skin lazy chair, was a relic of the missionary heyday here — the nineteen-seventies; several American missionary families lived at Bob-oto Mission then, and there'd been a functioning dispensary, a Protestant bookstore, a generator for electricity at nighttime, and even an airstrip for the Ubangi's missionary bush planes. The airstrip was pasture now, and home to half-a-dozen skinny, elderly goats belonging to the mother of Mbala Village's chief. The generator had rusted into a worthless lump of scrap metal. The other two houses were completely uninhabitable, the joists eaten through by termites; they'd collapse one day, and in less than a week kudzu vine would cover the brick and thatch rubble like a green shroud. I expected the old *goi-goi* chair to fall to pieces at any moment too, but determined I would enjoy it as long as it lasted. As I would enjoy that Rose of Sharon blooming there by the steps, if only for this one fleeting day. This morning three of the blooms were pure white, by noon they would be deeply pink, and by nightfall they would have turned a dark red, the frail petal-edges withered and transparent. And then of course dry season would be starting soon, if the teak tree behind the house was anything to go by; it was already losing its foliage, the base surrounded by fallen, faintly browning leaves....

All at once I didn't like the tenor of my mind, the way it had wandered mournfully off into "in the midst of life, we are in death" territory. This wasn't a funeral. My life here wasn't over yet, not by a long shot, and I'd had an idea. I locked the front door and jumped into the truck and roared off to Bosojala where I learned the *commandant* was at a meeting in Bosojala's commercial district with some of the town *commerçants* but would be back shortly. There was a guard on duty, the same one I'd met the first time I brought in The Rat Alphonse, only this time he wore an ancient Cardinals cap. He also wore red-flowered socks with clear plastic sandals.

"*Ah, Monsieur le Missionaire,*" he said with a smirk. "*Mbote.*"

"*Mbote mingi,*" I said politely, although his smirk worried me. "Is Alphonse still here, or have you let him out again?"

"Yes, he's still here, but not for long. The *commandant* will be letting him out when he gets back from his meeting. And most of the others who haven't anyone to bring them any food today."

"I see." I paused, then asked him if he knew how many people were in the jail at the moment.

"Sixteen," he replied.

I thanked him and then walked around the side of the concrete-block building. It was hard to believe that this small, boxy structure held sixteen people at the moment, and doubtless sometimes more. I figured it was miserably hot in there, especially since the roof was low, and made of that shiny tin stuff that soaks up heat and holds it like a cast iron skillet. Smelly too; the odor of urine seared the nostrils even from a distance. The building was surrounded by a large expanse of hard-packed red earth stained ashy grey here and there from cooking fires. Under the one lone tree, a mango tree that cast a wide circle of shade, a woman rested with eyes closed. Several feet away from her, two little girls giggled as they hopped their way through some kind of hopscotch game they'd scratched into the hard ground with sticks. I went over to the woman and asked if she was cooking for one of the prisoners. The woman said, "*Oui monsieur*, this morning I am resting, but this afternoon I'll be cooking for my brother."

I wondered what his crime was; it must be one of the "more serious" crimes referred to by the *commandant*, but naturally I did not ask. I did ask, however, if she'd be willing to cook a big meal for everyone tonight. "I'd supply all the food, and I'd pay you well for your trouble," I told her. "And of course you and your whole family could eat all you wished."

"Would there be meat?" she asked. "Real meat, not bits of sardine from tins?"

Her eyes were bright with longing, and they got even brighter when I said yes, there would. "Lots of meat," I went on. "Several chickens — four or five at least. And maybe even a goat, if I can get hold of one."

"A goat!" She stood up and dusted off the back of her faded cotton *liputa*. "This is going to be a *grande fête*! I'll be happy to cook, but you must understand that I'll need help. I can't do everything all by myself. I don't have enough time. I don't have enough cooking pots either."

I promised I would pay for cook's assistants and even buy her extra cooking pots if she couldn't borrow enough of them. To start with, I would drive her home to collect helpers and the cookware she needed, and then we'd stop at the tiny hut on the edge of the Bosojala business district which boasted the sign, "*Charcuterie European.*" (I doubted any European origins — doubted, too, that promise of pork — but as long as the proprietor could come up with one goat that wasn't too skinny or elderly, he could make all the hollow promises he liked.) The woman, Feliste, turned out to be a powerhouse of energy and efficiency; by eleven o'clock she and an army of assistants had already begun to cook.

By late afternoon the jail yard had taken on a genuinely *grande fête* atmosphere. Women and girls laughed and chatted as they stirred half a dozen pots over a half-dozen cooking fires, and voiceless *basenji* dogs, their noses twitching and muzzles dripping with drool, crept as close as they dared. A small table borrowed from the *commandant* was piled high with plates, bowls, spoons, forks, extra bags of rice to be prepared as needed. The centerpiece was a twenty-four-bottle case of Coca Cola, which children and adults alike came by periodically to admire. Even the *commandant*.

"Most of us haven't seen a Coca Cola for years, not since the war started and normal river and road transportation stopped," the *commandant* explained, stroking one of the glass bottles with the tip of one forefinger. "So this, a whole case, it's just hard to believe. *Incroyable.*"

I'd actually had that case of Coke for six months, ever since my last trip to Gemena, the regional capitol — when, by the way, I'd also purchased several cases of Primus. Primus was fairly easy to come by, unlike Coke, but I hadn't dared buy it closer to home. Since the *commerçants* in downtown Gemena didn't know me from Adam — to them, I could have been anything from an aid worker to a mercenary — I was able to lay in a year's supply without exciting comment or judgment. I'd drunk exactly twenty-four bottles of Primus in the past six months, but I'd almost forgotten about that case of Coke. To me, Coke was purely medicinal, something to settle my stomach after a bout of malaria or a touch of the Tropical Trots. I'd remembered it this morning at the Bosojala market where I was buying peppers, peanuts, and all the other fresh ingredients Feliste deemed necessary. I considered the twelve kilometer drive back to the mission to collect the Coke from my storeroom well worth the trouble.

"Except for our three very serious criminals, I'm happy to allow the prisoners to eat outside today," the *commandant* said. "Naturally we'll require a guard or two, but perhaps you wouldn't mind feeding them as well? In appreciation of their services, you understand?"

I said *pas de problème*, there would be plenty of food, and would he perhaps consider joining us too? In appreciation of his services, you understand?

Although the *commandant* did not actually smile, his upper lip twitched very slightly. He looked suddenly younger, less burdened, less self-important. "Yes, thanks. And I'll also bring my wife and children, if it's all right with you," he said. "In appreciation of their services, you understand. They keep me from going crazy in this life."

The rich smooth peanut smell of chicken *wamba* contrasted pleasantly with the sharpness of goat seasoned with hot Congolese *pili pili* peppers, and all at once I was flooded with a marvelous sense of well-being. Someone had brought a transistor radio, and several of Feliste's assistants were singing along with that grand old man of Kinshasa jazz, Papa Wemba. Two older girls had joined the little girls at hopscotch. The older girls laughed riotously as they clutched *liputas* loosened by their vigorous hopping, while the little girls, big-eyed with excitement, were busy drawing more squares as fast as they could. Everyone appeared to be in good spirits, even the jail guard with the red flowered socks and Cardinals cap. The whole enterprise seemed suddenly uncomplicated, even pure, and very much in line with the Parable of the Great Banquet in the fourteenth chapter of Luke, where Jesus says that when you throw a big party you shouldn't invite your family, your rich friends, your neighbors. What you ought to do, He says, is invite those too poor to recompense you by inviting you in return, and then God will reward you at the Resurrection of the Just. I began to feel downright impressed with my own generosity — after all, the goat alone cost me two days' salary — and when the guard brought me a chair to sit on, I took my seat with a proud sense of having been given my due as Official Benefactor. At five o'clock the prisoners emerged single-file, their progress monitored by two additional guards, and they all, guards included, cast avid glances at the cooking pots and nodded deferentially in my direction. Some actually smiled broadly. Fresh meat was probably well worth spending another day or two in jail, and from my point of vew, their good will was well worth feeding.

And then The Rat Alphonse appeared, bringing up the rear, and my sense of wellbeing evaporated like dew in dry season. His face, which was so extremely thin that his eyes, mouth and nose seemed to crowd a too-small surface, wore an expression of barely concealed amusement. It was as if he understood my efforts, as if he found me pitifully transparent. As if — and this is what really stung — he knew he had me where he wanted me in spite of my grand gesture.

"Coca Cola," said The Rat Alphonse musingly. "Strange you should bring that when Primus goes so much better with a hot *pili pili* pepper sauce."

The *commandant*, who had overheard, told him in a reproving voice to apologize at once. "As if any *missionaire protestant* would ever even think of buying beer. You should be ashamed of yourself!"

In the silence that followed I could hear the plaintive voice of Lokua Kanza on the little transistor radio propped against one of the protruding roots of the mango tree. He was singing one of my favorite songs, "Mboka," about how we should open our hearts, how we should do something about those in need. But I scarcely noticed. I was too busy wishing I had a Primus bottle in my hands right this moment. If I had, I'd have broken it over The Rat Alphonse's head.

෪෴

My sweaty palms grip the sides of the rough mahogany pulpit as I listen to myself prosing on in my anxious Sunday Lingala. I'm trying to explain the intricacies of poor Tamar's difficult domestic situation, and why she would have felt shamed and rejected by her dead husband's brother's refusal to have full sexual relations with her. "Onan had a duty to both Tamar and his dead brother, and God killed him because he wouldn't fulfill that duty," I say. "Levirate marriage — that is, the custom of the brothers or next of kin inheriting the deceased man's wife — was customary in Old Testament times."

I pause as I glance around the crowded church, but no one appears the least bit surprised by this information. As one woman shakes her head with evident pity for poor Tamar's situation, I grasp a fact I'm mortified not to have grasped sooner: a Congolese congregation, especially a congregation with a lot of older people in it, does not need the concept of levirate marriage explained to them. Levirate marriages have long played a role in the lives of many Congolese. "But of course many of you know all about that," I say hastily. "In Congo there is a long tradition of following through on your family obligations."

A muted hum of agreement encourages me.

"If someone is your brother, your *ndeko*," I say, "then you help him when he needs help. Like the Good Samaritan, you nurse him when he is ill. And you stand by his family as well."

The hum is louder now, and Mama Malia, an older lady who always sits in the front row on the left, stands up and does a little dance, wiggling her narrow hips with astonishing agility and waving her thin hands in the air. Completely taken aback, I stare at her. Mama Malia is the wife of a very senior elder in the church, and I have always thought her a shy, somewhat retiring person. When she sits down again I am relieved, but not entirely. I sense a new mood as several of the children sitting on the wide window sills giggle and point at her. At the back of the church, three men from the Bosojala jail slap their thighs and shake with silent laughter. My chest tightens. I have no doubt that if these men are once again at large, so is Alphonse. After all, the *grande fête* was two days ago already, and the leftover food won't have gone very far. Questions rattle around in my brain like dry seeds in a calabash: Why are all these men here in church? Do they expect me to provide another feast? And where is The Rat Alphonse? Ransacking my house this very minute, perhaps? There is no better time than between ten and twelve on a Sunday morning to do a really thorough job on a missionary's house, and I'm sure The Rat Alphonse knows it as well as anyone. I can't and won't delude myself about The Rat Alphonse; he made it perfectly clear on Friday that he is not finished with me, so I can't afford to hope I'm finished with him. I set my teeth and take a deep breath through my nose, willing myself not to rush the final moments of my sermon even though I want to sprint down the aisle and out the door and up the road to my house. I don't really care about my material possessions; he's welcome to all of them, with the possible exceptions of my computer and cellphone. I just want the chance to give him a really good concussion. Maybe then he'll forget about this whole Primus business once and for all.

"And that is probably the important thing about a text that most people usually remember for its sensational content," I say. "It is a reminder to all of us that failing in our duty to one another is a grave matter…"

I have planned to say a little more, but I never get the chance because all of a sudden Mama Malia is loudly praising the Lord for having given them a *missionaire* with a generous heart, a *missionaire* who feasts with sinners and evildoers just as *Yesu Klisto* did in the New Testament. They are all blessed by the example of this amazing *missionaire*, blessed and humbled, she says, and now she wants to dance in gratitude before the Lord. Yes, she wants to dance with joy and thanksgiving, like the prophetess Miriam after God drowned the Egyptians in the Red Sea, like King David before the Ark of the Covenant. And before I can pick my jaw off the floor, she is in the aisle dancing and singing, her hands fluttering above her head like birds. The jail men join in the dancing, and the little children scramble out of the windows, and pretty soon the whole congregation is kicking up their heels in a way that would have utterly scandalized the fundamentalist *missionaries* who built this church, who evangelized the parents and grandparents of these people, and who would never have dreamed of dancing. Who might, if presented with the choice of drinking or dancing, have actually considered drinking the lesser of two dreadful evils. I've never been in a dancing church in my life because American dancing churches tend to be weird charismatic places where people sing praise songs and speak in tongues, but I am afraid that if I don't join in the dancing I'll come across as a judgmental prude. I put my Lingala Bible down on the pulpit alongside my sermon notes, move into the aisle, and try to dance without looking like a complete idiot. I think about cutting grass because that's the only way I can manage to sway, to feel even the slightest sense of rhythm. Mama Malia and a few of the older ladies dance a circle around me, then spin away, clapping and laughing. Soon I'm dizzy from watching everyone spin and sway, sing and clap. I'm even dizzier from trying to do all these things myself. When Mama Malia vigorously slaps my hand with her open palm, I almost fall over.

It is a good hour later than usual by the time I get home. I'm dripping with sweat and I ache slightly in a few unaccustomed places, and I feel generally slap-happy. Nothing I find will surprise me, I tell myself as I insert the key in the lock. I am prepared to find that The Rat Alphonse has taken everything of value, even my hole-ridden socks. I am prepared to find that he's slit every single one of my screens just out of malice. I am even prepared to find he's still there, his head in the refrigerator, munching my few leftovers — a couple of chunks of boiled breadfruit, a baked yam, several slices of pineapple. What I am not prepared for is the sight of The Rat Alphonse standing at obsequious attention beside a table set for one. A half-dozen creamy frangipani blossoms float in a small glass bowl, and somehow, from somewhere, The Rat Alphonse has unearthed a white cotton dinner napkin.

"Ah, *Pasteur Alain*, I must tell you of the great thing that has happened," he says as he ushers me to my chair. "The Lord has convicted my heart and caused me to understand my sin and repent."

Usually I take a shower and change into fresh clothing after a morning in the pulpit, but I'm too bemused to say so. I permit him to push me gently down upon the hard wooden seat. "He has?" I say. "Really?"

His eyes meet mine squarely, frankly, and in his gaze I can see nothing but limpid sincerity.

"Oh yes, He has," The Rat Alphonse says. "And He has done even more than that. He has informed me that I must make restitution for my sin, and so He's called me to be your cook and your *boi moke* for free. *Gratuitement*."

I wonder what will happen if I say that there is a problem because the Lord has failed to inform me of Alphonse's new calling? What if I say that I believe the Lord is calling me to inform Alphonse that while He appreciates Alphonse's change of heart, Alphonse needn't feel obliged to prove it by becoming my cook? Or what about this: suppose I tell Alphonse that he's been sent to try my faith and he should just keep on robbing me until he's robbed me the seventy-times-seven that Jesus says I have to forgive him for? There must be plenty of possible responses I could make, but all at once my mind sputters and then stalls completely. Post-sermon exhaustion has set in, its severity compounded by a sleepless night. And now, reminded of my sleepless night, I am seized by guilt. I know perfectly well why I lay awake hour after hour last night: I was hoping — praying, even — for the chance to brain Alphonse with my wickedly heavy, three-battery flashlight.

I look down at the nicely set table, then up at the hovering and beaming Alphonse. Did he say anything to his fellow inmates? If he didn't, then I have to consider the dancing a spontaneous and genuine outpouring of goodwill, a kind of public thank-you that I know I don't deserve. But if he did, then the sudden lifting of an eighty-year ban on dancing, especially dancing in church, means something else entirely. Something I'm beyond being able to fully comprehend at this moment.

"I have made your favorite sardines and rice," Alphonse says. "I have prepared elephant-ear greens as well. Also a fruit salad with fresh papaya, mango, guava, and a hint of lime juice."

Alphonse will have to stay until I have a better grasp of what I am up against. One thing I do grasp already: Alphonse cannot be permitted to work for nothing. I will have to pay him, and pay him well.

"Thank you, Alphonse," I say, allowing him to unfold the napkin and drape it across my lap with a flourish. "You may go ahead and serve the meal."

Doing Good

As THE YOUNG BLACK WOMAN climbs into the front passenger seat of the VW Bug, Delia, crosslegged in the back, notes that her mother's ears are still ripe-tomato red. Her mother speaks to the young woman in her calm, warm, Sunday-morning voice but those ears, generally very pale with tiny gold freckles, tell Delia that her mother is very far from calm. Besides, it's Monday morning, when Delia's mother tends to talk a lot — getting Sunday out of her system till the next time, she says. Her mother grinds the car into gear and they are off, bouncing down the road in a way that the Bug is not accustomed to because in the city, in the white neighborhood where they live, the roads are well maintained. Delia twists around in her seat and watches the police officers lounging in the shade of a jacaranda tree scribbling in their notebooks. Really, she's amazed they can write, her mother says, adding that they are hillbilly hicks who like policing because cleverness is not required but brutishness is. Her father won't call them hillbilly hicks. He says insults solve nothing, and in all fairness one has to admit they've had a great deal to put up with from the British, who starved their women, children and old people in concentration camps during the Boer War. But he does agree they're a terrible cross to bear, especially for blacks and coloureds who certainly don't deserve it — and yet this too shall pass; world opinion won't allow it to continue indefinitely; one must try to take the long view and weigh one's committments and try not to act impulsively. Her mother always snaps back that the long view is infinitely more palatable when one is white, and her father always looks sad and even thinner as he says could they please have a little justice here, Elaine, because he is not a racist. To which her mother always replies that if he calls her Elaine just one more time she's on the next boat to Southampton. (Her mother prefers to be called Elly. Elaine, she says, is the mawkish choice of a Tennyson-loving mother who was silly enough to think the death of the Lily Maid of Astolat for love of Sir Lancelot was romantic. And romance, her mother sighs, is a snare and a delusion, and if she'd only understood that fourteen years ago she'd still be in England and not in this benighted place.)

The young black woman in the front passenger seat offers her passbook to Delia's mother, who waves it away, her ears now even redder. "Please," she says. "I'm not one of them. I don't need to see it. All of you should be free to travel wherever you like without ID."

Delia wishes she could have a look at it. Although much of what her father calls The Latest Injustice is about an increase in fares for black bus service, some of it is also about having to show passbooks, and she'd like to see what a passbook actually looks like. She'd also like to know the woman's name, but feels she can't ask if her mother doesn't, and her mother generally doesn't ask the name of any black person. Her mother knows black people only by their roles: cook, nanny, maid, washgirl, gardenboy. Delia leans forward curiously, but the woman is already putting it carefully away in her plastic carrier bag.

"Where would you like to be set down?" her mother asks.

"The typewriter repair shop on Pretoria Avenue, please," the young woman replies. "Shall you mind if I put on my good shoes?"

Delia's mother doesn't say anything for a moment, and Delia suspects she is slightly taken aback by the confidence of her passenger's Queen's English vowels. Then she says goodness gracious, of course not, in her most church-social, tea-pouring voice, and after a moment's hesitation the young woman reaches into the carrier bag and takes out a pair of black court shoes with the kind of heels that Delia knows are called kitten, though she doesn't know why. The shoes are very narrow, which must mean that the woman doesn't have the kind of feet Delia generally associates with the black women she sees most often, the ones who work in the homes on her street. Peering frankly over the passenger seat at the woman's feet, she is struck by their slim arched beauty. Nothing could be farther from the flat, callused, swollen feet of Delia's expectation, the kind of feet that splay out over the edge of dusty flipflops and boast the remnants of red nail polish in the same brave way that you will sometimes see a bougainvillea blooming out the windows of an abandoned house. Delia's mother glances too, then away, and Delia has the distinct impression that her mother is not pleased with her passenger. Her mother is always talking to her father about one's duty to The Oppressed but Delia suspects she'd rather The Oppressed had ugly feet. She also suspects that if she said this to her father, he would produce one of his rare but huge belly laughs even as he'd say, "Respect, sweetheart, respect!"

"My husband, Dr. Kempe, is the rector of Saint Michael's," her mother offers brightly. "I do parish work."

"How interesting," the woman says as she gazes ahead at the long convoy of cars all filled with black passengers and white drivers from the Liberal Party who support the black boycott of the buses. "Very rewarding, I'm sure."

"It isn't terribly interesting, really," her mother goes on. "I wish someone had warned me that being a rector's wife is mostly a matter of organizing the flower roster and playing gooseberry at teen events. You know, trying to keep them from kissing in broom closets or behind the baptismal font." And, she adds, exercising tact. "My husband thinks Thou Shalt Have Tact is the eleventh commandment. You simply wouldn't believe how much of my day is spent having tactful conversations, performing small tactful acts, even baking tactfully bland sponge cakes for church teas."

The woman glances at Delia's mother, obviously taken aback by the way her voice is climbing ever higher. She seems uncertain about the correct response, and after a moment pulls out a tiny mirror and a white plastic tube of lipstick. Delia watches as she applies it with a practiced hand. The colour is bright and bold as the cannas that bloom in the rectory garden, and Delia, who for the past several months has been memorizing The Song of Solomon during her father's homilies, finds herself thinking *Thy lips are like a thread of scarlet*. Then, frowning — thread really is not right for such full, beautifully shaped lips — Delia chooses another one: *Thy lips, O my spouse, drop as the honeycomb: honey and milk are under thy tongue*. Yes, better. Delia guesses this woman does not, like many black women, mop floors all day or feed garments through a washing machine ringer or change babies' dirty nappies. Probably she's a receptionist at that typewriter repair shop.

Although it isn't yet eight o'clock, the air has lost all freshness and the sunlight glares harshly down upon the convoy of cars moving steadily toward the city. Delia sticks her head out of the window and lets the wind blow through her hair. Her peter pan collar feels both damp and restricting so she unbuttons the top fake-pearl button of her blouse and pulls the sticky fabric away from her neck. As her mother is still talking — something about a new recipe for a tactful lychee fruit jelly, though why this woman with the blooming canna mouth should be interested Delia can't imagine — Delia decides she has enough privacy to peek down the inside of her blouse at her disappointingly flat and sweaty chest. She checks on the state of her chest upwards of a dozen times a day, hoping to be surprised by the sudden advent of curves. Secretly she despairs of growing breasts and fights a terrible envy of her best friend Eva who, although also only eleven, already has discernible swellings under her blouse and collapses to the ground in excruciating pain if she gets hit in the bosom by a volleyball or basketball.

Their passenger, Delia notes, has a nice bosom: not too big, certainly, but also not too small. Delia can't actually see the woman's breasts, of course — the neckline of her simple A-line dress is cut high — but she can always tell when women are wearing padded brassieres. Her mother wears one, and somehow both of her breasts always protrude with a pointy flawlessness that looks a bit unreal. Like side-by-side photos of Mount Kilimanjaro up in East Africa, she thinks, but without the giraffes in the foreground.

"I often wonder," Delia's mother tells her passenger, "what my life would have been if I hadn't married a minister. If I'd married a surgeon, maybe. Or a sailor, who wrestles with the elements."

Delia would find her mother's chatter mortifying if she weren't so amused by the very idea of her quiet, thoughtful, insists-on-seeing-all-points-of-view father as a dashing and muscular sailor who shouts orders to subordinates and physically struggles with potentially dangerous things like ropes, sails, winds, high seas.

"Or maybe a musician. I doubt musician's wives have to concern themselves with tactful Battenberg cakes and jellies and boring sausage rolls."

Delia finds the idea of her father as a musican — maybe a glamorous tenor like Mario Lanza, maybe the kind of gravelly jazz performer they have on Radio Bantu — even more entertaining than the sailor. As their passenger shrugs slightly, Delia notes that the colour of her dress is very becoming even though it's a shockingly bright yellow. Princess Margaret wore a hat that colour on her trip to Canada and her mother said it was regrettably showy and made the Princess's skin look like cheddar cheese.

On the left they are coming up to a lush stand of bamboo and yet another police vehicle. Delia's mother brakes slightly, passing the officer with what Delia considers unnecessary slowness. The officer writes down something on a note pad.

Thy two breasts are like two young roes that are twins, which feed among the lilies. That was one of the verses she'd sniggered over last Sunday with two other girls in the tiny lavatory by the kitchen of the Parish House. Delia had sat crosslegged upon the closed toilet lid and recited other favorite bits as well, about breasts like clusters of grapes, navels like round goblets, thighs like jewels, temples like pomegranates. Eva, precariously perched upon the narrow edge of what Delia's mother considers an unnecessary and even embarrassing bidet, read aloud about the hair like flocks of goats from Gilead, and Caroline did the part about thy neck as a tower of ivory, and then Delia had pranced across the floor grinning madly, lips pulled away from her teeth, saying "Thy teeth are as a flock of sheep which go up from the washing, whereof every one beareth twins, and there is not one barren among them." All three girls had clutched their sides, laughing helplessly, but somehow there were also those other bits, those strangely unnerving and enticing bits like *Open to me, my sister, my love, my dove,* and *Love is strong as Death, jealousy is cruel as the grave.* Somehow those things one could not say aloud; they were almost as personal as chapter seven, verse eight, about the little sister with no breasts, which Delia knew she'd be incapable of reciting without bursting into tears. As it was, she only recited the parts about roes and grape clusters so no one would suspect that breasts were a matter of extreme sensitivity.

"We need petrol," Delia's mother announces. "There's a place up here on the left."

Delia's mother pulls into the petrol station a bit too fast and has to slam on the brakes. The little building is strangely colourful: long orange stripes stain the white walls, years and years of rainwater having dripped from the rusty, corrugated iron roof, and the roof itself wears a thick green, purple, and white cape of blooming passion flower vines. While the black attendant fills the tank, Delia's mother heads for the ladies' lav. Delia wouldn't mind going to the lav as well, but she fears it might be rude to leave their passenger all alone in the car. So she sits quietly, head tilted against the back of the seat, and listens to the rhythmic sloshing of petrol and the clucking of chickens shaded by

34

a flamboyant tree with blossoms the color of the Boots lipstick Eva's cousin sent her from England. The distant but continuous grumble of thunder means a downpour later today. She spares a thought for Mrs. Thornton and her washgirl Mary next door; Mrs. T always has poor Mary do the laundry on Mondays no matter what the weather looks like and she's always complaining about how unlucky she is when it starts to rain before the laundry is dry. Vaguely Delia becomes aware of a low-voiced conversation between the woman in the front seat and a black man at the window with a long narrow face above his greasy blue mechanic's overall. He is telling her how sorry he is about her brother, that he has meant to write or come by in person for months now, that the Sharpeville tragedy will stir others to action, and she is telling him how much she appreciates his sympathy and that the kindness of others is seeing them through. She asks after his wife, his children, his Aunt Delphina, and then Delia's mother is getting back in the car with a great swishing of full pink-flowered cotton skirt, and the man backs quickly away.

Twenty minutes later the traffic is at a complete standstill. An accident? A roadblock? There's no way of knowing. And although they are close to the city limits, there's also no knowing when they'll get there. Delia is queasy from the smell of petrol fumes, three sweating bodies in a tiny space, and the penetrating odor of her mother's scent. (Most mothers Delia knows wear English scents like Yardley's April Violets but Delia's mother always wears the same concentrated French *eau de parfum* and enjoys telling anyone who asks that it is My Sin, by Lanvin.) Delia suspects her mother is sorry she allowed herself to get so exercised this morning. They'd breakfasted out on the verandah at their usual time, six-thirty. Her father was reading *Contact* magazine as he sipped his third cup of tea, and her mother asked him what on earth was the point of reading Liberal Party rhetoric when he didn't exert himself to do anything. He said patiently for the billionth time that doing something wasn't quite so simple as she seemed to think; he was responsible to his congregation for his actions, he begged to remind her, and as there was a great deal of disagreement among them about tactics for expressing views contrary to the government, he didn't feel authorized to do or say as much as he'd like to. "Remember that most Anglican congregations are semi-paralyzed in this way. It's not just St. Michael's."

"And since when does one need a consensus for moral action?" her mother asked. "Look at Bonhoeffer. And closer to home, look at Beyers Naude. They say he's starting to stand up to the Broederbond and the whole Dutch Reformed Church. If he can manage to do that, what's wrong with the Anglicans, for pity's sake?"

From the way his chair grated across the concrete verandah floor Delia knew her father was angry even though he said quietly that Beyers Naude was an honest and brave man, a man who seemed to be growing beyond his former racist theology, and he wouldn't be at all surprised if his body turned up in the bush one of these days. And the bodies of his wife and children. Then he looked at Delia as if he'd just remembered she was there and pressed his lips tightly together. After a moment he said to Delia, "Well, Little Limpopo River Eyes, I must get to work. Have a good day at school."

Delia rolled her eyes at him tolerantly. It was an old joke, that Kipling bit about the great, grey-green and greasy Limpopo River. Dove's eyes would be nicer. *His eyes are as the eyes of doves by the rivers of waters*. But she liked her father's old jokes; their predictability was somehow reassuring. And then her father headed off to his study, Delia collected her book satchel and got in the car, and her mother got in and slammed the door with exceptional vigour. She announced that they'd take a detour on their way to school. A detour out toward the townships to collect one of the bus boycotters in need of a lift. A detour that now, from the airless and increasingly dusty heat of the back seat of the Bug, seems it might take forever.

"I've already missed my first class, you know," Delia informs her mother. "What are you going to tell them? You know how they are."

"That you had a dental appointment," her mother snaps. "Don't fuss. You'll embarrass our guest."

Delia doesn't think their guest looks at all embarrassed. She just looks hot. And beautifully breasty. Delia guesses she is one of those women who had gorgeous grape clusters by the time she was ten. It's sickening the way some people are just born lucky. Delia sighs and stretches out flat on her back. She has a maths exam this afternoon and Mrs. Gordon will be merciless if she absents herself for a routine dental appointment. As long as she gets back for the exam Delia doesn't mind missing anything else. What she does mind, however, is having to listen to her mother's disgruntled Monday monologue, which is so much worse than usual because (so far, anyway) it is more than four times longer than usual. The drive to school generally takes twenty minutes; today they've been cooped up together for at least an hour and a half with no end in sight. Her mother is now complaining about Mrs. Patterson, who is agitating for a new kind of service on Sunday evenings that will be more casual, a service where there's no liturgy and anybody who feels like it can pray and sing and request laying on of hands for healing. Her mother tells their passenger that Mrs. Patterson should take herself off to the kind of church where that sort of thing goes on and let everyone at St. Michael's alone. Delia doesn't think it would be so bad; maybe she could request prayers and healing for her breastless state. If it really worked, it would be worth any amount of public embarrassment. Well, maybe not. She certainly doesn't want anyone doing a laying on of hands that involves actually touching her chest with about a hundred people watching. But perhaps she could ask for the laying on of hands and a prayer for healing without being specific about the nature of her problem. Perhaps that would be the better strategy anyway. After all, it's perfectly possible that some unfeeling people will think there are much worse things than being eleven without even the tiniest, faintest suggestion of bosom. They will, of course, be wrong. *Thy breasts shall be as clusters of the vine.*

"I meant to be a surgical nurse, you know," Delia's mother is saying. "I was a probationer at a good London teaching hospital. I was doing exceptionally well — matron said I had the makings of a really fine surgical nurse — and then what happens to me? A doctor of divinity student with a gorgous tan, that's what happens to me! A divinity student with a seemingly sunny disposition from a sunny land. A divinity student who grew up eating bananas and oranges, for God's sake, when for us they were still off ration."

Delia is so bored she's ready to take a nap. She knows all this dreary old post-war-austerity stuff by heart. Her mother's charming but ineffectual father whose death meant her once-middle-class mother had to "oblige" for middle class ladies who wouldn't dream of cleaning their own kitchens and bathrooms. Her mother's claustrophobia, which made sheltering in basements or the Piccadilly Underground station in the summer and autumn of 1940 a misery beyond description. Her mother's determination, once she began to think a year at a time instead of a minute at a time, to live in a country that didn't have wars, or at least not lately, and where she might bring up whatever children God gave her in peace and plenty. "All I wanted in 1947 was a home in a city that wasn't bombed to rubble, a home in a country that wasn't at war, and so I did it. I took a deep breath, packed my bags, moved halfway around the world. And then what happens to me in 1948? The Afrikaner National Party wins the election, that's what happens to me. And everything changes."

Delia touches her right nipple, which is about the size of a match head — only without, it seems to her, the potential for transformation inherent in a match head. She doesn't know why she thinks of such an explosive comparison — fire, danger, heat — but she does. Although she supposes the simmering temperature under the low metal roof of the car could account for it, somehow she suspects that it doesn't. She can't identify why; she doesn't even make the attempt. She suddenly thinks she may have heard of Sharpeville after all. She thinks her father mentioned it in a sermon, one of those sermons when many of the parishoners leave without shaking her father's hand.

"Well, now I'm stuck with another war of sorts," her mother says in a lighter tone, a tone tinged with resignation and a slowly returning good humour, "but at least there isn't any horrid Piccadilly station this time. And the people I know who have basements I could count on one hand."

Delia has never heard her mention this before. She's actually never thought about it, but it's true. Basements are a rarity here. Her knowledge of basements comes from American magazines where they are turned into something called "rec rooms" with hi-fis, televisions, a drinks bar, and lots of shiny pine panelling.

"I'll walk from here," their passenger announces abruptly. "It's only about three kilometers."

Delia's mother turns to the young woman, her hazel eyes widening with surprise. She says oh, but do you really…? I mean, the sun? The heat? And the young woman says it isn't so terribly hot, and is suddenly out of the car with her carrier bag and walking briskly down the road in her kitten heels.

Her mother says well, they've done their good deed even if some people can't be troubled to say thank you — and now, incidentally, the hillbilly hicks will have their car license number, and won't that shake her father up a bit!

Delia wonders what is so important about car license numbers but she doesn't ask.

Her mother sweeps on: "Oh, this really does look ridiculous, Dee. I feel like any moment you're going to tap me on the shoulder and say 'Home, James.'" She reaches across the empty seat to push open the passenger door. "Come up here with me."

Delia crawls out of the back seat, stands up and stretches her cramped arms and legs. As she slides into the front passenger seat, Delia observes that the young woman moving steadily past one stalled car after another has the kind of carriage that suggests enviable bosoms even from the back.

THE SMALL HONEY

I WAS READING CALVIN'S *INSTITUTES* and eating cornflakes when the moaning began. Softly at first, then sliding jerkily up the scale, higher, then higher still, with a gasping, "Oh yes, Lord Jesus! Yes, Jesus,YES !" I got up and closed the dining room window, but it didn't help very much because the apartment walls are by no means thick. (Trust one of the world's wealthiest religious academic institutions to be cheapskates about student housing construction.) I tried to concentrate on Calvin, but the moaning and gasping went on, now interspersed with broken bits of "praise song." That painful clenching started behind my breastbone, a clenching that felt a bit like acid indigestion and a bit like something Tums never even tried to cure. Snatching up my coffee mug, I headed for the hallway —*This time I knock on that door, this time I give Alicia a piece of my mind, I really do* — but there was Zekiel, sitting crosslegged on the doormat reading his *Math is Fun* textbook and slurping chocolate milk. He had his iPod ear buds in, his small head bobbing to a beat only he could hear, and after a moment I tapped him on one skinny hunched shoulder.

"Hi Zekiel," I said.

"Hi Ingrid." He pushed back the ear pieces and now I, too, could hear the hard, fast thump-a-thump. "Doing my homework out here this morning. Mom's talking to God again."

"Right." I sighed. "Seems like she talks to God an awful lot."

He stared at me, his pointy little chin raised, and I noted that his dark blonde lashes were so long that they clumped together as if they'd been spikily mascaraed. His father was said to be a Dallas Cowboys linebacker, but he'd gotten his mother's slinky, feline good looks. A lucky kid in my opinion since Alicia, a former Cowboys cheerleader, was a dead ringer for Scarlett Johansson. My heart, as they say, softened.

"Yeah, seems like she does," Zekiel said. "But so what." And then he hunched over his math and adjusted his ear buds again.

For a nine-year-old, Zekiel had the fine art of impassivity down pretty well, I thought. He wasn't much like the Old Testament Ezekiel, an excitable guy prone to ecstatic visions who once preached to a valley of dry bleached bones until all the bones got up and started dancing. Not much like his mother either — at least, not in that respect. The Seminary's token unwed-mother divinity student, Alicia belonged to one of those weird little sects that Texas spawns like cowboy hats and oil wells. Her raucous religious experiences would've impressed any of the prophets, major or minor, her annoyingly sleek appearance in skimpy spandex outfits no doubt providing an additional thrill. I went back into my apartment, wondering what made me so catty about her. Was it just my Midwestern-Scandinavian aversion to emotional display?

"Alicia needs therapy," my friend Danny had said. "And no excuse not to get it. I bet there's a one-to-one ratio of therapists to other supposed tax-payers in this filthy-rich town. Besides, the Seminary's insurance'll cover it."

"Oh, I don't know," I'd said.

"Well, I do. I read the policy."

"No, I mean that seminary's a kind of group therapy in itself," I'd said. "For some people, anyway."

"Blind leading the blind," he'd replied bitterly. "I've told Trixie, when she's in one of her 'I'm a stupid imposter and they shouldn't have let me in the program' moods, that she should find a therapist. But she says getting a really excellent one is too damn hard."

I'd heard this before, of course. It was one thing for us lowly Masters of Divinity students to find a therapist. For us (as the PhD candidates suggested in the nicest possible way) any middle-aged woman with empty-nest syndrome who had gotten herself a quick degree in clinical social work so she could mother somebody and draw a paycheck for it was perfectly okay. But for the really smart, the PhD-bound in Homiletics, or New Testament Studies, or — like Danny's wife — Systematic Theology, there was this dire and much-discussed problem of finding therapists with the right kind of PhD. Their therapists couldn't be traditional Freudians, of course, as psychoanalysis was too flagrantly un-Christian. But neither could they trust those therapists who made a point of calling themselves Christian, for fear they might have gotten their degrees at little fundamentalist divinity schools with no academic standing and believe casting out demons is a legitimate alternative to talk therapy. Consequently the PhD candidates tended to sit around and bemoan the situation, then affirm each others' mental health, and finally conclude they were best off without therapy anyway. I'd considered getting a therapist myself when my husband left six months ago, but the dozens of listings in the yellow pages had overwhelmed me. After Alicia had moved in next door, a second semester "freshman" M.Div. student, I'd considered it again, and this time more seriously. But I really couldn't see myself telling some therapist that my neighbor's horrendously audible Encounters with God had driven me into her office. She'd think, "Oh great, a divinity student so sexually frustrated that she doesn't just hear voices... oh no! This one hears Sex with the Godhead."

Seven-fifty already, darn it. I grabbed my car keys and rushed out the door. Zekiel was gone, as I'd expected; the school bus came by promptly at seven-twenty to pick up the multitudinous fruit of the Seminary's loins. Zekiel's mother's doormat, which I disliked for its royal blue announcement that any friend of Jesus was a friend of hers, had somehow migrated several feet down the hall. Gripped by a sudden fury of tidiness-is-next-to-godliness, I picked up the mat and centered it in front of her door, trying not to notice the handpainted wooden plaque which read, "Tongues Spoken Here," and ran down the stairs to my car.

I pulled into the Seminary Bookstore, where I was Manager of Shipping and Receiving, just in time to sign for a UPS delivery of twenty-two boxes. Second semester final exams so occupied me just now that I sometimes forgot summer school would be starting in a few weeks, but the UPS shipments didn't allow me to forget for long. I was pleased to note on the shipping label that these boxes contained all the back-ordered 1960s Liberation Theology texts we'd been waiting for. (It was funny how Liberation Theology was now old enough to be rediscovered, revised, and repriced for a new generation just before the last of the doddering old authors kicked off. Reminded me of my Minnesota high-school music club putting on "The Student Prince" because it was so antiquated that nobody had heard of it and thought it must be the newest, most avante-garde thing.)

"Hey, Post-Toastie!"

That was Danny Taber, my assistant and friend, who liked jeering at my unimaginative taste in food. Anything bland, anything colorless, and he knew I'd eat it like any average Scandinavian brought up on the prairie. I should never have spilled my dietary beans (ie. my love of cornflakes, mashed potatoes and rice pudding) to someone who doused his scrambled eggs with hot sauce.

"Hey, Post-Christian," I said, pleased. "You're here Post-Haste this morning! What's up?" I chose to work my half-time bookstore job in the mornings partly because of the UPS delivery, partly because of my class schedule, and mostly because Danny preferred mornings, and we preferred working together. He was a giraffe-necked guy from Alabama with sweet eyes and large ears, married to the most go-getter PhD student I'd ever met. His wife was going to be the first truly world-class female Karl Barth authority, or at least the first one named Trixie, and Danny was along for the ride, his self-described theology of God-Fearing Atheism and his jazz-piano-playing in grungy bars on Route One a deep, dark secret from the Seminary At Large.

"Yeah, I know I'm here a bit early, but I've got to leave early," he said. "I have to pick up Ninny at the vet."

Ninevah, alias Ninny, was Danny's adolescent cat. Danny had named her after that Biblical City of Spectacular Wickedness because he said just the name was welcome relief from genteel, proper "Pee-town", as he called it. Danny actually went so far as to blame his worsening asthma on the High Odor of Sanctity which wafted through the venerable trees of the Seminary campus.

"Why not call her Sodom?" I'd asked him. "She could be Sod for short."

"MAH sainted GRANNY, Ingrid!" he'd replied in shocked tones. "Ah just CAIN'T believe you-all think THAT kahnd of thing would go on HEAH!" (Ever since Danny found out that Famous Public Figures had worked with the Seminary's renowned speech therapy department, he'd spoken "Exaggerated Southern" whenever he remembered. Many of these Famous Public Figures — major network news anchorpeople, actors, and the like — were trying to get rid of regional accents, especially southern ones, which fact drove Alabama-born Danny to try to balance things out in his own eccentric way.) But it wasn't actually Danny's accent that surprised me now. It was because I hadn't meant to suggest what he was suggesting. Not at all. For as much as this school would have liked to feign a little open-mindedness, an awful lot of things that happened at Harvard and Yale Divinity Schools didn't happen here — at least, not in the open. It took over one hundred and twenty years for the Presbyterians to get back together after the North-South Civil War split, for one thing, so you knew even the most basic change could take a very long time. Besides, there was this large influx of tremendously conservative students from Korea who would never tolerate it. Which was exactly what you got for proseletyzing: a complete Frankenstein of a Presbyterian Church overseas that was so mired in the late-Victorian theology provided by American and U.K. Presbyterians circa 1900 that it now sent its own students over here in droves to disapprove and try to straighten everyone out. Religious colonialism home to roost, and richly deserved in my opinion, but — oh, Lordy! You couldn't help feeling that someone should have warned you about the theological conservatism when you were still seminary-shopping and not after you arrived for your first semester, all pantingly thrilled to stick your theological neck out just a little bit. You rather wished you'd just swallowed the substantial hike in tuition and gone off to Cambridge or New Haven instead. After all, what was another student loan or two, in the grand scheme of things? But you could never mention any of these fine distinctions about Ivy League theological education back home in Worthington, Minnesota. People would think you were about to turn into Garrison Keillor, who'd gone east and gotten himself a swollen head and never fully regained his position as Minnesota's Blue-eyed Boy.

"So listen, what's wrong with poor Ninny?" I asked. "Why did you have to take her to the vet?"

"She has sex on her tiny cat brain, that's what," Danny said — and then, apparently remembering to chew the stereotypical tobacco on the stereotypical porch — "Drahvin' us out of our tahny 'lil MAHNDS, she was, draggin' her belly and screechin' and moanin'! So Ah told her, 'It's tahm, gurl. Tahm to get you SPAYED!'"

I said I hoped the procedure had gone well. He said the vet said she'd had a mild allergic reaction to the anesthetic, which was why they'd kept her last night, but otherwise she was fine.

"Mah Ninny, she's a tough 'lil thang," he said fondly. "The vet told me she was pacin' feebly around her cage this mornin', impatient as all-get-out."

Then we unpacked twenty-two boxes of books about modeling Marxist values in the poor Catholic churches of Latin America. I pondered the irony of two dozen pastors from well-off congregations showing up for this particular Continuing Education course in their Brooks Brothers suits and their SAAB cars. They defended their affluence earnestly enough; I'd heard them last summer, and it had seriously annoyed that chip-on-the-shoulderish part of me that still felt like a low-class, low-income farm girl. "Well, you know, if I get a SAAB instead of an American car it'll run forever," they'd said. "This way I'm not supporting our extravagant throw-away culture." After which they'd arranged to hit the most expensive bar in town for twenty-dollar shots of extra-fancy single-malt whiskies.

"So, what's the latest on divorce proceedings," Danny asked.

I gave him a dirty look and told him to pipe down. If the administration found out about my change in marital status, I'd be thrown out of the Married Housing apartment complex. At the ripe old age of thirty-four, I didn't think I could stand banishment to the Singles Dorms.

"Sorry," Danny said, without contrition. "Okay then, how's Jesus's girlfriend next door?"

Some weeks ago I'd told him about Alicia. I'd given him the hilarious version, embellishing my story with distinctly rococo details, but now I found myself strangely guarded. "Fine, as far as I know," I said, and then raised my voice so anyone within fifteen yards could hear. "And how did the piano-playing go in Bart's Helluva Bar last night?"

So Danny gave me a dirty look, and we went back to work. Just as I was wondering how it was that the rarified air of this campus could both draw you together and set you at odds, Pat McGann, the divinity student in charge of Special Book Orders, walked in a full hour ahead of schedule. He gave us an exhaustive account of his meeting with the Pastoral Search Committee at Good Shepherd Presbyterian in Bakersfield, California, where he'd interviewed over the weekend. He told us that it was a Significant Pulpit of the most superior kind, having nearly eight hundred members who were all white collar types with six-figure incomes at the very least. The Search Committee wanted him to say yes, but he'd thought he should come home and pray about it first. I cynically interpreted this last as Drive-The-Salary-

Up Strategy, and Danny hissed in my ear that he supposed Pat was hoping William Sloane Coffin would kick the bucket over the weekend and free up New York's Riverside Church for him. I whispered back that William Sloane Coffin had long since retired and kicked the bucket as well, no doubt partly from the sheer rigors of fame. Besides, Pat was too Californian for a Terribly Terribly Significant East Coast Pulpit. The bankrupt Crystal Cathedral was more his style.

"Gee whilikers." Danny leaned against the work table and raised one sandy eyebrow. "Ah think ah should call Yale Div. and get some advahce about stahtin' up a witches' coven. Yawl are soundin' plenty witchy these days."

At that moment Dr. Isabell Thompson appeared in the doorway wearing an understated cream linen dress I'd seen in the display window of Talbots. Her caramel-colored Coach bag exactly matched her sling-back heels, and I was pretty certain her delicate blonde streaks did not come from a do-it-yourself bottle of supermarket stuff. She asked Pat, who was nearest the door, if he could tell her whether or not her summer textbooks had arrived. Pat, apparently dazzled, gaped at her with much less than his usual aplomb — and I reluctantly supposed I could understand why; Pat's poor little wife was so overwhelmed by new motherhood that I suspect she hadn't washed her hair or brushed her teeth in a month. Danny fell all over himself assuring Dr. Thompson that all her nifty little liberation theology books had come and that we could get more Next Day Air should we run out. Then Pat hastily added (from the vast experience of his three years here as a student) that no summer course had ever generated so much excitement before, or had such a staggeringly high enrollment. She preened a bit, then said modestly, "Oh, that can't be true. Why, it's such a privilege to try to fill Dr. Ernst von Gerhard's shoes. A whole year here and I'm still expecting to get the axe!"

Now this really was a bunch of malarkey in a steaming cowpat, as my ex-farmer dad would say. The Seminary was thrilled to get her, and somehow — via that peculiar osmosis common to academic institutions — everyone knew that the Seminary had shelled out a downright historic chunk of cash to lure her away from Emory. They'd also given her two research assistants and a gorgeous eighteenth-century house on Alexander Road. They'd even promised to finance the academic journal she wanted to co-found with somebody on the Emory faculty. (Rumor had it she wanted to call the journal Voices of the Downtrodden, and I figured she was going to have to go way out of this zipcode to find them. Maybe to Trenton or Camden, even.) But since Danny, as well as the repellent Pat McGann, appeared to be smitten by Dr. Thompson's charms, I figured I'd better shut up and try to re-habilitate that chip on my shoulder. After all, as my grandmother routinely said, "Ingrid, child, you're too defensive, too sharp. You suffer from such a winterish temperament that I worry for you." Gran had a summery temperament, of course. A temperament as bright as the fuchsia that Gran's neighbor, Bridie O'Malley, had brought her from Ireland, smuggling it through Customs in her enormous handbag. (In Irish, fuchsia meant "Tears of God," Bridie said — which actually wasn't one bit like warmly-human, laughter-prone Gran.)

"Everyone says great things about your classes, Dr. Thompson," I said nicely. "I'm looking forward to your seminar in the fall."

Dr. Thompson seemed ridiculously pleased and very ready to lap up more praise, so I said I needed a cup of coffee and headed down the hill to Wawa. When I came back she was gone, and Danny and Pat were having a distinctly barbed conversation about one of the Systematic Theology professors. Danny was saying he thought a license plate reading "Sem Doc" was unbelievably adolescent for a man in his late sixties, and Pat was saying he thought it was great and might do the same if he ever had the good luck to be tenured here. Deciding that the most urgent bookstore stuff was done, I went out on the quad, sprawled on a park bench beneath a maple tree, and studied Greek vocab for my Monday final.

"Oh sweet Jesus, oh yes! Oh praise God, yes, yes, YES!"

Alicia was off to an early start — and me? Oh sweet Jesus, I was in the most imminent danger of going off my head. Alicia's unseen Encounters With God made my long-defunct sex life seem even more defunct, and as for my spiritual life... but I didn't want to think about any of this at seven-thirty on a Saturday morning. I decided to drink my coffee outside, maybe admire the hydrangeas. I hurried past Alicia's door so fast that coffee sloshed onto the back of my hand. I stopped and studied the reddish burn mark spreading across my skin. It looked a bit like stigmata, and I wondered not-altogether-facetiously if I was marked for future sainthood. Then I decided that anyone living across from a woman who got it off with God every morning should qualify for sainthood without the nuisance of oozing Christ's wounds or being burdened by any other holy earmarks. And I remembered how Simone Weil's poor old mother had said of course her daughter was a twentieth century saint, there was no doubt about it, but had anyone ever thought what absolute pain and misery it was to be a saint's mother?

Out in the yard the hydrangeas were flowering with reckless splendor. They were that peculiar blend of pink and blue that indicates a confused soil. One bush had great bobbling blooms of bold Renoir pink, another had lavender, and then there was my favorite — that clean watery blue, the blue of oldfashioned airmail stationery, the kind that is so thin you can see your fingers through it. I sat down on a plastic lawn chair. Ah, peace! Ah, quiet! Ah, the blessedly silent abandon of green, growing things, and how very thoughtful of plant life to flourish and bloom without making a song and dance about it! Maybe I should make a sign, "This Is a Noise-Free Zone," and hang it in the hallway. But Alicia, Jesus-intoxicated as she was, would never realize it was meant for her.

I took a deep breath and exhaled it slowly, slowly, trying to relax against the hard straight chair back. All I'd ever wanted from this school was a sympathetic environment in which to pursue my questions about faith, and eventually (was this so much to ask?) acquire a respectable graduate degree in the process. I

hadn't expected to find myself shriveling up in the parched dry-
ness of Greek vocab and Calvin's *Institutes* — although I probably
should have anticipated the latter, given the Seminary's Scottish-
Presbyterian roots. And I certainly never expected to be almost
divorced, and living next door to someone like Alicia. I desperately needed a coping strategy. Maybe I could hang religious
icons all over my walls and use them as dart boards whenever
she started in on her noisy God-Encounters. I'd drown out all
that *oh yes, Lord, yes!* business with Gotcha! and Bullseye! It was
a pity that handmade icons were expensive; the Seminary Bookstore sold lots of them, so I knew that even the tiniest ones from
El Salvador or Russia could set you back a considerable sum.
But expense didn't have to be a problem if I made the dartboard
icons myself. I could schedule a pleasant, inexpensive frenzy of
paint, glitter, and glue, and call it Art Therapy. I could title the
whole collection "Ivy League Ladies," and then name them indi-
vidually: "Our Lady of the Nassau Street Shoppers," "Our Lady
of the Jaguar Drivers," "Our Lady of the Cashmere Clad Elite."
"Our Lady of the John Calvin Club." "Our Lady…"

"Morning, Ingrid."

It was Zekiel, and he looked about as forlorn as a child could
look. I said hello, and he sat down crosslegged in the grass and
started stripping the fat green leaves from the variegated hydrangea bushes. I said, "Hey, don't take it out on the hydrangeas,
Zekiel."

"Take what out?" he asked, genuinely puzzled.

After staring at him for a fascinated moment, I decided I'd go
for a walk around the housing complex. I picked up my coffee
mug and headed down the block. There were seminary couples
outside already, pushing strollers and walking golden retrievers
and hopping in and out of Volvo stationwagons and SUVs. None
of them looked like they were having strange and noisy encounters with God. Why couldn't one of them have moved in next
door to me? And then I saw Pat McGann sitting on a lawn chair
looking over some papers — his padded resumé, probably —
and turned back before he could see me. My apartment suddenly

didn't seem so bad. I'd just turn on the TV. Loud.

When I got to my building, I was surprised to see Dr. Isabell Thompson's distinctive baby-chick-colored Mercedes parked out front, and Dr. Thompson herself walking up the sidewalk, briefcase in hand. We walked through the main door together, and then she said, "Can you tell me which apartment is Alicia Johnson's? I have an appointment with her."

"One floor up, and on your left," I said.

"Thanks, I... "

"Oh yes, JESUS" — Alicia was apparently still going strong — "Oh yes, yes, and YES PRECIOUS LORD!"

I headed upstairs without waiting to see Dr. Thompson's expression, and let myself in my apartment. There was only one reason for Dr. Thompson to be here: Alicia was going to be interviewed as one of the Downtrodden for her new magazine, thus saving the elegant Dr. T at least one slumming-it trip to Trenton or Camden where someone might steal her car stereo and hubcaps, if not the car itself. If I were Alicia, I'd be royally pissed. Then again, Alicia might enjoy it. At the monthly Married Student Housing pizza parties, she'd been so frank with everyone about "The Bad Old Days Before The Lord Turned Me Around, Praise His Holy Name," that I had cringed for her.

As I was pouring a second cup of coffee, my cellphone rang. I figured it had to be my mother. She got up at five-thirty even on Saturdays and thought nothing of calling me by seven, central time. Her opinion, inherited from Gran, was that anyone who slept through anything so beautiful as a sunrise needed an iron supplement. Today she was later than usual, and I was grateful.

"Good morning, dear," she said brightly. "How are you?"

"Fine, Mom. And you and Dad? And Gran?"

"Oh, just fine. Fine."

Sure they were. My father lost the farm eighteen months ago. Some of the best land in southwest Minnesota too, rich and darkly fragrant as coffee, for which we'd had a land grant signed by Ulysses S. Grant in 1868. My father had done his best, working fifteen-hour days for years, but in the end the bank finally got it. He was so depressed — ashamed, too, although it wasn't his fault — that he spent most of his time on the living room couch mutely watching TV. My secretary mother supported them financially, and eighty-four-year-old Gran supported both of them morally. (Gran, with breathtaking good cheer, would drag them off to church or bingo games, and then back to her house for rice pudding and her famous Swedish meatballs made with ground veal.) Like hell they were fine, but who was I to judge my mother for withholding the truth? I wasn't exactly forthcoming myself.

The formalities over, my mother delivered one of her Worthington/Lake Wobegon news bulletins: Britta Nyquist (I hadn't forgotten Britta, had I?) had given birth to twin girls, Pam Gustafson had made a *tusenbladstarta* from scratch (just imagine peeling all those apples!) for the Golden Agers bingo night, the Einar Blombergs had lost more than five hundred dollars at one of those Indian reservation casino places (if I could believe it), and one of the Mitchell boys had West Nile virus. And Mona, Jeff's mother, had called from St. Paul. Jeff was dating the loveliest girl, Mona had told her, an English teacher at Minnehaha Academy. "But Mona also said that she still doesn't understand what happened between you two…" And my mother paused, waiting.

Oh, ask your own questions, why don't you, I thought, suddenly irritated. It was simple, wasn't it? Two years of Pee-town had made Jeff crazy. "Forget the Three R's," he used to say. "This place specializes in the Three P's: Pompous, Precious, and Pretentious." I couldn't blame him for feeling that way; he was here only because of me, and there wasn't much work opportunity for (or appreciation of) a canoe craftsman in Pee-town. New Jersey was no Minnesota, Land of a Hundred Trillion Lakes. What was he supposed to do, convince people to boycott Route One and commute by canoe to New York City? Tell them the portages would be such terrific fun? "Listen, Mom, don't take it personally but I have to run. Monday's my Greek final, and I've got to study like mad."

This impressed her. She said oh, of course, dear, I'm awfully sorry, and hung up. I stood there for a moment, my cell phone still in my hand and the weight of being the world's meanest daughter and potential Master of Divinity pressing against my breastbone. In my desire to atone, I decided to study all day even though I'd originally planned to spend the morning hiking along the canal and the afternoon rereading a favorite Henning Mankell mystery. So I alternated Calvin with Greek vocab until I was half-blind and wholly bored, and wondering how in the world I'd ended up studying systematic theologies and dead languages when it was the lives of people of faith that really interested me. St. Teresa of Avila, especially. St. Teresa, who had said that our souls are not poor hollow things but many-roomed crystal palaces, or great, rich, honey-filled beehives. I'd fallen strangely in love with the idea of having a honey-filled soul instead of my own winterish, skeptical one. I'd read and reread *Interior Castle*, smitten by the words, equally smitten by the perhaps predictable book cover, which was Bernini's rapturous St. Teresa in the act of having her soul "caressed by God." I'd thought to pursue soul honey — and here I was, a bewildered and hostile misfit surrounded by classmates in search of Significant Pulpits, by well-heeled pastors dabbling in the exotica of Latin American poverty, and by hoary (and horny) long-tenured male faculty more disposed to approve a dissertation topic if a female student would consent to a flirtatious dinner *à deux* at some restaurant out of town. (This last I had from Danny, who, on his piano gigs, had seen several of these odd couples skulking around dark corners of Route One hotel bars.)

At ten o'clock I finally decided I'd done enough Calvin-and-Greek penance. I ate Lean Cuisine lasagna while I watched Vicar of Dibley videos and tried to decide whether or not I liked the boisterous female Anglican priest. I'd never watched the show until — like many other seminarians I knew — I was given all the BBC videos by family members frankly desperate for holiday gift ideas. By midnight I was thoroughly tired of Dawn French in a dog collar. While she was at once fending off the sexual advances of a halitosis-afflicted parishoner and officiating at a wildly ec-

centric wedding where the flower girls wore Teletubbie outfits,
I fell sound asleep. When I awoke, my cell phone was ringing. I
picked it up and mumbled "hello" with groggy resentment.

"Post-Toastie, you'll get a crick in your neck sleeping in front
of the TV."

"How do you know?" I asked, startled. "And what are you
doing calling so late?"

"I'm on my way home from the bar," Danny said. "I'm outside your place. I can see the screen flickering, and your head's
all flopped sideways. Don't you ever close your curtains?"

I went over to the sliding glass doors that opened out onto
my little balcony and looked down at the street. Danny flashed
the brights on his old pick-up that still had the Alabama plates,
and I said into the phone, "You goddawful snoop!"

He replied that I'd cut him to the quick, and better take him
to an ER before his quick totally quit. I said he was crazed, and
he said oh no, just gently plastered from bar patrons buying him
shots of Jack Daniels all night. "Gotta go sleep it off," he added.
"Good thing Trixie's not here, or she'd be mad as hell."

"Where is she?" I asked.

"At a theology symposium," he said, slurring slightly. "In
New Haven."

All at once I imagined Danny sleeping it off in my own bed, a
pillow clutched to his enormous ears. He was so long and lanky
that his feet would hang over the end of the bed, and my summer
blanket wouldn't cover his bare toes — but I wanted him there. I
wanted to hear him snuffle and sigh in his sleep, wanted to smell
the light reassuring sweat of another body beneath the same covers. I wondered if he was a cuddly sleeper; cuddly sleepers were
the best kind to have around, especially if you weren't in the
mood for sex all that often. And he'd be a defense against — well,
just a defense.

"Now listen, you!" I said in my most sisterly tones, "Go
home. Before Security catches you parked drunk in the middle
of the street."

"Those old farts," he grumbled, and then — "Oh shit, speak

of the devil!"

I watched him pull off to the side as a dark van rounded a corner and headed in his direction. The guys who worked for Seminary Security were mostly retired military who loved using their crackly shortwave radios and exercising their small authority by giving students parking tickets even when their permits had expired only yesterday. I'd gotten one, so I knew.

"Ingrid," Danny said abruptly. "Can I come up?"

I was so taken aback that I said yes. Three minutes later he was in my galley kitchen, it was too late to reconsider, and I was trying to dispel the air of strangeness by bustling around — if anyone could be said to bustle wearing jeans so worn that they lived on the body like loose old skin. "Caf or decaf?" I asked as I reached for the box of Melitta filters in the cupboard next to the stove.

"I'd rather have more Jack Daniels," he said. "Or scotch, if you have any?"

I started to say that I didn't, and then I remembered Jeff's stash in the cupboard above the fridge; he'd packed in such a furious hurry that he'd forgotten a lot of things, and his Johnny Walker Black was one of them. "If your arms are long enough," I said, pointing up at the cupboard.

Danny extracted the bottle with a tall person's annoying ease. "Not much left," he warned as he poured a hefty slug into the wine glass I handed him.

"You're welcome to finish it." I said, shrugging. "I won't."

"Oh, give it a try. Live dangerously," he said, and took down another glass — which, pausing, he eyed thoughtfully. "Trixie would like this. She hates our wedding crystal since we moved up here. It's got all these big swoopy etched flowers, and most people here have plainer stuff. And plain is classier, she says."

"These belonged to Jeff's grandparents," I said flatly. "I've got to send them back."

Danny downed the scotch and poured himself some more while I tentatively sipped. It really wasn't so bad except that I felt like my tonsils were being cauterized. And the kitchen was too small.

"Come on," I said, heading for the living room. "Sit."

Lord, I sounded for all the world like I was giving orders to a dog. I didn't mean to, but somehow all my social skills had deserted me. Worthington and a decade of marriage had not prepared me for the intricacies of social intercourse under these circumstances. Back home, a married divinity student did not entertain another divinity student's soused husband in her apartment at midnight. Certainly she didn't ply him with even more alcohol and fantasize about cuddling together in bed. Well, naturally not. Worthington didn't have a seminary.

Danny followed me into the living room and sprawled beside me on the couch. I cauterized my throat a bit more, choked, and waited for him to jeer. Waited, too, for something I wasn't at all certain I wanted. So that, when he turned toward me and the old couch springs squeaked like terrified mice, I was too nervous to laugh.

"Ingrid," he said, and stopped. And swallowed.

I waited some more, my fingers cramping around the stem of Jeff's grandparents' crystal wine glass.

"Ingrid, she's screwing Sem Doc." Danny's brown eyes glazed with misery. "Right this minute, probably."

I set the glass carefully on the endtable. No doubt there were words appropriate for this, but I couldn't find them. I just sat there and watched the gentle tide of scotch lap golden against the interior of the glass.

"I could bust it up for the moment," he went on. "Literally. I mean, if I called the conference hotel, they could put me through no problem. He'd probably pick up — worried, you know, " Danny paused, swallowed. "And if I didn't say anything, if I just waited."

Yes. If he waited through several of Doc's urgent hellos and unspoken anxieties (what burned down? who is ill, dying, or dead?) Trixie might become unnerved enough to hiss, "Well, who is it, David?" — thus providing proof-positive in that Alabama accent so like Danny's. But on the other hand, maybe Trixie would suspect a trap and keep silent. Maybe, both dreading and expecting to hear Mrs. Sem Doc's voice, she would quietly edge Sem Doc away and press her own ear to the receiver. And then, when she heard nothing, what would she feel? Would apprehension tighten her chest until she went all breathless and lightheaded? Would she suddenly grow nauseated, her palms cold and her forehead slick with sweat — or would she be furious? And why on earth was I assuming that Danny was right? I rather liked Trixie, who was a born comic and added zest to any seminary social gathering. Certainly I admired her grit, her hardworking determination, but other things about her did annoy me. Her public reapplications of bright red lipstick, for example. Her pointy French manicures and lady-executive suits. And most of all, her habit of putting herself on a first-name basis with important academics, theologians or otherwise, like Cornel West, Phyllis Trible, and Elizabeth Schussler Fiorenza. "I waited in the post office line with Cornel yesterday, and we had such a great conversation," she'd say, or, "I ran into Elizabeth at Starbucks last week. She was down from Harvard Div. to give a lecture on democritizing Biblical Studies." Trixie would probably refer to The Great Karl Barth Himself as "darling Karl," if she thought there was the remotest chance anyone would think her ancient enough to have met him... Oh God, of course Trixie was screwing Sem Doc.

"Come on," Danny said, half-rising, grabbing my hand. "Let's do it. Let's call the Hyatt. We'll both listen. It'll be hilarious!"

I shut my eyes. "It won't," I said.

"It will too," he insisted. "Honestly it will. I promise!"

Danny sounded like a pouty three-year-old, and I couldn't bear it. I pushed him back onto the couch. I supposed I should ask him how long he thought it had been going on, and how he found out, and what he planned to do. If I knew Danny, he was frantic to talk, to tell all about his clever detection, recount all the dropped clues and his resultant gleanings, rid himself of every single detail, known or imagined. And so I waited, waited, and

at last the silence told me that I did not know Danny so well after all. This, too, I could not bear, for I wished — oh God, how I
wished — for the small certainty of knowing someone well. And
being known in turn. I sighed and said, "Come here."

He sagged into my outstretched arms, and only by the heav-
ing of his shoulders did I know that he was weeping. I smoothed
the bristly blond nape of his neck and stared at the bare wall across
the room and thought I really should make those Ivy League Ladies icons. Jeff had taken his framed map of the Boundary Waters
(Canadian side) and his poster-size blow-ups of his favorite canoe photographs with him, and I hadn't gotten around to filling
in the empty spaces yet. It occurred to me that "Our Lady of the
Name Droppers" might be a good first project, and one I'd really
enjoy using for dart practice. After a long while, after such a long
while that I'd developed a pain in my lower back and my legs
had gone numb from the weight of him, I said, "Listen, Danny,
do you want to stay here tonight?"

"Mmmm," he mumbled against my skin, then lifted his head
from the hollow of my neck and looked at me piteously. "Oh
yes."

*Oh yes, Jesus. Oh yes, precious Lord. Oh yes, oh yes, oh YES YES
YES.*

After silently damning the echo of lovely, golden Alicia to everlasting perdition, I said firmly, "You're too long for the couch,
so I'll take it. You can have the bed."

He nodded and tossed the last of his Johnny Walker down
the back of his throat. Then he stood, drawing me up with his
free hand, and we went into my bedroom. "Please stay for a bit,"
he said. So we lay down on my bed with all our clothes on, and
I held him so tightly that his rumpled hair tickled my ear and
his scotch-scented sweat dampened my arms and chest through
my cotton sweater. After long minutes his breathing deepened.
I allowed a few more minutes to pass before I tried cautiously
to move away, but Danny clutched me and rolled over so that
his legs pinned my hips to the bed. I knew he was still asleep —
knew, too, that his sudden hardness had almost nothing to do

with me, and would have mortified him if he'd been awake and sober. So it was quite a while before I tried again to move away, and this time he did not prevent me. He just moaned and burrowed his face deeper into my pillow as I covered him up with a cotton blanket. Then I tiptoed out and closed the door behind me.

The living room was littered with class notes I could be reviewing, and the kitchen was filled with dirty dishes. I could study, I could clean up, I could watch another Vicar of Dibley episode. I could even call Information in New Haven and track down Sem Doc and Trixie. Instead I poured the remaining scotch into Jeff's grandparents' glass and sat down on the couch. I'd just relax, try to go to sleep. In the morning everything might have changed, including my inchoate yearnings. And Trixie might be back, having "come to herself" like the Prodigal Son. She might show up on my doorstep saying that Sem Doc was history, that she'd seen the pickup out front, and that she absolutely had to see her darling Danny this very minute, if not sooner. Who could say? Even Jeff might be back. And I, even I, might genuinely want him the way he'd always wanted me to want him — if that made any sense.

After another few sips of scotch (really, it did kind of grow on you) I started thinking of other icons I might make. Probably I was more artistically inclined than I'd realized. My seven years as Activities and Crafts Director at the Applewood Manor Retirement Home in the backwater of Worthington hadn't exactly explored my talent or made use of my bachelor's degree in art history. Why not try a fun, possibly lucrative career in controversial religious art? It was an idea, and it was definitely in fashion. Only think of the Brooklyn Museum and Our Lady of Elephant Dung.

"Oh yes, Lord Jesus, YES."

I squinted muzzily at my watch. Surely it wasn't morning yet? Surely Our Lady of the Dallas Cowboys (oh, that was good, that was really good, I would make an icon out of one of those ultra-sultry, puckered-lip, glamour-mag photographs of Scarlett

Johansson and use scads of gilt stars and glitter) was not Encountering God at — at two a.m.?

"Oh Lord, yes! Sweet Jesus, YES!"

This was it, finis, the last and final straw. I got off the couch and went in search of the seminary phone book. I rummaged in the kitchen and looked through my bookshelves, I shifted and reshifted the paper stacks on my desk, but I couldn't find it. At last I looked at the list of emergency numbers on the fridge and called Seminary Security instead.

"Can I help you?"

"Um, yes," I said. "You can. I need a phone number for Alicia."

"Alicia who?" asked the terribly bored voice on the line.

After a quick shock of envy — did some people actually have the luxury of NOT knowing who Alicia was? — my mind blanked with fury. "Alicia next door," I snapped. "Just ALICIA, for God's sake."

Nobody had ever hung up on me that I could recall, and I was surprised even though I knew I deserved it. I began to pace around my kitchen. It wasn't easy to pace in a tiny galley kitchen, so I crossed the dining room and opened the sliding glass doors to the balcony and stepped barefoot onto the cool concrete. I could still hear Alicia, but only as a faint and far away murmur. The three-quarter moon silvered the trees, the cars, and the other apartment buildings, and I leaned against the railing gulping at the fresh air like a kid bobbing for apples.

"Hey, Ingrid."

A small head poked around the brick wall that separated Alicia's balcony from mine.

"Zekiel," I said, speaking extra-sternly out of a sudden fear that my articulation wasn't what it could be. "Shouldn't you be in bed?"

"I am. Mom's letting me try out my new sleeping bag tonight," he said. "Besides, shouldn't you be married?"

I stared at the child and found I couldn't see his face clearly. "I am," I told him. "Not that it's any of your business."

"The people downstairs say you shouldn't be living here because pretty soon you won't be married anymore."

I drew a defensive breath. "They don't know anything about it. "

"Yes they do. The people downstairs — the ones who live right under your apartment — they told us they could hear your fights. They didn't want to, but they could."

Oh hell. I'd thought the decibel-level of our arguments was very low — well, lower than Alicia's spiritual orgies, anyway. I'd also thought the people downstairs (both seminarians, and a wan spiritless pair who'd inexplicably and ornately named their little daughters Audrey Annabella Carrington and Radclyffe Rebekah Summerton) believed my explanation for Jeff's departure. I'd said he was offered a job back home that he couldn't pass up, and this year — my third and final year — he'd just have to come visit whenever he could get a cheap flight.

"The people downstairs… "

I said oh damn the people downstairs, and Zekiel giggled and said his mom would be surprised because she thought I probably didn't know how to swear. His mom figured I was a stuck-up Miss Priss like all the rest of them. His mom wanted to go back home to Texas where people didn't act like she should be awfully grateful that she's allowed to be here, and then interview her about her life and ask her all these nosy Oprah questions that make her so mad that she tells billions of really sappy un-Christian lies for the frigging fun of it.

"Does she?" I asked, fascinated.

"She sure did today!" He giggled proudly. "I heard her. But afterwards she felt kind of sorry for the lady, who got all worked up and cried and patted Mom's hands and told her she was this total heroine, like Rigoberty Somebody."

"Menchu," I said distractedly, trying to picture the self-possessed Dr. Isabell Thompson weeping. It was easier to picture her holding Alicia's hands. Alicia's slender fingers were straight out of an El Greco painting: elegant, elongated, and tipped with luminously-pale nails. "Rigoberta Menchu. A famous freedom fighter for the Guatemalan peasants, and a kind of theologian and Bible teacher."

"Whatever," he said, and I didn't have to see him to know he was shrugging those little buffalo-wing shoulders. "Anyway, then Mom told her the truth too, but she didn't tell the lady which was which. Jeez, did she laugh when the lady looked all confused! She just told the lady to pick whichever story she liked best, she didn't care, and nobody here would know the difference anyway."

I laughed too. Laughed wonderingly, trying to fathom both Alicia's lies and her frank self-exposure. Why hadn't I once — just once, in the past four months — considered having more of a conversation with her than a muttered hello in the stairwell? Had I feared she might transform me into a Holy Roller? Had I worried she could make me join Jesus's Little Harem against my will? Maybe it was something else altogether, something I might never genuinely want to understand, but one thing was certain: I'd badly underestimated Alicia Johnson. Hoping for more information, I said to Zekiel, "So tell me, which story did you like best?"

"You're just like her," he said. "Nosy."

Zekiel withdrew his head, and a lot of rustling and pillow-thumping was followed by a long zipping sound, then finally a sigh. Indignation pierced my gentle cloud of scotch. Dr. Isabell Thompson (Exeter, Amherst, Harvard Divinity) had ascended the academic ladder simply oozing Pee-town-like privilege. How could I — with my old Subaru, my Target clothes, my useless art history major from an obscure college, and my even-more-useless job history — be anything like her?

"You'd better go to sleep, Zekiel," I said, trying to get the last word even though I knew it didn't become me to one-up a child. "It's really late."

And then I just leaned on the railing for a while, contemplating Pat McGann's well-polished Volvo, which he always parked down in the cul-de-sac in order to minimize the risk of scratches. If his Significant Pulpit in Bakersfield, California, came through with the financial package he wanted, Pat would be upgrading soon. Maybe he'd even get vanity plates that read "Sig Pul," I thought, smiling snidely.

Moonlight glowed on the Seminary Day Care where Sem Doc's faded little wife, wearing a cashmere twinset, inevitably pastel, volunteered on Thursdays and Fridays. It glowed, too, on the Community Center where the Korean students took language classes, new moms took exercise classes, and weekend seminars were offered on people-managing skills and church budgets. A light wind gusted across the dark smoothness of the swimming pool where Summer Liberation Theology would have its end-of-session party. Dew glistened on the ninth green of the golf course, the soccer field, and the tree-lined canal where seminarians jogged in order to relieve stress and avoid the academic's spreading bottom and stooped shoulders... Oh, what a beehive this place was! What a crowded, messy, frantic beehive, the whole damn thing run by scurrying self-important worker bees too busy to taste the honey, even the smallest drop. Or maybe they weren't too busy. Maybe the relentlessly cerebral, nine-to-five business of the hive just destroyed all desire for the honey, made it seem somehow suspect, distracting, or even dangerous? As he'd emptied his sock drawer into a suitcase, Jeff had said, "I've tried to support you, I really have, but this Ivy-League briefcase religion is making me sick." (Energetic balling up of worn sock and direct hit to wastebasket.) "I don't understand why you're pursuing faith the Pee-town way, but then what else is new? I don't think I've ever understood what you're about, what you want. But I'm finally starting to get it. And what you want — well, it sure isn't me."

I pitched Jeff's grandmother's crystal goblet into the moon-splashed hydrangea bushes. The disturbed leaves closed over it, muffling the soft shatter in such a tactful Pee-town way that I wished I'd aimed for the street. Then I noted a small cat tottering precariously down the narrow curb — Danny's little Ninny, night prowling in her incorrigible way despite her recent surgery — and I was glad I hadn't. Just as I was about to go indoors, I saw two dark figures emerge from Pat McGann's Volvo, then head in opposite directions. The shorter of the two cut across the soccer field to a moon-colored Mercedes that had previously escaped my attention, and I was willing to bet my last dime that in daylight the car was baby-chick yellow. I went back inside. After slipping quietly into my bedroom, I peeled off my jeans and sweater, crawled under the covers, and pressed my naked breasts against Danny's spine. I cradled his back and shoulders in my encircling arms, hooking one leg over both of his. (See this, Jeff? See? I can too be spontaneously sexual and affectionate.) Danny was not sleeping so soundly that he couldn't be wakened and made willing despite the Jack Daniels and Johnny Walker. As my stroking hands moved lower, then lower still, Danny's breathing went fast and shallow and his buttock muscles clenched hard against my belly.

Oh yes, Lord Jesus, yes. Oh yes, God, yes. Oh please please God, make this the solution!

Oh no. Oh no, God, no. Morning. With Danny rolling on top of me, dropping his head into the curve of my neck and mumbling against my skin. With Danny's rumpled hair tickling my ear, Danny's sweat smelling of last night's scotch. Danny's bony ribcage crushing mine. With my skull percussive, my mouth dry, and my phone ringing like crazy from the pocket of my crumpled jeans.

I twisted my neck around and peered at the alarm clock on my bedside table. It was nine-twenty, and this time my "Oh God," was said aloud, with force. There was no way Danny could leave unobserved this late in the morning. It was Sunday, yes, but a lot of the Seminary's mothers and small children didn't attend church services regularly, due to earaches, colds, and flu bugs. Besides, different churches had services at different times, so you couldn't count on one mass exodus anyway. Often those attending a nine a.m. service arrived home again before those planning to attend at eleven were even out of bed. And who — who — was on that phone?

What if it was the wan couple downstairs calling to complain. "Your racket last night kept our little girls awake," they'd say. "You should be ashamed."

What if it was Trixie on the line, looking for Danny? "I was in Boston and I was missing him," she'd tell my voice mail. "So I just hopped the train back, and here I am. Except that here he isn't, and I saw his pickup in front of your building this morning, and I want you to know that I think you're a rotten, homewrecking, un-Christian bitch."

Pushing Danny aside, I propped myself up on one shaky elbow and waited for the beep before reaching for my cell phone.

"Ingrid, lovey, it's Gran here. Just thought I'd try to catch you before you left for church."

(Oh, darling Gran, who thinks I actually go to church like a proper believer. Bless her innocent heart.)

"Now listen, it's not important, so you don't have to call me back, but I just wanted you to know the most marvelous thing."

(What must it be like to find things marvelous? Gran is always doing that.)

"You remember those special glass panels I had put in for my plants last winter? Well, it was expensive and I felt a little silly because my fuchsia has just been sitting there looking half-dead for months, and now" — a quick gasping breath — "now it's just blooming like mad, and weeks ahead of schedule, and of course Bridie says it must mean something, because you know how Bridie is. Well, I guess that's it for me for now — my, how I hate this fancy voice mail stuff — and don't you overdo preparing for your exams. Your mother says you're working too hard."

I lay with my eyes closed, picturing the cascade of blood-red Tears of God from the gigantic potted shrub on Gran's living room floor. Probably Bridie had a dozen theories ranging from the semi-scientific (new plant food) to the fanciful (it's finally quit being homesick for Galway) and she would doubtless make Gran listen to all of them. But Gran would be supremely uninterested in anything except the fuchsia's wonderful boldness, even abandon, in blooming so extravagantly and early. It was the kind of mistake that Gran admired. The kind of mistake that was not a mistake, but an achievement of the most conscious, deliberate kind. A consummation, even. And she would tell Bridie so.

Danny moaned and opened his eyes as I leaped out of bed and grabbed my bathrobe. I ignored him, thrusting my arms through the sleeves and half-tripping over the long ragged hem in my hurry. And then I was out the door and in the hallway banging on Alicia's door with such urgency that the "Tongues Spoken Here" plaque crashed to the floor. And then Alicia's door was opening — and opening so abruptly that I lost my balance and fell against the doorframe — and Alicia herself was standing before me, long blonde hair loose and full red lips parted. She wore a tight white tank top and sky-blue spandex shorts, and she looked all sleek and blessed, all lissome and delicious and ecstatic as high summer: Bernini's St. Teresa in streamlined modern dress. And even as my peripheral vision filled in the details — the Sunday-clad couple from downstairs gazing up the stairwell in perplexity, barechested Danny standing in my doorway blinking like a sleepy giraffe, Zekiel peering curiously at me from around his mother's gently curving hip — my interior vision offered up a completely different picture. A picture of prodigal daughters having come to themselves, and also come together, in the far country of Pee-town. Prodigal daughters laughing as they closed the Subaru's trunk lid and then bundled Zekiel into the back seat with his iPod and his collection of soccer balls. Prodigal daughters holding hands as they pulled slowly away from the Seminary's married housing complex and headed for Route One.

Bereft of speech yet strangely certain, I stood in the doorway until Alicia put her arms around me and drew me inside.

EAU DE PARADIS

CREAM-COLORED BOOTS, wispy blonde tendrils, and — oh dear — a Burberry plaid miniskirt she probably wears because she had a similar one in high school in 1974. She'll want — really, this is so easy it's boring — a girlish perfume. Yves Saint Laurent's Baby Doll, probably, though it's beyond me why anyone pays good money to smell like weak lemonade. Then again, a girlish dress sense sometimes goes hand-in-hand with a taste for aggressively sexy fragrances. My money's on Chanel's heavy spicy Coco — or, if her vamp instincts involve tuberose and are of the come-hither-and-do-it-NOW variety, Dior's Poison. But no, she's passed both Chanel and Dior, she's heading my way, and Baby Doll it is. Why don't people wear good old-fashioned spikenard ointment anymore? Wonderful stuff, spikenard, but does anyone come into Saks and ask for it? Not in my lifetime. ("I'm sorry, madam, but Baby Doll has been discontinued. I think you can still find it online. Try Fragrance.net.")

Black raw-silk sheath dress, sleek black chignon, cranberry-red lips from Nars or maybe Trish McEvoy. And oh, what delectable little Jimmy Choo heels! She's a bit more of a challenge, but the category is clear: classic and pricey. Very pricey. Clive Christian No.1, if she knows that it is advertised as the most expensive perfume in the world. Or Joy, if she's heard Jackie O. wore it.

Just for fun I'll show her that limited edition Baccarat bottle for $1500. ("Thank you madam, and may I congratulate you on your choice? The Baccarat is a collector's item.")

Oh Lordy, look at *this* one — thin-lipped, thin-bodied, tweedily genteel in a vintage mulberry-colored Jaeger suit. All she needs is the famous flamingo brooch, and the Duchess of Windsor is back from the grave. Unquestionably Youth Dew time. How did she miss the Estee Lauder counter anyway? Ah, Emile's with her. She must be Somebody. Or Somebody's Wife.

"Magda, darling, would you assist *mademoiselle* with a Caron perfume? Narcisse Noir, I believe."

Oops. Miscalculated this time. And how attentive Emile is, smiling fiercely and flattering her with *mademoiselle*, his hand hovering at her withered elbow. He can't stand her. He'll imitate her. Mercilessly.

"Delighted to be of assistance," I murmur, and Emile heads back to Lancôme with the insolent swagger of a model. His trousers drape fluidly from his narrow hips, and his buttocks have elegant but well-defined curves. He must be working out again. I only hope his little Marty is as appreciative as I am. I tell the Duchess of Windsor that Narcisse Noir is one of my personal favorites even though this is absolutely not true. The sweet, festered-lily stink of Persian black narcissus makes my nasal passages shut down. Besides, I dislike any perfume made with even synthetic civet. But the bottle design is from 1912, and ravishingly gorgeous. Late Art Nouveau.

"Well," the Duchess says with a slight flare of her thoroughbred nostrils. "I don't like it at all, frankly. I just buy it out of loyalty to Ernest Daltroff. He was devoted to my grandmother and created the perfume with her in mind."

"Ah." I feel rebuffed for my polite lie. I also refuse to be impressed.

"I don't care for scent in general," she says. "I never have."

"Ah." I now decide the Duchess of Windsor is One Unholy Bitch. Really. Because the fact is, good scent has genuine spiritual meaning. Where do people think the high-church love of incense comes from anyway? The great Christian tradition. The "odor of sanctity." The sweet smell that distinguished the personal presence of saints. The delicious floral perfume of St. Veronica Giuliani's stigmata that permeated her entire cloister. The trademark scent of violets that clung to the tomb of St. Catherine de Ricci for years after her death even though her body was encased in a lead coffin. Everyone knows that warlocks, wizards, and all the exceptionally evil emit a horrible smell. Noisome Philistines! And then there's poor St. Catherine of Siena who almost died of suffocation in the malodorous presence of a notorious sinner and had to be carried from the room... Okay, I know the Duchess doesn't actually smell *bad*, but her lack of appreciation isn't much to her credit. At least her disgust of scent in general means she doesn't like — or worse yet, wear — the appalling Thierry Mugler Angel. I tend to think one whiff of Angel and poor tender-nosed St. Catherine would've given somebody an outraged slap.

"Are there any fragrances you like at all?" I ask the Duchess as I wait for her American Express card to ring through. "Even just a little?"

"Only one," she says, and an impish, albeit thin-lipped, grin cracks the lacquered perfection of her makeup. "The sweet smell of success."

Disarmed, I burst out laughing. How wonderful it is, this excuse for laughter. And how equally wonderful this sensation behind my breastbone: a great sparkling flood released from some deep river-vein of joy. I know I often talk like work is Hell, but I will freely confess that I'm just conforming, just trying to keep my little euphoric surges under control. And, more importantly, unnoticed. I don't want other people to realize that for me the Saks perfume department represents mountains of myrrh, hills of frankincense, orchards of fruit, and beds of herbs and spices. I don't want to realize it myself, most of the time. Because I do have mixed feelings about who I am and what I do. Given the choice, I'd rather be a person of more serious, substantive talents — a history professor, maybe, or a medical doctor in a developing country. A Brain or a Heart has infinitely more gravitas than a mere Nose.

"It wasn't *that* funny." The Duchess's voice is dry, but her grin widens delightedly as her eyes meet mine. I can tell she is not in the habit of making people laugh, and is pleased with herself. For a frivolous moment I think maybe Saks is actually so far from Hell that it's Heaven — and I feel again that occasional, eerie rending of some important veil. Though peculiar (and it is always, inevitably that!), my rent-veil sensation is not so rare that I'm thrown off balance by it. But today there is more. Today I hear something as well. A voice, a distant voice, speaks words that seem directed at me — or maybe someone very close by: "This day you shall be with me in Paradise." I glance up at the high white ceiling, half-expecting to see deep fractures zigzag down the plastered arches and bright bulbs explode from the tactful recessed lighting. Half-expecting to hear a gusty drumroll of thunder and the glorious blare of a dozen trumpets. None of this happens and I feel a little ridiculous that my legs have gone weak at the knees. I hand the glossy little shopping bag to the Duchess, take a deep breath, and say, "When you invent a perfume called The Sweet Smell of Success, count on me to buy a bottle."

"That'll be in my next life, when I'm reincarnated as a perfumer," she replies. "You know how some people are tone deaf? Well, I'm scent deaf. I was born that way."

As I watch her head for the escalator, I lean my elbows against the counter. We're not supposed to do this for fear of smudging the glass or endangering expensive merchandise — and God forbid the manager sees me! — but my legs are still wobbly. Besides, I get nervous when people make jokes about reincarnation. I realize they don't mean anything by it, that it's just part of casual modern discourse. But I still don't like it. Last year one of the bigwigs from Guerlain was here to lecture on "The Perfumer's Art," and he asked several us to try to determine the composition of one of the more obscure Guerlain scents, Vol de Nuit. My ability to do this ("Top notes are definitely bergamot, orange blossom, mandarin, lemon. Then jonquil — I think that bitter greeny note must be galbanum — and then aldehydes of some kind, oak moss — um, a little orris, very high quality and probably Italian orris- ") had excited him into offering me a job on the spot. "You are a Nose, Mademoiselle!" he had cried. "The first real Nose I've encountered in twenty years. We need you in Paris!" I was flattered, even briefly tempted, until he said, "You must have been a perfumer in a former life. A French perfumer, *naturellement*. Maybe even our great founder, Pierre-Francois-Pascal Guerlain himself." He seemed so perfectly serious, even fanatical, about this possibility that a coldness shivered down my spine. I rejected his offer so emphatically that he was offended and gave me a lecture on the irresponsibility — the immorality, *enfin*! — of squandering a remarkable gift.

"Magda, my love, my sweetest one, my dove."

I start, whisk my elbows off the glass, and glare suspiciously at Emile. He doesn't usually waste his fulsome endearments on his colleagues. He's too tired out from catering to the expectations of a certain kind of lady shopper by fulfilling a certain stereotype of gay behavior even though he isn't gay. ("How they do adore feeling titillated and daring and tolerant all at once!" he says. "And how I adore the way my sales go up, even though the act gets tedious.") I wonder what he wants. Lancôme must be really slow today — and why not, since the whole store is — but I think he's up to something.

"Planet Magda must be a really interesting place," he observes. "Did that old Narcisse Noir bat get to you or something? Her suit was as ancient as she was, I swear. And talk about Eau de Mothballs!"

"Don't be ridiculous," I snap, suddenly much offended by the mindless arrogance of the young, the unlined, and the gorgeously fit. "That was just good oldfashioned Pears soap. I know the difference, I promise you."

"Of course you do," he flares back. "Mademoiselle Magda of the Magnificent Nose!"

Poor Emile. There's nothing he'd like better than a glamorous job in Paris with Guerlain, and he hasn't forgiven me for casually rejecting an opportunity he will never have. Emile is wonderful with color, appreciates the infinite subtleties of different beige-toned foundations the way an Eskimo is said to distinguish variations in snow, but he's hopeless with scent. Once I actually heard him tell a client that Lancôme's floral semi-oriental Trésor had "a sort of fresh green smell, like a newly-mown lawn." I like him, though. And I like his little Marty too. They were high school sweethearts and ten years later they're still going strong, which is pleasant to see in our world of short-lived loyalties. But that doesn't mean I'm in the mood to hear him trash old ladies just because they're old. I'm not as young as I used to be either.

"Spikenard," I say meditatively. "For some reason I woke up today thinking about spikenard."

Emile's beautifully arched brows lift, and he says, "What's spikenard?"

"An aromatic plant substance from way back when," I tell him. "They used to put it in expensive ointments or perfumes. Just imagine: once upon a time you went to your friendly neighborhood apothecary and said, 'Listen, mix me up a little jar of spikenard cream, would you, Gaius Octavius Augustus?' And no snotty, critical people like us intimidated you with unbelievably high prices or bewildered you with hundreds of choices or openly jeered at your fashion sense." Emile looks hurt, opens his mouth — and I rush on. "Now don't take it personally, Emile. I was just thinking how it used to be, that's all."

"Like you really know, Mrs. Methuselah!" Emile snorts. Then he pats my arm and says, "Never mind, Magda darling, my dove, my sweet. I'm going bonkers too. It's the lack of customers. First dry sunny day in weeks, and nobody wants to be inside. Including me." A significant pause. "Especially me."

"So that's it," I say gleefully. "You want to take a long lunch, and you want me to cover for you."

Emile looks both pained at my bluntness and embarrassed by his own transparency. He explains that, well, as a matter of fact, darling Marty has the day off. Darling Marty has just called from Whole Foods where she has picked up brie, paté, and french bread. They've both been just absolutely perishing for a picnic, he tells me soulfully. And he'll make it up to me, of course — doesn't he always? — so what do I think?

I think he and Marty are lucky, adorable, and straight out of the Hebrew poets. *Rise up, my love, my fair one, and come away. For, lo, the winter is past…*

"Come on, Magda. Please? Pretty please?"

I surface. I say, "Yes, all right, if you really are perishing." And I hope to God I haven't been mumbling from the *Song of Solomon* out loud.

Emile rushes off to phone Marty. I sell a bottle of Fracas to a frail-looking older man in a conservative suit and cannot help speculating about his private life. Then there is a long lull, broken only by one irritable young woman who just can't *believe* we don't carry Paris Hilton's Tease and goes off in a huff. Emile leaves with a grateful wave, and I divide my time between Fragrances and the Lancôme counter. Even so, there isn't enough going on to keep me busy, so I amuse myself by spraying Caron's Parfum Sacré on my wrist and taking judicious sniffs. A fairly good quality rose absolute, musk, incense — hmm, can that be a tiny hint of pepper? — and, ah yes, myrrh. I do so love myrrh. It isn't used in scent as much as it could be. Though there is Oscar de la Renta, I guess, and Jil Sander No.4. Serge Lutens' gorgeous La Myrrhe, of course. I wander back to Lancôme, catch a glimpse of myself in a makeup mirror and decide my face could do with some color. I try a tiny dab of the new highlighting cream Emile is so enthusiastic about on my browbone, then apply a little orchid-colored shadow on my lids. I admire the results in the hand mirror. It's gratifying to realize I could still turn heads if I felt like making the effort. I don't feel like it though, not as a rule, which annoys all the Saks makeup gurus who palpably itch to get their hands on my makeup-free face. Emile says I'm not living up to my advertising potential and one of these days the management will probably apply a little pressure. As I study my face from another angle, guiltily pleased that my cheekbones are still to-die-for (not that anybody ever did, of course, but certainly some very extravagant things were said), I tilt the mirror just a little to the right. And feel all the blood, all the warmth and color, leave my face. *Oh Duchess, no. Please no.*

For there she is, my Duchess, standing close up against the wall with the built-in shelving that holds all the marvelous Annick Goutal fragrances. There she is, ostensibly examining one of the larger trademark cream-and-gold eau de toilette boxes in her right hand while her left hand slips a smaller box into the inside lining of her unbuttoned Jaeger suitjacket. There she is, about to be caught — although she doesn't know it. For I can have security here in ten seconds. If, that is, they aren't already on their way. The Duchess can have no idea about that huge bank of video screens in the Security Room downstairs. Nor can the Duchess realize that the new Head of Security, for all the disaffection suggested by his greasy ponytail and ragged black jeans, is a tremendously earnest thief-catcher who likes nothing better than watching those screens right through his lunch hour. ("He doesn't trust us," his two assistants tell anyone who will listen, which is why we all know so much about the new Head. "He's so afraid we'll miss something that he doesn't drink fluids all day so he won't have to break for a leak.") The Duchess is about to be arrested for stealing perfume, and the Duchess is — or so she claims — scent deaf.

Instead of discreetly pressing the alarm, I leave the Lancôme counter at an unhurried pace. I cross the shining floor toward her, and even from a distance I see the galloping of the pulse in the chic scrawniness of her neck. My hands are trembling so much that I clench them behind my back like a guilty child, and I have no idea what I will do or say until I stop in front of her and ask very quietly, "Which one, Duchess."

"Folavril," she replies.

"Why?"

"It smells like pomegranates."

"No it doesn't," I say, taken aback. "It's jasmine. And mango and tomato leaf."

"Maybe. But it's pomegranate too. All at once I could smell

it." The Duchess is suddenly and strangely radiant. "I could feel it in my nose, taste it on my tongue — like champagne. And it's fabulous."

She's right. I can smell it myself now, and it is fabulous, and it is definitely pomegranate. Invisible waves of pomegranate swirl around us so that I am dizzied. *How much better than wine is the smell of thine ointments*...isn't that how it goes? I think so, yes... *The pomegranates have budded, the orchard is pleasant with fruit, with camphire, with saffron, with spikenard*...

Striving for the prosaic, I say, "How much did you spray on yourself anyway?"

"None," the Duchess replies simply. "I just sniffed it from the bottle."

Never in my life have I been at such a loss. Never have I been so uncertain about the rightness or wrongness of things. Why should the Duchess experience this — this miracle? And why should she celebrate it by stealing? Since our vigilant Security has not arrived after all, judgment is up to me — and I am no fit person to do it. I have never been the judging kind, which may be the main reason why I haven't aspired to one of those substantive Brain and Heart professions. No, I ought to qualify that; I am the judging kind, really, but I don't judge out loud and I don't judge with a view to punishment. The very thought sickens and disorients me. I know how it feels to be judged *out loud*. I even know what it is to grow *comfortable* with the role of The Judgee, to feel that I have actually found my proper niche in the world. Honestly, you should have heard those men on the subject of my spikenard ointment wickedness alone. A flamboyant display, they said. A prideful gesture with no true repentance behind it. A sinful waste, they said, when with good management forty orphans might have lived for forty days on that money. And they picked up the lustrous shards of the alabaster jar and waved them accusingly in my face...

"You're not going to faint on me, are you?" There is wonderment in the Duchess's old blue eyes as she grips my arm.

The veil is well and truly rent at last. And I am furious.

"No, I most certainly am not," I tell her firmly. "I'm going to aid and abet. I'm going to be an accessory — or whatever it's called."

"Why?"

"Because I think He's got an absolutely rotten sense of humor. I was standing right there when He told the thief on His left that he'd be with Him in Paradise. And me? What happens to me?" I stab my breastbone with my forefinger. "Well, I'll tell you. Saks happens to me, for God's sake! A Nose happens to me! Century after century of Saks — or its equivalent — and here's what I'd like to know: Is the Saks Fragrance Department any kind of substitute for Paradise?"

The Duchess's lips twitch as she says, "I shouldn't think so, dear."

I can't tell if her twitch is from amusement or nervous alarm, and I don't much care. I sweep on, tumbling my feelings into words: "He was always saying I took myself and my sins far too seriously — but even so! To play a joke like this on me, century after century — why, it's mean. It's perverse. Under His circumstances, I'd even say it's thoroughly deviant behavior, don't you agree?"

"I don't really understand perverse or deviant," the Duchess says calmly. "This is the most deviant few minutes I've ever spent in my life, and I suspect it doesn't even count since it was sort of an — an hysterical reaction. Because I honestly never did smell anything before, and this pomegranate-"

Her voice is almost reverent, and I stare at her for a moment. Stare at her hard, and pityingly. However privileged, however well-connected and respected, the Duchess has missed out. She has never used her favorite mortar and pestle of Egyptian marble to make the best spikenard ointment in Israel. Never scampered across the steep green hillsides of Capri gleefully collecting the spicy wild carnations exclusive to the island. Never picked French jasmine by night, sightlessly following the blissful scent from bloom to bloom. Never made her own attar of Bulgarian rose in her own Balkan castle stillroom, her fingers redolent and her spirits high for days afterwards. Never been apprenticed to the monks at The Farmacia di Santa Maria Novella, perfumers to the Medicis, and entrusted with secret recipes and priceless essences. Never been the artist behind the Empress Josephine's favorite musk cologne. Never helped the great Balzac create his own customized scent. Or Sarah Bernhardt. Such a terribly demanding and finicky woman, the Divine Sarah, but once I steered her in the direction of *rose de mai*, she was as sweet as...

My God, I *have* been a Nose at Guerlain.

I give the Duchess's thin arm a gentle pat. I tell her to enjoy her purchase. I tell her that if she should ask for me next time she comes in, I'll give her a free 2.5 ounce tube of Annick Goutal's Eau d'Hadrien lotion, which smells like a Sicilian lemon grove with a few cypress and grapefruit trees thrown in.

And as she heads for the exit, I say aloud, to the ceiling, "Alright, very funny. And maybe You were right. If you are penitent — truly and really — I might, just might, forgive you!"

THE EISENHOWER JACKET

IF I EVER GET MINE, the odds are it won't fit. Reidar Jonsson, the tailor on Clark and Summerdale, says men with my rangy build always wear clothes well, but he can never resist adding that it's a pity I'm so shortwaisted. At least he is more tactful about it than Mother. "Built like a spider, you are, Nils," she says. "All legs and no body. So unlike your *pappa lilla*, who was exceptionally well-proportioned even though he wasn't a tall man." Yes, it's inevitable: someone will have to remove a good two inches from above the waistband. But I won't let just any tailor do it, and I'll keep the strip of spare fabric too. You never know when a piece of good thick wool will come in handy — like now, for example. I could wrap it around my head for warmth. It would be better than nothing.

Hours pass, perhaps many of them, perhaps not. I cannot guess how long I have hunched within the spreading shelter of these snow-weighted branches, nor can I guess how long I will have to do so. My watch broke when I slipped on the near-frozen creekbed. Daylight seems so long ago, and the darkness so unending and complete. Not that there'd have been a moon anyway, but if the atmosphere had been clearer the radios might have worked in spite of heavy forest and rugged terrain. And if the radios had worked, I might have had a better sense of where

I was and avoided that goddamn creek (*fy-da!* my father would have said in a sweet tone of gentle reproof, for shame!) full of large slick stones. I figure I'm very close to the hamlet of Sadzot, maybe a half-mile south of Briscol, but I can't be certain. My only certainty is that I've lost the rest of the 2nd Battalion, or they've lost me, and there's nothing to do but to try to sit tight and make it till morning without freezing. My CO will think I'm a *dumbom*, and I don't wholly blame him. And O'Connor, if he's still alive, will seize the opportunity to fire a few more rounds from his arsenal of Sven-the-Slow-Witted-Swede jokes.

A small gust of wind sends a few clumps of soft, heavy snow down on my bare head. I reach up one gloved hand to brush it away, but do so with as contained a motion as possible. Above all I must keep still, so that no one will hear the faintest crackling of iced-over snow and suspect my presence. The atmosphere may be dense, moisture-laden, and the night darker than the inside of a suitcase, but I know that every soldier in this bit of forest is just as much on the defensive as I am, just as afraid for his life. I am as likely to be shot by another American as I am by a German. I wriggle slightly against the rough, unyielding trunk of the great fir tree. My gratitude for the low drooping branches is is almost as deep as the snow; they remind me of hiding behind my mother's fullskirted apron, something I haven't thought of in twenty-five years. Later in the night, when staying alert is more difficult, I'll set myself the task of sawing off a few of the smaller branches that crowd my head and force my shoulders and upper back into a forward curve. I'll have to do it with my pocketknife, and very slowly so as not to risk any audible rustlings. But there is time. Time to try to make sure all my actions are performed with the proper care and caution.

A distant shout, a burst of gunfire — but from which direction? Southerly, perhaps? I'm not sure. I wish I could smoke; even that tiny warmth would mean something to my fingers and face. But of course it isn't possible. I'm just going to have to huddle against this tree trunk and feel for all the world as if I'm back in the church pews of my childhood, restless in body and fatigued in spirit. And my swollen knee throbs hotly on despite the cold, despite the occasional frigid gust of wind, despite the knapsack I've placed carefully beneath it to bear some of the weight.

The CO says General Eisenhower doesn't approve of nicknames, but what does he know? Has he actually met the General? Has he heard the General say "Wool Field Jacket, M-1944" with his very own ears? That tailor O'Connor found to cut down his woollen coat to an Ike jacket did a fine job. A snug fit at the waist, but full enough in the shoulders to allow for freedom of movement — and he even got the pocket flaps right. I think the color is wrong though; it's a bit too yellow. Mine will be a cross between nut-brown and juniper-green. And I think I'll postpone any alterations till the war is over and I can take it to Reidar Jonsson. A good fellow on the whole, Reidar. A member of the Harald Viking Lodge, and famous for having gone on several dates with Gloria Swanson before she left Andersonville, met Charlie Chaplin, and got famous herself. Reidar used to attend the Swedish Mission Church, so he must know about what went on, but he's never acted like my family is a matter of local gossip. Yes, I would trust him absolutely with my jacket.

From out in the darkness comes a faint but disturbing sound. Animal or human, I cannot tell, but it's something between a moan and a whine. The very hairs on my head would stand to attention if they weren't so damn frozen. Strange how at the age of thirty-five I still feel I ought to apologize to my father for saying damn — not that I believe in eternal damnation and hellfire. If there is a hell, I'd bet it's cold rather than hot. But I am sure there isn't; such a concept goes against my atheistic grain.

I have the foolish thought that it might be a St. Bernard out there in the soot-pocked snow bearing a small container of revivifying spirits. I permit myself a small fantasy: three St. Bernards carrying three different aquavits flavored with that Holy Trinity that I, like many self-respecting Swedes, do genuinely believe in: dill, cardamom, and caraway. Caraway's my favorite, really. Fiercely aromatic. The alcohol would warm me, however temporarily, and the smell would keep me wide awake.

I issue a few reminders to myself: Nils, wiggle your toes. Flex the calf muscles on your left leg. Twist your torso slowly to the left, then to the right. Shrug your shoulders three times.

Any colder and I'll be one of the poor stiffs I've seen scattering the blackened snow for the past few days. Even in the darkness I can still picture them, especially the small ones wearing long coats too big for them. The Germans must be desperate if they're sending little boys to the front lines, but it's meagre comfort. The little boys have better guns than we do.

What would be comfort, and not at all meagre, is a hot meal. My last meal was many hours ago, and even then it wasn't much, and it certainly wasn't hot. The one lone chocolate bar in my knapsack isn't going to keep me going for long. At least it's decent chocolate. I won it off Gary, that new recruit from Gary, Indiana, whose real name I somehow never learned because we played cards in silence. Sometimes you talk and sometimes, dizzy with fatigue and cold, you can't open your mouth if your life depends on it. Two nights ago we were pretty talkative, having been joined by O'Connor's best buddy with the 28th Division. He'd survived December 16th, the first day of the German assault, because a Belgian farmer had given him shelter after he got separated from his unit. "What's more," O'Connor's buddy told us, "His wife gave me two bowls of the most delicious soup." Raptly, you might even say reverently, he had described a thick split pea soup studded with great chunks of potato, carrot, celery. "There were leeks in it too, and herbs and spices I'd never tasted before," he went on. "Even — and I swear this on the Holy Virgin — bits of dried lavender. You know, that stuff girls keep in their bureau drawers. It was the most spectacular soup on earth." After such a grand claim, battle had been joined on the matter of spectacular soups. I mounted an attack, waving the banner of my mother's rutabega soup. O'Connor counterattacked. "Food like that stinks of peasant poverty," he said. "It's the kind of food people get nostalgic about when they don't have to eat it any more." Then he boldly advanced the merits of cabbage soup, drawing fire about pots calling kettles black, and after that the fellow from Louisiana, the farmer from Iowa, and the Bostonian radio operator seemed on the verge of hand-to-hand combat over a peppery shrimp-and-okra soup, corn chowder, and oyster stew. Faces reddened, eyes glistened, hands waved and gestured. And then we'd all suddenly lapsed into a strange and hostile silence, as if too much had been said. Last night, of course, we talked very little; and when at midnight the attack came, I had the odd thought we'd all somehow sensed it coming and chosen to husband our energy.

I wrap my arms around my torso and hug myself hard for a long shivery moment. Rumor has it the 289th Infantry's going to be getting a shipment of Ike jackets soon, but how many will get to the 2nd Battalion is anyone's guess. The General sure does look snappy in his — although you have to wonder why he's always got his hands on his hips. Maybe he's just comfortable that way, or maybe photographers just routinely catch him in the act of giving some poor SOB a tongue-lashing. But I've noticed that his tie is always beautifully knotted, exactly the right amount of it showing above his top jacket button. And the waistband button never seems to be straining like it does on some people — that fellow from Gary, Indiana, for example, who's got enough fat to keep him warm in just a singlet. How do they decide who gets them first, anyway? It can't be based on need; my M-1943 field jacket — no, let's call it what it is, an M-1943 windbreaker — is the shabbiest in the battalion. The thinnest fabric too, even with that double-layer wool-blanket lining I sewed into it last month. (The stitches are unravelling already; why Mother never taught me to sew I'll never know. In a war, men need sewing skills almost as much as they need strong chests, good vision, and feet that aren't flat.)

The silence is of such a blown-glass purity that when I hear again that faint moan I am jerked into an almost intolerable state of fear. So abject a sound shouldn't terrify me, and yet it does. Every childhood fright ever endured rises up within me, and ghosts surround me, great apocalyptic ghosts prophesying humiliation, loss, and doom from which I cannot possibly be saved.

At the age of eight I was, in fact, thoroughly and publicly saved. I don't choose to think about it much, but my father's dummy saved me at an evangelistic service at the Swedish Mission Church in our Chicago neighborhood, Andersonville. It was nearing eight o'clock in the evening, but because of the recently instituted War Savings Time, I could see the still-bright sky outside. A summer sky daubed here and there with pink and green above flat apartment roofs sealed with heat-softened, mildly odorous pitch.

"Now listen, Nils," Mother hissed. "Keep your eyes on your father and set an example!"

And I did just that, watching him with an avid absorption. My father's presence in our own church was a rarity. His presence in general was a rarity, as he was much in demand as a travelling evangelist. But here he was now, this evangelist, this Reverend Nils Forsberg Senior who was also my father, seated upon a chair on the platform just a few yards away. His fine blond hair flopped across his forehead and the one-sided smile on his thin face radiated warmth and good will.

"Oh dear, he's forgotten his hair pomade again," Mother said in a resigned whisper.

I scarcely heard her, so fierce was my concentration, so deep my awe. For my father could do more than preach the Lord's Salvation and Second Coming. My father could talk like a completely different person, his tones high and sweet as a child's, and all this with his mouth shut!

"I'd like to introduce my young friend Harold," my father was saying. "Harold is delighted to be with you this evening" — an attentive look at the blond dummy seated on his knee — "Aren't you, Harold, my boy?"

And Harold, fortunate Harold, sat there completely at ease in his blue striped summer suit — an exact replica of the one my father wore, both made by a local tailor — and beamed all across his wide wooden face.

"It's a privilege to serve the Lord in my small way," Harold said, his red mouth opening and closing with a magical, abrupt energy. "Welcome to Child Evangelism Night! How do you do, children?"

Childish giggles seemed to float up like clouds against the sanctuary's sky-blue ceiling. I giggled too, even though I knew my father was making Harold talk. Harold couldn't talk by himself; he was just a doll (albeit a blessed, witnessing doll) who accompanied my father on his journeys all cooped up in a black leather suitcase with a miniature wardrobe that my mother kept clean and freshly ironed. But I had never actually seen my father and Harold work together, and I was captivated by the obvious affection between them. My father smiled at Harold, bounced him on his knee, pretended to ruffle his golden painted hair. My father spoke in a rich warm voice, not the tired, gravelly voice he soothed with honey-sweetened tea whenever he was at home between engagements. I leaned forward and curled my hands over the varnished top of the pew in front of me as my father and Harold talked about Shoeless Joe Jackson's yellow-bellied decision not to go to Europe and fight. About local architect Mr. Frank Lloyd Wright, who had just scuttled off to Japan to build the Imperial Hotel and avoid the war. About Jane Addams' trip to the Hague and her interfering efforts to stop the war altogether. About fellow evangelist Billy Sunday who had recently said, "If you turn hell upside down, you will find 'Made in Germany' stamped on the bottom." And, most particularly, my father and Harold talked about all those brave men fighting the war from airplanes. Harold, bouncing up and down with glee, expressed a desire to fly airplanes and shoot down German pilots when he grew up.

"But did you know, Harold, that even young boys and girls can be brave and fight wars too?"

Harold said no, he didn't, in his highest, squeakiest voice, and my father said he would explain it and Harold must listen very carefully like the bright boy he was. So my father told Harold all about Spiritual Trench Warfare and how boys and girls had to Hold Fast the Line by crawling through the No-Man's-Land of temptation, by returning Enemy Fire, by struggling bravely Over the Top despite the danger.

"And who do you think this Enemy is, Harold?" my father asked.

Harold said nothing, and as the silence continued my father's face went long and grave. The snufflings of summer colds ceased, and even the adults held their breath. I watched Harold droop ever so slightly upon my father's knee.

"Harold?" My father's voice had lost its cozy warmth. He sounded grieved, distressed. "Put your thinking cap on, my boy!"

Even Harold's black bow tie seemed to slump with shame, but still he said nothing. The first shadows of evening crept across the hardwood floor, inched up the platform riser, up my father's black leather pumps, up his striped pant leg toward poor Harold. In another second the shadow would obliterate Harold's large blue eyes, his round rosy cheeks, his red mouth. I could not bear Harold's silence, the imminent destruction of Harold's brightness and glory. Panic blurred the suited figures on the stage and the ceiling seemed to press down upon my chest, but somehow I was on his feet. "It's Satan, Harold!" I was shouting, clutching the curved pew before me with sweating hands. "Listen, the Enemy is Satan!"

The three ringletted Sholund girls across the aisle collapsed giggling upon each others' shoulders, and the next moment the entire congregation had joined them. I sank back onto the hard pew and stared at the floor so I wouldn't have to see my father's well-mannered fury or my mother's embarrassment. Why had I made a fool of myself for stupid old Harold? Stupid old Harold didn't need any help from me. Dummy or not, Harold had my father's complete attention. And all at once Mother's thin hand gripped my upper arm. "Never mind, Nils *lilla*, " she told me. "Some people are just — just profligate with their laughter."

Although uncertain of her meaning, I was heartened by her rare sympathy. I glanced up at my father and was at once relieved and astonished to see that he was laughing along with everyone else. Then I had a dim suspicion that my father had to be good-humored about it or the laughter could be turned against him. He could end up looking far from "God's Proven Hero in the War for Souls," which was Pastor Reinhold Lundeen's respectful title for him.

After what seemed a very long time, the laughter subsided save for an occasional snort, and my father observed to Harold that King Solomon once said, "Laughter doeth the soul good, like medicine," and he was sure Harold liked a good laugh as well as anyone.

"I should think so!" Harold exclaimed, and went off in a high-pitched fit of silly giggles that I would never get away with in a million years.

"But now, Harold, now we are going to settle down and be very serious," my father said in a gently reproachful voice.

"Yes, indeed!" Harold said, nodding his head. "We're going to talk about how you children can counter Satan's attacks." And he went on to describe the field of battle, the shells and hand-grenades of temptation that Satan sent our juvenile way ("For aren't we all tempted to lie, to covet, to be insolent to our parents?") and the defeated, faithless children lying senseless in the desolate spiritual landscape. Harold's high voice quavered with sincerity and my father watched and listened with grave attention.

"The first step toward victory is up to you, boys and girls," Harold said. "You need to accept the Lord Jesus as your Commanding Officer and pray to Him for strength and guidance."

Both Harold and my father looked suddenly very military, like General Pershing in the newspapers, and I realized I would follow them anywhere. I would even cross those barbed-wire-infested fields in France, hide in those mud-and-rat-ridden trenches, make daring rescues of fallen comrades. Whatever they asked of me, I would do to the utmost of my ability. And now, at this very moment, they were asking me to come forward, to forsake sin and publicly enlist in God's army.

"Who among you children will be the first to join us at the

Front?" Harold asked, fixing me with his bright blue eyes. "Who will dare to be bold and brave and committed, despite 'the terror by night and the arrow that flieth by day?'"

"I will," I shouted, and headed for the center aisle, scrambling over Mother's narrow, black-clad knees. "Please, Harold. Please let me be the first!"

And I was. My father smiled, and my father's dummy glowed with happiness all the way down to his tiny, made-to-order, patent-leather shoes.

I suppose it must be a very high-class sort of tailor who makes the General's uniforms. And the wool used for his jackets is probably a quality of wool I've never even seen before. A whole inch thick, I shouldn't wonder. Maybe even soft to the touch, like the CO's. The CO, now, he knows enough to give his a good, thorough brushing. That idiot O'Connor doesn't bother with brushing even though I've told him the fabric will withstand the weather better if he does.

Will the sleeves be long enough? Yet another disadvantage of being built like a spider. If they aren't long enough, that strip of fabric some tailor will have to remove from around the waist might come in handy. Though I must say I don't want to look like I'm wearing one of Mother's crazy quilts, all random bits and pieces. In photos, at least, the General never looks anything less than natty.

That unearthly moaning has stopped at last, and I consider poking my head out from my fortress of branches. A stupid notion, there's no doubt about it. I won't be able to see anything unless I use my flashlight, and that could bring gunfire from anyone still alive and able to pull a trigger. But a pressure is building in my chest, a pressure I have been warned about and know I must resist if I want to survive. Don't do anything impulsive, I remind myself; impulsive acts are dangerous acts. Breathe in deeply, hold that knifelike air, hold it, hold it — and then breathe out. Do it again. And again. Then a few more exercises: flex those toes — especially the ones on the left foot, the ones that have, in the past few days, taken on a sickly mushroom pallor beneath the grime. I can't help thinking my father had it easy in Cuba all those years ago; I'm sure I'd rather have malaria than frostbite any day. Not that my father actually got malaria. All he got was a ball in the shoulder after a few weeks and then a hero's welcome back in Andersonville where every Swedish family with unmarried daughters wooed him with homemade potato sausage, veal meatballs in cream sauce, and *tusenbladstarta* dripping with applesauce and cinnamon. My mother won. Anyone who's eaten her *tusenbladstarta* understands why, but it was her marzipan cake that I loved most as a boy. I can see her now, grinding almonds with her mortar and pestle, mouth compressed in a tight dry seam but temples damp. Her rare and rising joy was wonderful to see: slowly, slowly, her mouth would soften, take on a slight upward curve, and at last she would begin to hum — always hymns, of course, but the bouncier ones, the ones with Swedish folk melodies. *Var store Gud* was her favorite even though she sang alto in the church choir and the last line had a few high notes that many sopranos couldn't reach. My mother beat butter and sugar in time to her humming, cracked eggs with an energetic flourish, even tapped one foot as she sifted flour. The cooling cake scented the whole house with vanilla, a thick butter-fattened vanilla. I didn't want to wait. A slice, mamma? Just one? You know better than that, Nils *lilla*. Your father gets the first slice, always, no exceptions. And so I waited, and after the cake had cooled completely I would sit at the kitchen table, my mouth running with anticipatory juices, watching my mother decorate the glossy marzipan surface with wild strawberries. As I watched the faint spreading pinkness from the strawberries, I wondered if, while my mother's back was turned, I might be able to give it the tiniest lick with my tongue. Once before I had managed it, licking the marzipan with such fervor that I'd left a slight depression which I'd glossed over with spittle on my index fingers and a few more strawberries from the back yard. Later I took a shamed glee in watching my father choose the piece of cake with the most strawberries. Had I known he would do that?

I wriggle my spine against the tree trunk and worry that I am feverish. Perhaps my knee has made me feverish, perhaps exposure (what I wouldn't give to have my steel helmet, but it's somewhere near that creek). Perhaps it's just the thought of marzipan cake. I find I'm also slightly aroused. O'Connor is always talking about sex, working himself into what he calls a blue balls frenzy by reminiscing about various girlfriends and his own stamina, but I sometimes get hard thinking about food. Even foods I'm not fond of, like devilled eggs and blood sausage. It's odd to be reminded, if only for a moment or two, that my body is a source of pleasure as well as pain. For so long pleasure, especially sexual pleasure, has seemed a pre-war fairytale best forgotten.

A tremor in the earth unnerves me. What is the cause? Surely the panzer division at Grandménil isn't on the move at — what — two, maybe three, in the morning? It could be bombers, I suppose. Last week the fogbound sky was empty of bombers, but in the past few days the sky has been slowly filling up again. Allied Flying Fortresses, mostly. But O'Connor, who is always somehow in the know, says not to get our hopes up because the Germans have just successfully tried out a new kind of aircraft, a bomber that is jet-propelled. I hope this is just O'Connor's bleak imagination at work but I cannot deny the German gift for innovation. Yesterday I saw several dead German soldiers wearing uniforms that were white from head to toe. They blended so beautifully into the snow that I very nearly tripped over them. It was the blood amid the white that stopped me at the last possible moment from treating them like a great mound of snow to be trudged through; a seeping red had stained the snow beneath an improbably-bent leg, from which protuded a thick, jagged bit of bone.

Now I wonder if the tremor I felt was exterior. Perhaps it came from within me, a shuddery shiver of the kind I strive hard to repress. I can't afford those kinds of shivers; they are weakening, exhausting, make me want to sleep. Once I give in to them, my chances of surviving til morning will be significantly lessened.

I am now certain the tremor was internal, and cold-induced. When I get my Eisenhower jacket I'm going to mail my M-1943 to the bastard who invented it. I hope he burns — no, freezes — in hell for all eternity. I hope he ends up being terrorized by the Great Red Dragon with seven heads and ten horns in the twelfth chapter of the Book of Revelation. I hope that the hideous Beast rising out of the sea uttering blasphemies swallows him up, that the Wormwood Star falls on his head, that the Abomination of Desolation pays him an indescribably painful visit. (What is the Abomination of Desolation anyway? I can't remember.)

Pressure is building in my chest, building, surging, climbing, until I am convinced that my whole body is swelling with it. My chest feels twice its usual size, and so does my neck, my head. Even my tongue has thickened in my mouth. My skin can't sustain the pressure, and the beating of my heart has become a great throbbing in my ears. I must act — I must.

I do not remember grabbing my flashlight and rising up and hurling myself through the branches and into the waist-high snow. I do not remember the scourge of the wind in my face, the sharp-as-gunshot crackle of ice, the starless blackness above. Even the pain in my knee, a pain so sharp that I pause to spit bile onto the snow, I do not remember. I am just suddenly out here in the open, a target with no regrets, scanning the landscape with my flashlight.

The loneliness of the open space stuns me after the snug intimacy of my shelter, but I know that dwelling upon this is unwise. I shine the flashlight boldly amid the icicle-hung branches above, then search the glittering shadows at ground level — but nothing stirs. The soldier lying face down approximately four yards away doesn't stir either. I lurch toward his body, fall down beside it, rummage through his pockets. One pocket contains a small flask, which I unscrew and hold to my lips, flinching at the touch of cold metal but imagining the fiery warmth even before I swallow — and oh yes, those St. Bernards are welcome to go rescue someone else now. I have no idea what I'm drinking, nor do I like it; the taste is harsh, heavy, completely unlike the transparent purity of herb-flavored aquavit. But I savor the heat spreading into my chest and tingling down my arms and legs.

I sit beside the dead soldier and swallow another great draught of his liquor. I wonder if it is schnapps, of which I have heard much, or perhaps jagermeister. No doubt he could have told me, as he wears a full-length German officer's leather great-coat. I stroke the leather, noting its fine quality and thickness even through my glove. The coat would fit me. After a moment's pondering, I decide I'd rather wear a German officer's greatcoat for the rest of the night than almost certainly freeze to death in my inadequate M-1943 with the improvised lining. The man is dead, after all — he must be — and anyway, if he isn't, he's the enemy. He's supposed to be dead. Because I need both hands, I switch off my flashlight and lean it up against the soldier's booted ankle. In darkness once more, I strip off my gloves and stash them in my pockets. Then I grope for the coat buttons, undoing all eight of them with fingers gone clumsy from cold. That accomplished, I put my gloves back on and tug at one sleeve. Impatience rises within me — removing a coat from deadweight is more arduous than I'd have expected — but finally I turn the soldier's body roughly onto its left side and yank the arm from the sleeve. All my strength is needed to tip the body facedown, then onto its right side, and I pant in quick breaths that freeze in my throat. At last I drag the coat free. Remembering the flashlight, I reach for it and find it has been dislodged. I dig about in the snow near the body's booted feet, but the flashlight isn't there. I lift one heavy foot, feel the space beneath, then lift up the other. I am enraged. I hope the obstructive bastard finds himself in my father's hell with the Abomination of Desolation. After giving the corpse a swift hard kick, I turn away, the dead man's coat hanging over my right arm. I will first return to my tree — no, I will first put the coat on, then return to my tree. The coat fits well, I find, and I turn up the collar. The sensation of warmth is so immediate that I am suffused with a new optimism. Possibly there is a god after all — a god who will rescue me from *the arrow that flieth by day and the terror by night.* Especially the *terror by night.*

Suddenly realizing my actions have been foolhardy in the extreme, I am tempted to rush wildly away from the corpse. Instead, I force myself to think carefully about direction: it is a matter of just a few yards, but I want the right tree, I want my tree. I also want my knapsack. I recall that I approached the corpse's feet first, so I must go back the way I came. I move cautiously, quietly; why risk being shot now, just when my chances of surviving the night have improved? When I have located my tree, I crawl under the lowhanging branches, my teeth clenched against the shooting pains in my knee. I ease myself into a seated position, then set to work arranging my knapsack so that it supports my knee and my lower thigh. I am slightly ashamed of having wished the Abomination of Desolation, a phrase that has always conjured up vague but terrible images, upon my dead enemy. At least I haven't wished upon him the Great Red Dragon with seven heads and ten horns. All that apocalyptic garbage from the Book of Revelation which, according to my father, should have attended the year 1925, the seventh anniversary of Armistice Day.

Wriggling my back into that spot between the lowest branch and a knotty protrusion, I think about my M-1944 Eisenhower jacket. When I get it, when it's been re-tailored to fit properly, I'll have a formal photograph taken. Bjorklund's Studio on Foster Avenue is probably the best. I'll give one to Mother since she likes that kind of thing. And — silly of me, I know — it'll be bigger than the photo of Father that she keeps on her nightstand, the one of him in Cuba.

The seventh anniversary of Armistice Day was earnestly awaited by my father, who had spent the years right after The Great War studying the Revelation of St. John the Divine and the Book of Daniel. He peppered ordinary conversation with references to the King of the South, the three score and ten weeks of this or that trial and tribulation, and the Ships of Chittim — whatever they might be. He had ceased to hold evangelistic meetings except on an occasional basis, and my mother quietly began to run a little bakery out of her kitchen in order to make ends meet. My father spent whole nights on the living room couch, the dummy Harold beside him, making endless numerological calculations. "Now, verse twelve says the Abomination that maketh desolate will be a thousand, two hundred and ninety days," he would say. "But verse thirteen says a thousand, three hundred and five and thirty, which — if you subtract —- no, no, that doesn't work, do I mean add? Or maybe divide?" Many nights I shut out his mumblings by sticking my head under the pillow.

At last my father's studies yielded a firm prediction: the Second Coming would occur sometime between Armistice Day, 1925, and the very end of that year. In the early summer of 1925 he reproached my mother for making a twelve-month supply of strawberry-rhubarb jam. "It is a faithless act, *alskling*," he said gently. And when in September I began to save for a bicycle, he worried that I'd deserted the Lord's Army, that I no longer considered Jesus my Commanding Officer. "Nils, my son, you won't be permitted to bring your bicycle to Heaven," he said. "I fear you've become enamored of the things of the world at the very moment in history when you should be focused upon the things of the spirit." I assured him that I was not a deserter, and that I only wished to buy a bicycle. I did not tell him that enamored was exactly the right word, but had absolutely nothing to do with the bicycle: I was in love with Ingrid, the oldest of the ringletted Sholund girls, and deemed it unfair that the Lord should even think of returning before I got to kiss her. Since she was sixteen and I just fifteen, I needed time — and both God and my father seemed determined that I should not have it.

As November approached, my mother committed the sin of mulching her roses, and my father, who now never left our home but read or prayed most of the hours of the day, wept with sorrow. My father scarcely spoke to either of us during the final weeks of December, and on the last evening of the year, while all our neighbors celebrated, we sat around the dining room table in silence, waiting. I was hungry and resentful, my father having decided that food was a mundane consideration when any moment we would be swept up into the air to meet the Lord. My father sang his favorite hymn about the Lord's return, "*Snart randas en dag*," over and over again in such a loud, rapturous voice that I thought surely the neighbors would complain. (They didn't; they'd all avoided us lately.) My mother sat quietly, wiping her eyes; I could not guess the meaning of her tears, for she cried at many things and always had — communion services, baptisms, handmade gifts, the first wild strawberries.

When December 31st, 1925, turned inexorably into the first moments of the year 1926, my father closed his eyes and ceased to sing. My mother and I dared not move, dared not even look at each other. After several minutes my father opened his eyes again and informed us that the Lord had extended a grace period to the world. "Just as He did so often for the Israelites of old, the Lord is choosing to withhold judgment just a little longer. It is a gift, a second chance," he said — but the radiance of his one-sided smile had dimmed, even slightly soured. "And I must say that a reprieve is certainly necessary when even my own family has shown such a lack of spiritual maturity, not to mention so little enthusiasm for His return." My mother quickly assured him that she would make every effort to "mature," but then suggested that perhaps it would be wise for him to return to more regular work now — if the Swedish Mission Church still wanted to support his ministry. My father gave her one terrible look, then ordered both of us off to bed so that he could pray in peace and quiet. My mother and I obeyed, cowed by his anger and our own spiritual inadequacy.

In the morning my father was gone, the dummy Harold with him, and I dimly understood that he had risked a great deal and lost. Although the Swedish Mission Church made heroes of its evangelists, my father had crossed the line between a Man of Faith and an eccentric, and the way back was fraught with humiliation. I felt humiliated myself, not so much because my father was mistaken but because he had left us. And as time went on, my mother's behavior, both in private and in public, was a humiliation to me as well. She chose to believe that God had taken him up to Heaven, just as God had snatched up the saintly Enoch in Old Testament times. And why? Because my father, like Enoch, was too good for this world, too good to die in ordinary mortal fashion. "The Lord knew his soul and judged him ready for the world to come," she would say to anyone who would listen, apparently never noticing the pity in the eyes of friends, neighbors, and bakery customers. And in 1927, when Ingrid Sholund married the oldest Engebretson boy, I liked to think that my father was responsible. Ingrid had not wanted to ally herself with the family of a Hero of Spiritual Warfare who had become a disgrace and an embarrassment; it had nothing to do with me.

Warfare, spiritual and otherwise, is a misery that nighttime only accentuates. There is no escape from the misery. No escape from darkness and dark thoughts. There is a reason the Psalmist said, "Joy cometh in the morning." Nobody in their right mind would find "joy cometh at night" convincing. Warmth is helpful, German alcohol is helpful, but it is not joy and never shall be.

Perhaps the closest I've ever been to joy was the realization (and this made some years ago now) that while I might not possess Faith, I have kept faith. I have not deserted my mother.

I hope I shall not do so now.

Tiny needles of light dance between the snow-covered needles of my fir tree. The action has plainly moved elsewhere, for the silence is deep, continuous. I remove the German officer's overcoat. I cannot risk wearing it now that daylight has arrived and I must make a move. While I regret the lost warmth, it can't be helped. The locals are far more likely to help me if I'm not wearing a German uniform.

The swelling in my knee has gone down slightly, I am relieved to see, and I dare to hope it will bear my weight. I sling my knapsack over my shoulder and crawl slowly forward while the disturbed branches drop clumps of snow on my head, shoulders, and back. Cautiously, I stand. My knee protests, but the pain is bearable. In the distance are two stone cottages, and one has smoke coming from the chimney. In the foreground is my dead German, and it occurs to me that a German revolver would be useful.

As I approach the body, I see what I could not see in the darkness. The body is wearing an Eisenhower jacket. A beautiful Eisenhower jacket, brand new, unblemished. I look at the dead man's face, at the bullet hole rimmed with frozen blood on his forehead. He is not from my battalion, I note; he is a complete stranger — but all the same, and only if I am very lucky, I will have to live with this. I am oddly tempted to see what lies beneath the jacket. Maybe there is another uniform, and another, and yet another still. A Doughboy uniform from the Great War, perhaps, or the infantryman's blue sack coat, a coat like my father wore in Cuba. So many different uniforms are possible: khaki ones, green ones, grey, butternut, even silly-looking plaid ones. A British soldier told me about a gurkha regiment that wore yellow, back in the nineteenth century, and if I hadn't seen pictures in history books I wouldn't have believed the medieval uniform of the Hospitaller Knights of St. John: bright red surcoats with enormous white crosses on the front.

Turning away, I trudge through the sooty snow toward the stone cottages.

Spiritual Warfare

On Sunday night our dinner conversation went like this:

Me (brightly): Have you ever read Pope Gregory I's account of the woman who became demon-possessed by ingesting a lettuce leaf?

Tom: No. Pass the broccoli, if you don't mind.

Me: Well, here's what I want to know — which part of the lettuce leaf had a demon on it? I mean, it's an interesting question. Maybe the demon was just clinging to the surface, like a drop of balsamic vinaigrette. Or maybe it pervaded each little lettuce molecule. What do you think?

Tom: I think there are much more important things to think about, and so do you. By the way, are you still planning to help out at the Food Pantry tomorrow evening?

Me: Yes, and what a good thing we don't stock lettuce. Just think how sad it would be if Chicago's needy and homeless had to cope with possession on top of everything else. You'd be overrun with requests to perform exorcisms.

Tom (rubbing the bridge of his shapely nose): Oh for God's sake, Melissa, give it a rest.

But I couldn't give it a rest. And because I couldn't, Tom took his coffee into his study and closed the door.

This was our dinner conversation on Monday night:

Me: The historian Josephus wrote about this guy Eleazer who used a magic ring to draw the demon out of the victim's nose. I wonder if it hurt.

Tom: We'd better leave no later than six-thirty. Can you be ready?

Me: No problem. Well, I suppose it all depends on if there's more than one demon. Sometimes people have lots of demons, and every single one has to be exorcized. St. Dominic delivered a man who had blasphemed the Blessed Mother and the Rosary from 15,000 demons, and that would have to be really hard on the nose, if he did it Eleazer's way.

Tom (with an effort at playfulness): Why, oh why, did I marry a reference librarian?

Me: Why, oh why, did I marry a minister?

Tom (after significant pause): Because even as a dog returneth to his vomit, so a fool returneth to his folly. Proverbs 26, verse 11.

Me (feelingly): Thanks a lot. Now listen, do you have candles for the Big Event?

Tom: I don't know that candles are necessary.

Me: Of course they are. Especially if the candles were blessed on the Feast of St. Blaise.

Tom: Who on earth is St. Blaise?

Me: Some Armenian dude who died after "suffering divers tortures," according to this saints' website I looked at. He's supposed to be good for throat troubles.

Tom (abruptly pushing back his chair): We better get going. That old guy — you know, the one with Tourette's — will be waiting outside, and it's pretty chilly.

Me: How do you know it's Tourette's? Maybe he's really got a demon. Maybe you should offer to exorcise it for him. Yes, that's what I think you should do. That would be the responsible thing to do.

Tom: I think I'd rather you didn't help out tonight after all. Kelly and I can manage on our own.

Of course they could. Nothing would make Kelly, a classic preacher-groupie with hungry eyes above a sweet smile, happier.

What kind of dinner conversation we'll have tonight is impossible to predict.

This whole thing came about so suddenly, so unexpectedly. Last Sunday I was lazing away the afternoon on the front porch with a cup of coffee and an old P. D. James mystery. I had that strong sense of well-being you get on the first really hot spring day of the year in Chicago. The occasional gust of wind was mild, good-natured, and the people passing by on the sidewalk were barelegged, barearmed, and smiling. When Tom came up the steps and told me he'd been asked to perform an exorcism, I laughed. "And on such a beautiful day too!" I said. "What a shame."

"I'm serious," he said. "Barry Sutton. He thinks his problem is possession. He thinks he's got a demon that needs to be exorcised. And he wants me to do it."

I stood up and looped my arms around his neck and kissed him. "Oh Tom, darling." No one knows better than I do how difficult it is for Tom to say no to anyone, no matter how unreasonable the request. If lonely old Mrs. Wheeler decides she needs someone to talk to at three a.m., she thinks nothing of calling Pastor Tom. If the cheapskate Bergman family needs a dogsitter, they ask Pastor Tom because he won't expect to be paid. Last year our church janitor, pleading lack of time due to his twenty-hour-a-week job, actually got Tom to do his taxes for him. Tom is always being taken advantage of, and this I resent on his behalf since he's too nice to resent it himself. The fact is, Tom is a much nicer person than I am, which is one reason I love him; he'll do just about anything to make other people, including me, happy.

Tom kissed me back. The kiss started out as a casual peck, but suddenly it took an urgent turn. His big hand stroked my naked upper thigh. "Aren't these pretty short shorts for a forty-something pastor's wife?"

"Not this pastor's wife." I might be forty-something — well, fifty next year — but I've still got reasonably good legs and I see no need to hide them.

"Thank God," he said devoutly, a distinctly carnal gleam in his eye.

We were both moving toward the door, he in his relaxed, post-Sunday-service mood, me in the possessive, you-can-look-but-he's-all-mine mood that sometimes comes over me after watching other women lust after him. (In any given church congregation approximately thirty-five percent of the female population and ten percent of the male has the hots for a male pastor. Some people see clergy as a sexual challenge, others are attracted by authority figures, and still others simply yearn for articulate, sensitive individuals who are interested in matters of the spirit — which is fair enough, in my opinion.) Once in the house, I slid a hand down inside the waistband of Tom's dark trousers. I heard his quick intake of breath with that pleasurable blend of sensuality and comfort you feel only when you've been with someone for a long time. As Tom unbuttoned my blouse, my nipples hardened into tiny sensitive pebbles.

"Maybe he just needs some decent sex," I said.

"Who?" Tom looked at me foggily.

"Poor Barry Sutton. Before his wife died he never seemed to have any kind of depression problem."

Tom murmured agreement while he nuzzled my neck and the base of my throat, and then — to my horror, and to the abrupt eradication of all sexual desire — Tom said, "That's why I agreed to do it."

Tom has decided that the exorcism should be done on Friday afternoon. Tom wants it to be Friday because Naomi, the church secretary, is off that day. He knows perfectly well that Naomi, who is not only a superb secretary but a forthright woman, would not approve. I know exactly what she'd say: "Pastor Tom, the Catholics have exorcisms, and some Christian fundamentalist sects have exorcisms, but we aren't Catholic, and we aren't a sect. We're just a boring old Main Line denomination with a fondness for dead white guys like Luther and Calvin. You must be out of your mind." Tom doesn't want to hear that from her, especially when he's already hearing it from me.

This was dinner on Tuesday night:

Me (in a sprightly tone): Did you know that there is an International Association of Exorcists? Father Gabrielle Amorth, the Vatican's top exorcist, is the president emeritus.

Tom: Yes, I do know. I've been doing a little research myself.

Me: Did you also know that Father Amorth heads up a Vatican training program for potential exorcists? And that he has his own special exorcism room in the Vatican? There's a bed in it with straps for tying down those who are violent. He says he's treated more than 70,000 cases. I wonder how many that works out to per day.

Tom: Oh, for pity's sake, Melissa. Don't be sensational and disgusting.

Me: Me? I don't think you understand the — the — visceral quality of this whole thing. I think you're grossly underestimating the psychological and — oh, I don't know — maybe even the spiritual repercussions.

Tom: And I think Barry is entitled to try another kind of "therapy" if he wants to. He's been on all kinds of meds and none of them have worked. He can't take pleasure in anything; he can't work; hell, some days he can't even get himself out of bed! Why shouldn't he feel a bit desperate? Why shouldn't he try something else if he wants to?

Me: Well, in that case don't you think Barry is entitled to an exorcist who actually has some faith in the process? I know I'd feel a lot more confidence in the end result if my exorcist truly believed in what he was doing.

Tom (patiently): I think Barry is entitled to an exorcist who knows him, who honestly cares about him as a person. He said that if I wouldn't do it, he'd use one of the exorcists he's found on the internet. That could be anybody. A criminal. A wannabe voodoo queen. Some weirdo Wicca woman.

Me: At least it wouldn't be you. And I have to say I think it's tacky to get all sexist over it. In Wicca no spirits or things or people are inherently evil, so exorcism is pretty unlikely.

Tom (standing up and slamming in his chair): Now why do I have this feeling you're spending your entire work day digging up little tidbits to make me feel in the wrong? You could at least try to be constructive, you know. This isn't exactly fun for me. I mean, it was never my life dream to perform an exorcism.

I admitted, albeit silently, that Tom had a point. I wasn't being constructive. I wasn't being helpful. But then Tom didn't have to be so damned helpless either. He was supposed to be Barry's spiritual adviser, not Barry's little tool.

Me (snidely): Well, when you do it, be sure to follow Roman Ritual and place your right hand on Barry's head. I hear the demon might come after you if you use your left hand instead.

Just a week ago I'd never have believed such a conversation between us was possible. Tom and I have always been of the same mind when it comes to issues of faith. We believe in the Christian tradition, the central importance of the life and teachings of Jesus Christ; however, neither of us would be personally devastated if major events in Christian history — the Virgin Birth, perhaps, or even the Resurrection — were proven without doubt never to have happened. The symbolic value of those events would remain the same. At Princeton Seminary we were part of the "liberal fringe," politically as well as theologically, and we've happily stayed in the same Chicago parish for fourteen years because it's very much a liberal fringe parish. Tom spends about ten percent of his time writing sermons and ninety percent doing counseling and organizing social services. The Food Pantry, which is open three afternoons and evenings per week in the church basement and provides free meals and canned goods for our area's needy and homeless, is Tom's brainchild and favorite ongoing project. And while I work fulltime as a reference librarian for a local branch of the Chicago Public Library, I volunteer with the Food Pantry because I too think it is important. Our church members are interested in Amnesty International, rehabilitating Congolese and Ugandan child soldiers, and providing AIDS sufferers with antiretrovirals. They are not interested in evangelism or the more finicky issues of theology and doctrine. This is the last church congregation to expect a pastor to perform exorcisms, and Tom the last person I'd expect to do one.

Wednesday morning I walked to the library, in part because it was a beautiful day, in part because I like to think things through while walking. I passed the Lutheran church of Jenny Lind fame (she visited it back in the 19th century on a singing tour and donated a lovely paten and chalice) and admired the daffodils in a yard across the street. Tom had done a "blessing of the home" for the Weldon family, who lived in one of the houses on this block; he privately called it "Christian feng shui," but it seemed a perfectly nice way to celebrate their settling into a new house with a new baby. I had no problem with that.

I was happy to note that two workmen were finally repairing the library sign. The "l" had fallen off "public" over a year ago, much to the delight of the more ribald among our library patrons and staff. The whole neighborhood had fallen into the habit of saying "the pubic library," and I rather thought the habit would be hard to break.

As I entered the front door I glanced around at the library patrons and noted that many of our regulars had already arrived. Old Mr. Svenson slouched in his usual chair at the long table by the Fiction Section, his hearing aid whining; Mr. Rizzi mumbled to himself as he flipped through the new Sports Illustrated; and pretty Mrs. Zeinab was hunched over her English-as-a-Second Language homework. Several hundred years ago, it occured to me, all three of these patrons might have been considered good candidates for exorcism. Mr. Svenson was something of a scholar of Swedenborgian mysticism, and I spent a lot of time getting him obscure texts on everything from alchemy to cosmology via interlibrary loan. Mr. Rizzi was schizophrenic, and much troubled by voices. And Mrs. Zeinab's long skirt, long sleeves, and meticulously tied headscarf identified her devotion to a faith that was not Christian. Who knows what might not have happened if they'd been dropped into Salem, Massachusetts — or any of a thousand less famously judgmental towns, come to that?

While I tracked down a new book for Mr. Svenson about the relationship between Swedenborg's thought and the Neoplatonic conception of the world soul, I fretted over Barry Sutton. Just knowing he wanted an exorcism made me feel like calling 911 and begging them to commit him to a mental health institution. Certainly it put me off a little matchmaking scheme I'd had in mind. (Our circulation librarian had lost her husband two years ago and was now finally interested in dating again; I'd thought they might hit it off, both being quiet, book-loving people.) What frightening extremes of emotion Barry must suffer besides low spirits, or surely he wouldn't consider exorcism appropriate. Did he really believe God, through Tom, could exorcise him of his grief? His rage? His despair?

All this would be less upsetting if I didn't have the particular religious background that I do.

Dinner on Wednesday night went like this:

Me: Have you read Bob Larson's *Book of Spiritual Warfare*? Besides giving basic exorcism instructions, it offers little practical tips for a better exorcism experience.

Tom: You know I haven't.

Me: He suggests that during the exorcism you should have some light, healthy snacks available, and maybe some nice CDs of Christian "praise" music.

Tom: My God, why did I tell you I was going to do this!

Me: Yes, why? You might have known how I'd react.

Tom: How was I to know you hadn't gotten over your whacky fundamentalist background? You haven't talked about it for years now.

Me (angrily): Well, I'll talk about it now then, shall I?

Tom: I'd rather you didn't. I'll be late for the church board meeting.

I couldn't help thinking that all those people in the pews who lusted after Tom, assuming that his Sunday pastoral robes covered a sensitive soul, were dead wrong.

Tom is right about one thing though; I don't talk about it anymore. It's ancient history. The fact that I grew up a preacher's daughter in a fundamentalist sect in southern Illinois called the Apostolic True Believers doesn't seem real even to me. But it is a fact, and the faith ruled our lives even though I sensed from early childhood that my generous-spirited parents had trouble conforming to an ungenerous, even mean-spirited, theology. When I was seventeen the sect became bitterly embroiled in a dispute over End Times interpretation, half the members believing that the Anti-Christ was Pope Paul VI, and the other half that the Anti-Christ was Francois-Xavier Ortoli, then President of the EU's European Commission. My father (to his credit, and somewhat against the odds, since most people raised in strange little sects leave when they're young or else not at all) decided this was the last straw and it was time for the Stoltz family to leave the Apostolic True Believers. For the last twenty years of his professional life my father taught English in a private high school where he felt fairly safe from theological controversy.

In the early days of our relationship, the discovery that Tom planned to go to seminary dismayed me greatly. I told him why, explained all about the Apostolic True Believers, and he'd understood as much as anyone raised sect-free by agnostic parents can. He'd reassured me that he considered Christian ministry a sort of sanctified social work for people who liked Bible stories — and that I could appreciate. I had always loved Bible stories myself. Not only that, it seemed to me that a lot of Jesus's ideas about how human beings ought to treat one another had stood the test of time; I'd forgotten that Jesus also cast out demons, and authorized his disciples to do so as well.

Our conversation at dinner last night, Thursday night:

Me: Just for your information, Vatican Exorcist Reverend Amorth says that one should avoid directly rebuking a demon. One is supposed to say "May the Lord rebuke you," not "I rebuke you." Demons tend to find "I" language from humans arrogant.

Tom (sighing): Who said I was going to be arrogant about it?

Me: Personally, I think just doing it is arrogant. I also think, in your case, that it's patronizing, given your disbelief. But what Amorth means is that arrogant humans tend to annoy demons, make demons act out in hostile, even angry ways. What will you do if tomorrow afternoon you find yourself confronted by an angry demon?

Tom: Tell it to take two aspirin and call me in the morning.

Me (acidly): Very funny. Did I ever tell you about the time our Chief Bishop in the Apostolic True Believers performed an exorcism during a morning worship service?

Tom: I honestly don't remember. Maybe you did.

Me: He rebuked the demon, and very directly too. As I recall he told the demon to remove himself and his minions — yes, minions — to the Pit.

Tom: And did they go?

Me: How the hell should I know? What I do know is that the girl was on drugs, and this is how her family chose to deal with her addiction. My father brought in the Chief Bishop, as exorcisms were his department. Her family marched her down to the front of the church and sat her down in a chair, and held her there. The Bishop stood over her and said his rebuking piece about the minions.

Tom (reluctantly): What happened.

Me: The girl laughed. She kept laughing until her family took her out of the church. I didn't know her — I was only twelve and she was in high school — but I do know that she died of an overdose just two years later. Tell me, Tom. What do you expect to happen tomorrow? What sort of outcome do you hope for?

Tom: A lifting of Barry's depression. He genuinely believes that his depression is a form of possession, and it is true that his depression does possess him in a really terrible way. So that's why I am willing to help him in the way he wants to be helped.

Me: And you don't find medieval tools repugnant?

Tom: Well, of course I do. How could I not, with an eminent shrink for a father? But so far the modern tools of pharmacology and talk therapy aren't working for him.

I couldn't help thinking that Tom looked just the tiniest bit pleased about this. Tom had always freely acknowledged that his choice of profession was in part a way of distancing himself from his loving but somewhat overbearing father; for the first time it occured to me that competition might also be a factor — but I decided I'd better leave that alone, at least for now. Besides, I was more concerned about something else.

Me: I'm beginning to wonder how far you will go to please your congregation members, to make them happy. Suppose Kelly, whom we both know is a preacher-groupie and hopelessly infatuated with you, decides her only route to happiness is having sex with you? Will you go ahead and screw her even though it goes against your principles, your beliefs?

Tom: That is a really offensive thing to say, Melissa.

Of course it was offensive, but he'd offended me first. And the images in my mind further offended: Tom, decked out in his best vestments, solemnly placing his right hand upon Barry's head. Tom, stern-voiced, addressing an invisible spirit of evil and ordering it back to Hell where it belonged. Tom, my honest Tom, assuring poor vulnerable Barry that he was now liberated from "the wiles of the Prince of Darkness who roams the earth seeking the ruin of souls." Frankly, I wanted to throw up.

This morning I did something I never do: I called in sick. I had already dressed for work, even made my tuna salad for lunch, when I suddenly found myself incapable of carrying out my usual routine. I couldn't pretend that this was a Friday like any other; it just wasn't possible. So I stayed home with the flu, the first time I have ever used "flu" as a euphemism for marital discord. Tom went over to the church offices before eight; he didn't even drink a cup of coffee, just said he'd go by Starbucks on Ashland

Avenue. He didn't kiss me goodbye either. That was fine with me. I wasn't sure I wanted to kiss a man who performed exorcisms. On Thursday I'd read about the case of Anneliese Michel, a twenty-three year old German woman. She died in 1976 shortly after a course of exorcisms, and her parents and two priests were found guilty of manslaughter due to negligence.

As the hours passed I grew more and more edgy. By lunchtime I'd drunk four cups of coffee, done the laundry, cleaned all the bathrooms, and started in on the kitchen. When I realized I was actually considering pulling out the stove and cleaning behind it, I decided I'd had more domesticity than was good for me. I'd go for a walk instead. After a few aimless blocks, I headed toward the church. I didn't want to see Tom; I did want to see if the church as I knew it, as I experienced it, was still there. And it was, of course — a squat, homely structure made of blonde stone that could use a good sandblasting. The white lilacs by the main doors were just beginning to bloom, and I inhaled their heavy sweetness with gratitude. I followed the concrete walkway around the side of the building, then took the stairs down to the basement entrance, which was also the Food Pantry entrance. The door was locked, naturally, but I had a key. In a moment I was inside and had flipped on the light switch.

The room held six card tables and twenty-four folding chairs. Storage shelves filled with canned goods lined one wall, and I idly wondered why it was we always had so many industrial sized tins of lima beans. Maybe next time I cooked for the Food Pantry Café I'd use some of them up in a Brunswick stew. Brunswick stew was good comfort food, and healthy too, if you went heavy on the veggies. I reorganized the shelves a bit — really, it made no sense to mix tins of evaporated milk with tins of soup and stewed tomatoes — and then I sat down at one of the tables to wait. The Food Pantry was directly underneath the front of the sanctuary; if anything happened, anything really noisy and alarming, I would hear it. I would be able to do something.

Around one-fifteen I applied a little lip gloss. Around one-thirty I ate the wrinkled packet of stale M&M's at the bottom of my purse and reapplied my lip gloss. At one-forty-five I asked myself what it was I expected, or feared, to hear anyway: the devil incarnate, seeking whom he may devour? I asked myself what I thought I'd be able to do. Was I in any position to rescue Barry, either from his ravening demon (should it actually turn out to exist) or from his disappointed hopes? And what about Tom? I had already tried to rescue him from what I considered an irresponsible action, an action in bad faith. As for me — well, I was beyond rescue. I was also somewhat hoisted with my own petard. I had jeered, however gently, at all the parishoners who yearned after my husband, who pedestalized him, and now I too felt betrayed. I mourned my own lost faith in him as much as I mourned his feet of clay.

A distant door banged. At the sound of footsteps and low voices above me, I stood up. I could not witness this, even from another room. On my way out I grabbed a giant can of lima beans. When the can wouldn't fit in my purse, I tucked it under my arm.

We are eating dinner. We are not hungry, but we are eating anyway because habit consoles us.

Tom: Excellent stew.

Me: Good.

Tom: Thanks for making it.

Me: It wasn't difficult.

Tom: Lots of fresh vegetables.

Me: Except for the lima beans.

Tom: Oh, right.

Me: I stole the lima beans from the Food Pantry.

Clearly discomfited, Tom looks directly at me for the first time since he got home this evening. But he does not ask me if I went over to the church this afternoon; he does not ask me what I know, what I heard. Nor does he ask why, when we can afford all the vegetables we could ever possibly want, I stole the Pantry's lima beans. Tom returns resolutely to his stew, and I know he is hoping that a little calm, a little silent mutual reflection, will restore our marital equilibrium.

I tell myself that I am relieved Tom wants no further explanation. After all, I have no explanation. I only have a hunch, an inkling, that we are, all of us, needier than we know.

Peaceable Kingdom

I NEVER HAD A GODDAMN FARM in goddamn Africa at the foot of the goddamn Ngong hills. That's what I'd like to tell her. Yes, I would. You write pretty stuff, Karen Blixen, I'd say. All of it is just terribly pretty — the grass gleaming with dew like dim silver, the African new moon lying on her back, the flowering of the plain like a new frock — but you know what? I'm sick to death of your pretty writing about your six thousand acre farm with your own personal savanna and jungle when all I've got is a back yard the size of two beach towels.

In a few minutes Phoebe will climb down from the roseapple tree, put her diary back in the Lu biscuit tin, and stash the tin at the back of the cookhouse woodpile. The woodpile is safe, both for her diary and her one other secret thing, the *mbangi*. Only Mattieu messes with the woodpile, and he can't read English. (The *commandants* still let Mattieu come to work every day, although they always make a huge production of searching him when he arrives, then searching him again just before he leaves.) If the woodpile ever gets low enough that Mattieu notices the biscuit tin, he will certainly open it to see what's inside — but then, perhaps a little amused, perhaps a little sorry there aren't actually any biscuits, he'll put the tin back where he found it. Books are only interesting if they have pictures, Mattieu says, and even the cover of Phoebe's diary is perfectly plain. Unless, of course, you count the toad-colored splotches of mold that look like something from her dreaded Modern Bio text about cell reproduction.

I'm not sorry about the swearing. It's just on paper. In public, I'm nice. If you have the bad luck to be a white girl in Congo in 1964, you'd better be nice. That Karen Blixen though, she didn't have to bother with niceness. She didn't have to bother with being under house arrest either. She could do whatever she liked. She could go flying with her hunter-aviator boyfriend, and — since she wasn't a Mennonite, Super Leftie Variety — she could dash around with guns and shoot lions, buffalo, antelope. She could even go to wild European parties and live it up smoking opium and chewing *miraa*, or barge into the Kikuyu villages and be treated like a queen. MY Kikuyu, she always used to say. And then she gets so famous that a little bit of Kenya is named "Karen" in her honor. Just imagine a piece of Congo called "Phoebe!" Having a normal name would probably help (so stupid, being named after some saintly lady in the Early Christian Church) but I don't really know. I suppose it's kind of an art, having a life like that.

Phoebe peers through the leaves of the roseapple tree, pushing one small branch aside. She is conscious of the gentle resistance against her palm, the small return pressure. If she cranes her neck ever so slightly forward, Phoebe can see right over the top of the house to the tiny fringe of front lawn, the red gravel road, the green sloping bluff, the blue-grey Congo river. And of course she can see the *commandants* — the rear view, that is. They are sitting under the mango tree, heads tipped back, guns glinting in the grass. The short one, the one who's been here since the whole thing began, is wearing dark glasses even though he's in the shade and anyone can see that a rainy season shower is in the offing. Phoebe hopes a tarantula bites him. Since tarantulas adore crawling around in overgrown grass, there's a fairly good chance that one will oblige. Unfortunately he is broad and very heavy; a tarantula that might kill her would probably only make him a little sick and feverish for a day or two. Phoebe can't imagine calling him MY Congolese. She wonders what his name is anyway. None of them will say. They all just want to be called "*Commandant.*" This makes the title so meaningless as to be ridiculous, her father says, adding, "Not that military titles of any kind aren't just plain stupid to begin with."

Although Phoebe doesn't risk the spindly upper branches, she is high enough to see around the long green strip of island which looks, at ground-level, like the other side of the river. From this vantage point she can see quite a lot, can almost believe she is free of Bolala-Mission-turned-*Commandantville*, but of course she is not. She thinks enviously of the Baroness Karen dashing all over East Africa having a good time and decides that the only things they have in common are Scandinavian blood and awkward, practically Victorian, clothing.

When all this is over and I get back downcountry to the Leopoldville American School, I'm going to find some library books that have nothing to do with white women zooming around Africa acting like it's fun to be here. No more Baroness Blixen, that goes without saying, but also no more Beryl Markham in flying suit and goggles. No more Mary Kingsley describing moonlit nights from a canoe on the Rembwé River. No more Joy Adamson rattling around in a Land Rover filled with lions either. I'm going to read books about Russia.

Having finished the hour-long morning exercise routine they've deemed necessary to surviving *commandant* rule, Phoebe's parents are sitting on the tiny back patio in rotting *goi-goi* chairs. They talk softly, which makes it harder for Phoebe to follow their conversation from the roseapple tree. The whole world seems to have gone quiet in recent weeks, what with no traffic on the back path and the Millers gone altogether. Even the Davidmans are reduced to whispers, which is a startling change since they used to be so annoyingly audible, whether they were practicing French and Lingala, arguing, or — usually very late at night — giggling and growling suggestively. The Davidmans arrived just a few weeks before the Rebellion started and the *commandants* showed up; Phoebe figures the poor things only recently realized that screen windows and windless nights mean you can hear a lot of what goes on, whether you want to or not.

"You still haven't told me how it went," Phoebe's mother says gently, leaning forward in the *goi-goi* chair.

"That's because it went nowhere. I was calm, I tell you. I was respectful. I was even eloquent, and it was useless." Her father whacks his fist down on his khaki-trousered knee. "Talk about cutting off your nose."

"Oh, now honey!"

They're doing it again. Taking turns. This time Phoebe's father is angry, and Phoebe's mother is being quiet, reasonable, the Peaceable Kingdom Mennonite. That's her parents' thing, the Peaceable Kingdom. They believe in it. They've got a print of one of Edward Hicks's Peaceable Kingdom paintings in every single room in the house, and Phoebe supposes she should just be grateful that they don't have one for every single wall. This Edward Hicks, an American Primitive painter and Quaker preacher from Pennsylvania, did almost two hundred of them, all based on those verses in Isaiah about how the wolf shall dwell with the lamb and the leopard lie down with the kid and the lion eat straw like an ox. Reverend Hicks was the best kind of visionary, her father says, but Phoebe thinks he was a nutcase. Some of his animals give her the creeps. That placid-looking lion in her bedroom is a complete fake; you can practically see those meat-hungry incisors behind the sweetly-golden muzzle. The smirking lamb beside the lion looks like it had a lobotomy, which is pretty sad considering it was a sheep to begin with. And the leopard in the dining room looks like it hasn't slept in a week, all frantic and wild-eyed and fur-on-end.

"Those poor kids, Norma. They've already paid their tuition.

The Lord only knows how they scraped it together, little as it is!" Her father's voice is rising dangerously. "And these *commandants*, if you please, won't let me walk two hundred measly yards so I can teach my classes!"

"Shhh, dear, I know. I can't teach my classes either."

"They won't pass the state exams. All their hard work, all our hard work, and they're going to flunk!"

This is so completely and irrefutably true that Phoebe's mother does not argue with him. Everyone knows the students can't afford the imported French language textbooks that would enable them to learn on their own. They have to depend on their lecture notes, mimeographed hand-outs which they pore over nightly by lamp or candlelight, and the little two-hundred volume library that a Mennonite church in Lancaster, Pennsylvania paid for. At least once a week her father says, "Now if we could only interest the U.S. State Department in education instead of military nonsense, we'd have all the books we need in no time." But of course the State Department isn't interested, and now the library's been locked up for fear of looting.

"Well, you never know. Maybe tomorrow the *commandants* will see sense and change their minds," her mother says brightly. "Listen, dear, how about a cup of Nescafé?"

Phoebe knows the coffee strategy is doomed. Her father has the really oldfashioned Mennonite's horror of stimulants. Unfortunately they've long since run out of the rosehip and camomile *tisanes* that her mother buys at Madame Boussard's grocery. They've even used up the very last of the wild lemongrass that grows along the cookhouse wall. All they've got left is the powdered Nescafé they keep on hand for visitors. Her mother's mid-morning efforts to soothe him won't succeed any more than her father's will early tomorrow morning when the *commandants* won't let Congolese women come to the door to sell eggs, sweet potatoes, bananas, pineapple. "Okay, fine!" her mother will fume. "We can live out of cans for a while longer, I don't care. To tell the truth, I love cans. But where do they think those women are going to get any cash income, I'd like to know." And then, by ten o'clock, they'll trade off again.

"It's too hot for coffee," her father says. "I'd do some more jumping jacks and sit-ups but it's too damn hot to live."

ॐ

He swore! My father actually swore! But he's right. Today even my knees are sweating. Definitely Russian novels, as soon as I can lay my hands on some. Frozen steppes and all that. Vast frozen steppes where you can just wander free for years and years without ever meeting a soul.

ॐ

"Maybe we could write out our lectures, mimeograph them, and ask Mattieu to deliver them to the students," her mother says. "Or what about that nice Catholic catechist who lives next to the school? "

"You know perfectly well Mattieu would just get in trouble. So would Father Sebastien — I mean, since when are the local military going to trust a Batetela, even if he is a priest?" His sigh is loud and impatient. "Try to be realistic for once, Norma."

Phoebe sympathizes with his irritation. Her mother's wilful hopefulness is one of her more obnoxious traits, Phoebe thinks. Her mother frequently says that she's sorry everyone finds it so maddening but she has to be that way; it's part of her deliberate, ongoing struggle not to be a Scandinavian-American-Depressive-turned-African-Fatalist.

"Hot or not, I think some more jumping jacks would do you good," Phoebe's mother says. "Or you could run a few laps around the back yard."

Phoebe's father stomps indoors, the screen door slamming behind him. Phoebe's mother flops back in the *goi-goi* chair, pushes her sunbleached hair off her forehead, and sighs. At this moment she looks depressed in the most thorough-going Scandinavian way; even from this height, Phoebe can see how her mother's chin and shoulders slump in toward her chest, her thin arms hanging limp at her sides. Her mother frequently says that she thanks God Phoebe won't suffer from it like she does since her father, being of mostly-Dutch extraction, has a healthy, good-humored Dutch phlegm plus a *soupçon* of the practical Swiss ability to take life as it comes. Her father says that her mother's cultural categories are too rigid and unenlightened for words. Phoebe says oh, what's the difference anyway, it's all European isn't it? But her mother always gets the last word: "Europe is the most tribal place on earth, and has the World Wars to prove it. As for Scandinavian depression — well, someday, Pheebs my love, I'll take you to an Ingmar Bergman film. Then you'll understand why I enjoy living thirteen thousand miles away from your grandparents, may the Lord forgive me."

"*Eh, dit - tala! Nalongi esili!*"

Phoebe peers across the roof to the front drive. Although the *commandants* have their backs to her, Phoebe can tell they're engaged in a pissing contest by the twin sparkling arcs above the red gravel road. The short guy, the gleeful speaker, is evidently winning and she looks quickly away. Ever since their arrival the *commandants* have taken every possible opportunity to waggle the contents of their unzipped trouser fronts at her. That first day she tried to be polite, even friendly, going over to where they sat in the shade of the mango tree and introducing herself. And they'd both responded by inviting her to take a look at their impressive *nsokas*.

How much you want to bet Karen Blixen never had to see genitals she didn't want to see? She thought she was so tough, but I wonder if she'd still think so if she had to be here now, in the crazy 60s. Shoot, she was such an old-fashioned lady that she made her poor Kenyan servants wear white gloves when they served dinner. But I'm forgetting. I don't suppose she much wanted to see her Danish husband's genitals either. Not after he went and gave her syphilis.

The Davidmans never come out of their house at all these days. Phoebe sometimes walks to the very edge of the property nearest the Davidman house and glances casually through the windows. There's never much to see. Just Mr. Davidman in shorts and no shirt, his thin naked chest glistening as grossly pale as the underside of a dead Nile perch. And Mrs. Davidman drifts around in the kind of slinky nylon nightwear most Mennonite missionary women wouldn't dream of buying. The Davidmans are British, and they are replacing the Millers at the mission secondary school. He teaches algebra, geometry, and calculus. She teaches French and English language and literature, and clutches half-empty teacups to her chest with both hands, the way small children hug their stuffed toys.

The Millers' house, which is directly behind Phoebe's, still smells of burnt thatch, burnt furniture, burnt everything. The school board had planned to get it fixed up again real quick. They seemed to think, Phoebe's father said, that if it looked normal, everyone would forget about what happened and it would cease to be an embarrassment. Fat chance. The scandal was so bad that the school probably would have had to close down for a while at least. In that way, the Rebellion was a kind of backhanded stroke of luck, her father said once, and her mother said oh, Jonathan, for shame! As far as Phoebe is concerned, the lingering stench of burning has its uses and could even be considered a blessing.

The thunderheads are piling up like gigantic grey balloons above the river. In a few minutes Phoebe will no longer be able to see around the islands, and then the river will lose its high, late-morning gloss. It'll look like a huge sheet of dull pockmarked steel, and about thirty seconds after that, the rain will hit. The *commandants* will pick up their guns and run for the front porch and shiver until Phoebe's mother brings them a Thermos of coffee and two mugs. ("Heaping coals of fire," she calls it, "Not that they realize, and not they they aren't just doing their job, but I feel better.") Phoebe will retreat to her bedroom, where she's memorized every crack on wall and ceiling, and reread more Africa books, since that's all her family's got except for one hideously boring biography, *Menno Simons: The Myth and the Man*. Maybe she'll reread *The Nun's Story*, about that Belgian nursing sister in Congo before the Second World War. At least that poor woman understood about feeling fenced in.

Wonder what the *commandants* would do if I just walked off down the road. Would they shoot? Would it be worth it? Probably not. But maybe I should try it tonight anyway. I know those guys don't stay awake. The short, fat one snores like a metronome, especially after a few cups of palm wine. He didn't miss a beat even when I shone the flashlight through the living-room window at him last night.

Phoebe watches her mother stand, shake out her long full skirt ("I realize long skirts are out of fashion, darling, but we must be culturally sensitive") and look up at the sky. She folds up the *goi-goi* chairs and puts them just inside the kitchen door, as she always does when she knows it's going to rain. Rain will make the antelope-skin lazy chairs rot faster, and these are getting pretty rotten as it is. And not just rotten, but worn to a fragile transparency in places. Phoebe finds the transparent places a little horrifying, a kind of last humiliating gasp of some poor *nkulupa* who had no idea it would end up being a chair. Phoebe's mother does not like the idea of having them replaced before it's absolutely necessary. Neither does Phoebe, although she wonders why it is sometimes so much easier to feel compunction for a dead antelope than, say, thousands of Congolese and the handful of Europeans dead or held captive upriver by the Simba Rebels.

Karen Blixen thought shooting animals was really fun. She wrote about it all the time — the thrill, the glowing sense of power, etc. She liked doing it so much she even wrote some idiotic poem about it while her boyfriend skinned the lions they'd shot. That's the Great White Hunter life for you — and here's poor me, stuck with two *commandants* parked on my few measly yards of front lawn. Stuck, too, with having to climb trees at the advanced age of twelve-and-three-quarters in order to have any privacy.

Dad says that Karen Blixen and her buddies saw themselves as Owners rather than Guests. Dad says we are Guests in Congo, not Owners, and we have the rights and the rules of a Guest. I've never figured out what the rights are, but rules? — Oh yes, those I know!

1) Be polite no matter what gestures, what pinchings and proddings, come your way.

2) Pretend nothing's wrong, that you aren't upset, scared, or angry. Especially angry, since *commandants* have guns.

3) Heap coals of fire if you (or your mother) get the chance, and try to ignore the coals that are piling up all hot inside you.

4) Remember what the Congolese have suffered at European hands in the last hundred years. American hands too, your father says. Your little sufferings aren't worth mentioning, and you know it — so DON'T.

Guest? What total crap. After the last fifty-three days, Byron's "Prisoner of Chillon" is more like it. (Must know more British Lit than I thought. Wouldn't Mrs. Davidman be impressed?)

Rain spatters her face in the large drops that presage a real downpour with a harsh, sideways wind off the river. All in a moment the rain is blinding, torrential. Phoebe descends the suddenly slippery tree, but her caution ends there. She does not follow her parents indoors. Her mother, who worries about Phoebe feeling unhealthily cooped up, has agreed that she doesn't have to come in unless there's lightning. Phoebe's long hair hangs upon her shoulders in a dark wet cape, and she twirls around on her bare feet, streaming face tilted upwards and eyes closed. She zigzags around the perimeter of the back yard, deliberately stepping outside the property line since she knows the *commandants* are drinking her mother's coals-of-fire coffee in the shelter of the front porch. She takes great skidding leaps in the wet grass, then runs around in ever-decreasing circles until she collapses in a dizzy heap, uncertain what has drenched her more, rain or sweat. Lying there panting and sodden, she remembers the diary in her pocket. Now the cover will be entirely toad-colored — but who cares.

After she's caught her breath, after her back has begun to itch from ant-bites (God knows what kind of ant: red, black, fire, army?) she stands up. She reaches inside her shirt to scratch her back, aware that this is a bad strategy since welts have already risen on her skin and scratching will only aggravate them. It's still raining but without much conviction, so she wrings the water from her sodden skirt, pushes her wet hair away from her face, and heads for the woodpile. The rain-pummeled grass deposits burrs and other debris upon her skirt at nearly knee-level, and she mourns the conscription of Michel by the Congolese National Army. (Her father did try to cut the grass once, but he was hopeless with a machete. When Phoebe laughed, her father scowled and said, "Okay, girl, YOU try!" After a disastrous attempt that ended with Phoebe taking a slice out of her ankle, Phoebe's mother had said brightly, "I vote we have a natural savanna habitat for the duration." And so they had, stepping cautiously as the grass grew longer, realizing that insect and reptile wildlife would all too soon assert their rights.)

The diary is replaced in the Lu biscuit tin, the packet of *mbangi* removed and pocketed, and Phoebe heads back to her tree. Because it was a colder rain than usual, Phoebe rubs unaccustomed gooseflesh from her arms before grasping the lowest branch and swinging her considerably-hampered legs upwards. She settles in the tree's midsection where the leaves will provide the most dense shelter, pleased she has remembered matches. Mattieu has told her she's too young to *mela mbangi*, really, but these are unusual circumstances; he's sorry she's all cooped up like this; and she should know there are ways of escape that don't involve walking down the road and getting shot. Mattieu grows the stuff himself ("Regular gardening, that's women's work, but I have a special talent for this") and brings it to her wrapped in newsprint and tucked away in the bottom of his cracked old shoes, which the *commandants* never bother asking him to remove. When they check him over every morning, they're looking for something larger, something metallic, like a revolver. They know Phoebe's father was in the American Army in World War II and they call him "*capitaine*" even though he has begged them not to; they don't seem to believe that he was a chaplain, that he hates weapons, that he would never ever bribe Mattieu to smuggle one for him. As for Phoebe's mother, the very idea of having a gun in the house would throw her into one of her Gloomy Scandinavian Specials for days. And as for Phoebe — well, she thinks of *mbangi*-smoking as a sort of gun substitute. It gives her a thrilling sense of power, of adventure, although she has no intention of writing a bunch of stupid poems about it like Karen Blixen.

She takes out the plastic-wrapped packet of *mbangi*, shakes a small portion into a large dried leaf, and rolls it as Mattieu has taught her. Lighting up requires several attempts since the Chinese matches that corner the Congolese match market have heads with a nasty habit of snapping off and landing somewhere on one's skin, creating small black scorch marks. She draws the *mbangi* deep into the back of her throat, holds it, then lets it escape though her nostrils with a slow harsh sweetness. After a few more inhalations and a few smothered coughs, she begins to enjoy the small delights of her treed position: the returning sun dappling the dark and dripping roseapple leaves, the fat black ants skittering comically across the wet tree bark, the pistachio-green roseapples beginning to redden in beautiful stripes. Mattieu is welcome to every *franc* and *centime* of her allowance when his home-grown hemp can bring all the small things of her circumscribed world into pleasant, not claustrophobic, focus. Butterflies seem to beat their wings with the same ponderous languor as the huge hornbills hovering above the teak tree in the Millers' yard. Leaves loosened by the wind land upon the ground with an audible thud, she would swear it, and the very air quivers and swells and sings like one of those portable pump organs Baptist missionaries cart around in Ford pickups from village to village. She wants to sing herself, throw her voice into the dripping brightness, the billowing expectation. The small of her back melts blissfully against the tree trunk while the cramping fury in her chest eases, then falls away. Even the Millers' house, fire-stained and roofless, seems purified and lovely from the abrupt rainstorm. From her vantage point, Phoebe can see the blackened spot on the living room floor where Mrs. Miller lit the fire. The spot glistens gently, innocuously, as harmless as poor little Mrs. Miller seemed when Phoebe and her parents escorted the Miller family to the Coquilhatville airport three months ago and put them on an Air Congo DC4 to Léopoldville where they could catch a flight to Europe and then America. "Angélique is a gorgeous woman, there's no question," Phoebe's father said as they watched the plane taxi down the heat-softened tarmac. "Incredible Luba bone structure. But committing adultery with your childrens' babysitter... Dear Lord, Norma! Miller must have been insane." Phoebe's mother had cuffed him lightly on the chin, "Beautiful, yes, but do keep in mind the insanity part, won't you?" They had laughed and kissed with an enthusiasm that Phoebe found reassuring.

Recently Mattieu told Phoebe that besides being the Miller children's *mobateli*, Angélique was the village *mwasi na pité*. She had her fun, he said, and made money at the same time, lucky woman. Anxious to appear sophisticated and worldly — well, as worldly as a Mennonite missionary girl could decently get away with — Phoebe had laughed at Mattieu's comment and his wink-and-nudge manner. Now, though, Phoebe wonders about the fun part. She wonders if Angélique found Mr. Miller's white American *nsoka* as alarming as she herself finds the black Congolese *nsokas* so frequently displayed before her. Phoebe hasn't actually seen a white *nsoka* before, her father being a modest man who never goes to the bathroom in the night without pulling his trousers on. But the very idea of Mr. Miller's — well, fun just doesn't enter into it. Mr. Miller is a repellant little man with greasy grey skin, grey stubble on baggy jowls, and small rheumy eyes beneath wiry brows. Why Mrs. Miller should mind his defection so much Phoebe can't imagine.

As Phoebe burns her thumb and forefinger on the very last

blissful puff of *mbangi* (oh, what a gorgeous day, calloo callay, hip hip hooray, even if the river's a tad lopsided and rain is dripping down the back of her own silly-happy neck), a green Mercedes-Benz truck bounces into view. It stops at the Davidman house, a few men in *Armée Nationale Congolaise* uniforms climb out and speak to the *commandants* stationed there. After a moment, the *commandants* and one of the ANC-uniformed men walk up to the front door. After a few more moments during which Phoebe strains her ears to no avail, (quick, my happy little ears, detach and zoom-zoom over there and sit-sit on the window sill and listen-listen-listen!) the *commandants* collect their guns, wrap their few belongings in java print cloth, and climb into the truck. The driver starts the motor, and with hideous groanings the truck draws up to Phoebe's house. (Oops, better pay attention now. Un-silly that brain and don't giggle. Something more important than fan belt trouble is going on here.)

In a very few moments the *commandants*, who have begun to seem permanent fixtures in Phoebe's front yard, collect their bits and pieces: blue-speckled tin drinking cups, playing cards, sunglasses, two blankets, and of course, guns. They join the other men in the Mercedes-Benz.

Phoebe's mother bursts out the back door, her latest Gloomy Scandinavian Special apparently over. She cups her hands around her mouth and shrieks, "Pheebs! Pheebs, sweetie, are you up there? I KNOW you're up there. Listen, Pheebs, it's over!"

For once Phoebe is not angered by the graceless nickname. She gazes down upon her mother standing on the verandah. Her mother is radiant, her fine blonde hair glowing in the post-rain brightness, her feet bare despite the possibility of ringworm, hookworm, and jiggers. She looks ready to dance. Dance around the world in that long, culturally-sensitive skirt that actually does protect her because she's not a kid but an adult with the power to pass or fail people, to hire or fire them, even to buy or not buy what they have to sell.

"Come down, Pheebs. Now! Your dad's going to make sure the pickup still runs and then we're going into town to shop. "

Phoebe dabs herself with the tiny Air France sample of Miss Dior that she keeps for just such emergencies, and even puts a tiny dot on her tongue. She clambers down slowly, still aware of a gently happy focus on the details — the soggy silver tree bark, and the golden spatter of sunlight on her arm.

"Pheebs?"

"Coming, Mother," Phoebe calls, dropping from the bottom branch so clumsily that she falls forward onto her knees in the deep grass. The *mbangi* has affected her more strongly than usual, she realizes. She is too dizzy to stand. Mattieu, who has joined her mother on the verandah, is looking at her with obvious alarm.

"Hurry up, darling, I can't WAIT to get out of here," her mother is saying, fortunately too distracted to notice anything amiss. "Now where's my notepad? I've got to make a list. Madame Boussard's shop first, then the market — oh, I'm buying every eggplant and pineapple they've got! — and then when we get back, we should pop in on everyone else and see how they've managed. Listen, Pheebs, run over and ask Dilys Davidman if she wants to come along."

"Do I have to?"

"Quickly now!" Phoebe's mother says, then bursts loudly into her favorite silly post-gloom song. "MARES eat oats and DOES eat oats and little lambs eat I-I-IVY!"

"Can't Mattieu do it?" Phoebe rises from her knees slowly, carefully. So far so good. Then she turns to him. "Please, Mattieu, would you?"

Mattieu looks at Phoebe's mother with an inquiring willingness. Phoebe knows he's worried that she, Phoebe, is in danger of exposing herself and therefore him. But her mother, the expat adult employer, overrules: "No, Mattieu can't. I've had it with sardines and tuna, so he's off to the village to find us a fresh chicken. He's going to do it up special with fresh peppers and a bit of *ndunda* on the side, bless his kind heart."

Mattieu's modest smile has an anxious edge. Phoebe, who dislikes spinach greens anyway, on the side or not, opens her mouth to protest further. Her mother, obviously both annoyed and bewildered, forestalls her. "Well, for pity's sake!" she says. "It's your first step off the property in over seven weeks. After all your whining I'd think you'd want to!"

Willing herself into a state of steadiness and balance, Phoebe walks next door. Although her brain is still bemused and her limbs relaxed, her knees have only the faintest wobble. She climbs the back steps and knocks on the wooden frame of the screen door. There is no response. After a moment she peers in the large kitchen window and observes that the Davidmans are chasing each other around the dining room table and that they are naked. Totally naked. Mrs. Davidman is laughing, her little breasts bouncing and her arms pumping as she crashes into a chair. Mr. Davidman is right behind her, and Phoebe can actually see his *nsoka* springing up and down like a Slinky toy. As she'd suspected, the pale doughy color is no improvement — in fact, it's quite a lot worse — and Phoebe leaps back from the window, her heart pounding with disgust. She can't imagine what they are thinking of, acting like this, but Mattieu has told her that everyone reacts differently to a *crise*. "I talk to the other cooks, who tell me what the other white people are doing. And you, Phoebe, you alone have *originalité*." A pause, weighty with approval. "No one else on the mission is smoking *mbangi*." And this has pleased her very much — though she does sometimes wish the price of originality wasn't quite so high. The full amount of her monthly allowance is going to Mattieu, who says it really isn't enough and she's getting a bargain.

Phoebe has no desire to interrupt the Davidmans' celebration, but she knows her mother is in a hurry to shop, shop, shop and will be growing impatient. So she knocks on the screen door again, this time with a loud, proper *ko-ko-ko*, and then retreats to sit on the top step. After some moments Dilys Davidman appears in a striped cotton robe that is much too large for her, creases of aggravation above her long nose.

"No, thank you, I'll go to town later," she says, then pauses and subjects Phoebe to microscopic scrutiny, her creases deepening. "If school starts up again next week, I think I'll have my English Language students read part of De Quincey's *Confessions of an Opium Eater*. What do you suppose they'll make of it?" Her green eyes are very direct, but kind, even concerned. "Why don't you sit in? I know you're a reader."

Phoebe smiles blandly. "By then I'll be back downcountry at school, I expect," she says, and hurries to her own front drive where her parents are waiting, the pickup motor already running.

"I'll ride in the back," she announces, and in a moment they are off. She stands on the rusting truckbed clinging tightly to the metal rack, her wet hair whipping behind her, and her rain-soaked blouse plastered to her goose-pimpled skin. A women's choir is practicing in the church, which seems somehow larger than it used to be, and the gardenia bushes in the old mission cemetery are heavy with creamy white blooms. Several Congolese men are busy re-thatching the Anderson's molting grey-brown roof with fresh thick grasses of palest yellow. The palm-lined road into the city of Coquilhatville stretches before them without bend or curve, and Phoebe's father steps on the gas.

How exhilirating to be in motion once again! What joy in speed, in open road! As for the tangled scents carried by the wind — diesel fuel, wet greenery, frying peanut oil — however did she manage without them? There is just one problem: Phoebe is starving. *Mbangi* has this effect.

Madame Boussard has her ear to the radio even as she rings up people's shopping. Her thick nose twitches, her bright red hair sticks up like an electrified bird's nest, and Phoebe notes that her black skirt is the shortest one yet. Is it possible, Phoebe wonders, that Madame still doesn't understand that in Congo women may bare their breasts but only prostitutes bare their legs? No, it isn't possible; Madame has lived here most of her life. Just now Madame is conversing loudly with Miss Mildred McCracken, the mission bookkeeper.

"Such madness this morning!" Madame shrieks. "All over at

last, and now people everywhere are dying to buy things! I had a dozen South African and Rhodesian mercenaries in here wanting Chanel #5 to bring home to the *bonne femmes*. It is just like the GIs in Paris in '45. *Incroyable.*"

Phoebe wonders what is responsible for the avid gleam in Miss Mildred McCracken's pale eyes. The Chanel #5? The GIs? The mercenaries?

"White mercenaries," Phoebe's father mutters with quiet revulsion. "What on earth was Kasavubu thinking?"

"He was thinking he'd better take any help he could get," says Phoebe's mother as she heads for the fresh produce section. "And you can drop the high moral tone, Jonathan, my love. Your Swiss ancestors did a great job of providing the Vatican with all the mercenaries they could use, if I remember my European history."

Phoebe and her father follow in the billowing wake of her mother's long flowered skirt.

"That was centuries ago," her father says. "The Swiss have changed. Besides, you can't provoke me today. I'm unprovokable."

Her mothers grins. "Good," she says. "That means I can shop forever. And buy fancy silly things like *cornichons* and selsify and — oh — chocolate-hazelnut paste to slather on French bread."

French bread. Phoebe's stomach rumbles.

"Listen, you shop all you like," her father says. "I'm off to see if the Post Office is still functioning. I should get telegrams through to the folks. They're probably half-crazy by now."

Phoebe's mother doesn't seem to hear; she has reached the fresh produce and is examining — no, fondling — a large and delicately green European apple. Phoebe's father grins and retreats through the throng of white women grabbing things off the shelves gleefully gabbling in French and English:

"Oh Martha, look! Ox-tail soup! And aged Gouda cheese, unless my eyes deceive me. Isn't it marvelous?"

"*Voyons! Les oignons. Les carottes…*"

"What joy, Rachel, Hero rosehip jam. Apricot too…"

"Ah Madame, quel plaisir de vous voir!"

Phoebe can't bear all the bodies and noise after the weeks of quiet. The crowded store sounds like a giant convention of weaverbirds at dawn — screech, cackle, caw — greedily stripping the palms bare of greenery. Madame's screech is loudest of all, louder even than her staticky radio. Madame is the Weaverbird Queen, and Phoebe doesn't care if Madame has got Gouda and rosehip jam. She craves fresh French bread from Antoine's Boulangerie down the street. Yes, French bread is the single food item she has missed most in these past seven weeks, and she can't believe she didn't realize this before. Even without chocolate-hazelnut paste, even without the tiniest dab of butter, French bread will restore that pleasant blurry edge of *mbangi*-induced happiness.

She hurries out the door and into the street, pushing past clusters of white adults talking, laughing, hugging, even crying. The hungering hollowness in her belly is expanding rapidly; any minute it will spread to her brain or maybe her heart. Head down to avoid anyone who might wish to speak to her, Phoebe rushes into the hot fragrant gloom of the bakery just in time to hear Antoine himself, dark face dripping with sweat, announce that there will be no more bread for at least thirty minutes. "Please please will you all leave!" he is imploring. "Or at least form a line outside, perhaps? My shop is an oven just from the crowd!"

Antoine's customers have no intention of leaving, Phoebe can see that. Afraid of losing their place in line, they all hold their ground so firmly that the few successful customers can't get to the exit. There is a lot of pushing and shoving and irritated exclaiming as the stubborn mass of white and black bodies resists motion. Wedged uncomfortably just inside the doorway, Phoebe doesn't want to leave either. She isn't sure she could leave even if she wanted to, for she is hemmed in on every side. A sense of oppression builds behind her breastbone. Her heart feels crammed in too small a space while her stomach feels more miserably empty than ever. When a tall Congolese man, one of the lucky customers who met with success, squeezes slowly past her with a string shopping bag bulging with French bread and several small round brioche, Phoebe's sense of suffocating hollowness gives way to something else. She doesn't put a name to this something else, but she is acting upon it as she gives a sudden fierce tug to that portion of the bag where the string has unravelled. She is acting upon it as her nimble fingers tear the hole wider and the still-warm brioche slips into her hand. Phoebe watches the man's oblivious back with a rageful joy, her fingers digging into the brioche's delicate crust. She is about to slide it in her skirt pocket — for once in her life she is grateful for her long, baggy skirts — when a strong hand grips her wrist and gives it a painful twist.

"Give it back, *mademoiselle*."

Phoebe finds she is staring into Angélique's beautiful and implacable face. Her mouth goes dry, wordless.

"It's dangerous to do a bad thing in a bad time," Angélique says in an urgent whisper. "Especially if you are caught. Give it back. Now."

The next few seconds pass in a mortifying blur as Phoebe runs after the man, brioche in hand, and explains that it fell out of the hole in his bag. He takes it from her with unsuspicious gratitude — or at least she thinks he does. She thinks his smile is genuine and his vigorous handshake sincere, but as she watches his retreating back, a brand new idea suddenly forces itself upon her, an idea as merciless and true as the Congo sun. This unknown man, victim of her thievery, cannot afford to disbelieve her. If she's heard her father say it once, she's heard it a million times: "The leftover channels of colonial power are as strong as ever, just subterranean." It would be difficult for him to get redress even if he had actually seen her steal the brioche. He would need money and connections that his worn teeshirt and shabby trousers suggest he does not have. Antoine's Boulangerie is most likely the only place where he rubs shoulders with whites and the wealthier Congolese because even the poorer people in Coquilhatville buy bread now and then. Phoebe does not know what to do with herself. She stands in the middle of the dusty street and wishes one of the potholes would open up just a little wider and swallow her whole.

"Come here."

Angélique has taken her hand in a more kindly grip and is hauling her down a side street. When they reach the relative privacy of the Catholic schoolyard, Angélique pauses in the shade of a still-dripping mango tree and looks at her sternly. "*Mademoiselle*, you could have caused a real palaver. Don't you realize? Don't you have any sense?"

Before Phoebe can reply, Angélique sweeps on.

"I shouldn't have bothered with you," she says, her dark eyes slitted in disgust. "You're a *mondele*. You have all the money in the world, and you aren't starving. Why, you aren't even hungry!"

"I am too hungry!" Phoebe snaps, aware that she sounds like a petulant five-year-old and hating herself for it. "Terribly hungry. You don't know!"

Angélique looks at her furiously, and then her eyes slowly widen in amused comprehension. "So the rumor is true," she says. "Oh, that Mattieu really is *mabe mpenza*. He has been absolutely wicked ever since he worked for the McCracken woman — and yet, who can blame him? Old enough to be his mother, that McCracken woman, and a *nguma*. *Professeur* Miller told me about her."

Baffled, Phoebe stares at Angélique. Missionary ladies are always respectfully referred to as *madame* or *mademoiselle*. Whatever can Miss McCracken have done to deserve to be called a python when the disgraced Mr. Miller retains the dignity of *Professeur*? Phoebe knows that Mattieu worked for her at one time — knows, too, that Miss McCracken was brought before the Mission Discipline Board several years ago, and that her parents suspect she hasn't got a True Call to mission work. "Why is she a *nguma*?"

Angélique shrugs, then sighs deeply. "Because she would swallow a man whole — but never mind. It isn't a matter for children. Nothing much is in these hard days. Now if you are so terribly hungry, come with me. I have some *makatis* at home."

Half-running to keep up with Angélique's long strides — everything about Angélique is very long, including her legs

— Phoebe notes that Angélique has subtly altered in the three months since the Millers' departure. The Luba cheekbones Phoebe's father admired are sharper than before, the hollow part beneath them now even hollower. Inky shadows stain the skin under her eyes. And there's something else: while Phoebe knows that many Congolese have distended bellies due to parasites and malnutrition, Angélique's belly has always been flat. Her belly now presses hard against her orange-flowered *liputa*.

Too ravenous to mind that the little fritter-like *makatis* are cold and slightly greasy, Phoebe bites into her sixth one with enthusiasm. The sweetness of cooking banana lingers on her tongue while palm oil smears her lips and fingers a bright yellow-orange.

"Better?"

Phoebe looks across the small table at her hostess and nods. "Yes," she says. "Much better."

"I'll get you some water," Angélique says, picking up a tin mug and heading for the door. "*Makatis* always make one thirsty."

Her hunger assuaged enough to permit a little curiosity, Phoebe looks around the tiny dark one-room house. The walls are whitewashed mud brick, the floor is hardpacked earth, well-swept, and there is one tiny glassless window. In a corner stands a rolled-up sleeping mat tied with a length of dried vine. The only furnishings besides the table and two chairs are two wooden crates stacked on top of one another, open side facing out. The bottom crate holds a few pots, pans, and plastic dishes, and the top one a blanket and several lengths of java print cloth. Angélique's one ornament is a Dutch KLIM powdered milk tin filled with pink-and-cream frangipani blossoms.

Since her parents make a point of living more simply than most expatriates — more simply than other Mennonite missionaries, even — Phoebe is used to spartan surroundings. She actually dislikes houses with lots of rugs, decorative pillows, and cluttered end tables. But the bareness of Angélique's walls unnerves her, makes her worry that the *makatis* she just ate may have been Angélique's dinner. If Angélique really is, as Mattieu claims, a *mwasi na pité*, then the job must not pay well. And now she is going be stuck with a baby — maybe Mr. Miller's, maybe not. Probably Phoebe should pay for those *makatis*. But even as she thinks this, Phoebe realizes that she hasn't a single *franc* or *centime* to her name. She's given it all to Mattieu — a fact she'd have remembered sooner if Antoine hadn't run out of French bread. (Not that Antoine would have embarrassed her or even denied her the bread. Like most Congolese shopkeepers, Antoine would have said, "*Likambo te, mademoiselle*. Just take it and pay me next time." This knowledge discomfits her further.)

When Angélique returns with the water, Phoebe makes an impulsive offer. "I'll bring you one of our pictures, if you like," she says. "We have lots. Way too many, really."

"Pictures of what?" Angélique asks.

"Well, animals mostly. Sheep, cows, leopards…" and then she pauses, for Angélique is laughing. Laughing so hard that she is doubled over, clutching her sides. Phoebe stares at her, slightly stung that Angélique sees her generosity as some kind of joke.

"Oh no, *mademoiselle*. No animals, thank you," she says at last, wiping her eyes. "Not when we spend most of our lives trying to keep animals out of our houses! A picture of Frank Sinatra though, that might be nice. Or *Madame* Kennedy. Or *le bon pasteur* Martin Luther King."

"We don't have any pictures of them," Phoebe says, a little on her dignity. Who is Frank Sinatra? "Just these five animal pictures, one for every room. There's one in my room right above my bed, and it has…it has…"

It has (oh, can it still be the effect of Mattieu's *mbangi*?) materialized right before her astonished eyes on Angélique's whitewashed wall. Definitely the *mbangi*, she thinks — and may even have said out loud, for Angélique is looking at her very oddly. But there it is, the Peaceable Kingdom from her own bedroom, and clear as ever, familiar, both disdained and beloved. Then she notices the difference. Although the animals are still animals, they have also assumed human identities. That goat, still smirking, still rolling his large lustful eyes, has developed

Mister Miller's grey and unappealing features. And that big-eyed, slim-faced sheep is Angélique, but without any sheeplike stupidity; she is simply trapped between all the larger animals. Mattieu is the thin but handsome wolf, sly and resentful, while the mild-eyed bear who utterly fails at looking alarming is the short fat *commandant*. The snake in the corner has Miss Mildred McCracken's thin neck and lipless but rapacious mouth, and as for the leopard pair — well, they are her parents. Unmistakably. Although the reclining leopard seems disheartened and weary while the standing leopard appears stern, even fearsome, both have an air of wisely presiding over events of significance. They look sure of themselves, confident of the well-thought-out integrity of their opinions. They look (and Phoebe admits this most reluctantly) downright smug.

But what about me, she wonders. Where am I? How do I fit in? Please don't let me be that idiot child sitting beside the serpent's hole. Please don't let me be that sweetly-smiling lion either; the smile is nice, but the eyes are…furious. Enraged. Slightly dizzy, and more than a little fearful she may be introduced to a Phoebe she has never met and will not like, Phoebe closes her eyes and leans her head against the rough chair back. The animals recede from her mind's eye, but the landscape behind them remains solidly in place. A great fissure splits the dark foreground, ominous clouds fill the skies above the river, and in the lefthand corner there are weaverbird-like people talking talking talking.

"Are you all right, *mademoiselle*?" Angélique asks.

Phoebe nods slightly.

"Listen, you're just tired — and with reason. It was a big day, an important day."

Phoebe notes that Angélique's voice is soothing, reassuring. She's speaking as she might speak to an infant, not to a girl just a few years younger than herself. Phoebe cannot blame her.

"And you hadn't seen the world for a while, you know. Not really."

"No," Phoebe says, her eyes still tightly closed. "Not really."

BIATHANATOS

THAT MOMENT BEFORE JACK TOLD ME was our last fine moment. Constance had taken all the children to see some triply-tal-
ented, flame-eating, juggling, baiter of bears near Temple Gate,
so in that moment we were enjoying a delicious rarity: privacy.
No small child tugged at my skirt or coughed with phlegm-rid-
den gusto, no older child complained about having nothing to
do or banged doors with sullen venom. "Take them, Con. And
take these two pennies, one for you and one for sweets," Jack
had said as he hurried all seven of them them out the door. So it
was just Jack and me, and because there was as yet no need to let
out the waistline of my gowns, the only hint of anything infantile
was the weak, uneven stagger of spring sunlight across the polished floorboards.

I'd overheard Jack arranging things with Con early this
morning. "Your mother needs a little respite," he'd told her. I
had paused there in the hallway, so profoundly touched by his
consideration that my eyes blurred with sudden tears. Jack knew
better than anyone of my afflictions, although I had yet to make
my new Announcement. And I, on the other hand, knew better than anyone how he hated to part with his few, hard-earned
pennies. What a marvel that after our sixteen years together he
could still desire time alone with me — even desire it enough

to indulge the children in sweets and amusements he could not altogether approve of, or often afford.

Having fairly danced through my morning chores, I now relaxed upon the settle amongst half-a-dozen embroidered cushions, my feet up. I watched Jack assume an oratorical position beside the mantelpiece, his chest ballooning slightly and shoulders well back. He wore his divinity robes with the conscious air of the fledgling Man of the Cloth, and I regretted once again his abandonment of the fashionable attire which had accentuated his narrow hips and long, well-muscled legs.

"Ann, my dear…" he picked up the blue and white Netherlandish candlestick he'd sent me from his continental travels five years ago. "Ann, I have long…"

"A moment, love," I interrupted, watching those hands, those oh-so-clever hands, toy with the candlestick, turn the candlestick slowly, caressingly. "Why not a little sense of festive occasion. A cup of Malaga wine, perhaps? And then, well, the sun is out, and the afternoon warm and dry. I wish…"

But even as I spoke, I was not certain what I wished for. I didn't fancy any amorous frolicking. I didn't fancy a staid marital stroll down Drury Lane ducking the slops from the second floor windows either. Perhaps the placid intimacy of the expanded moment was all I really wanted, the chance to enjoy together the faint glow of April light upon the brass-nailed trunk by the window, upon Con's half-completed embroidery (dear me, the girl's unicorn was so badly proportioned: head too small, haunches enormous, legs too spindly), and upon the pewter tankard so crammed with narcissi that leaves and petals slumped onto the table. And dear Jack — yes, yes, today I was thinking of my husband as dear Jack again, not the other names — smiled at me with sudden heartstopping radiance, his dark eyes crinkling and his soft moustache lifting buoyantly, and my momentary calm gave way to that terrible disturbance which I recognized as hope. That particularly tenacious kind of hope that makes women keep watch out their windows past midnight for tardy lovers or grubby messenger boys bearing brave and unlikely explanation.

At the age of thirty-three, I did not wish to suffer this hope again, and yet suffer it I did.

"Malaga wine?" Jack's delightful smile widened. "But I thought we had only ale. Yesterday you said…"

"I'd forgotten about this bottle," I told him.

Jack did not need to know that I'd made a special trip to the Melton Lane wine merchant this morning, or that the bottle I'd purchased was of a quality beyond our means. "This shipment arrived just yesterday," the merchant had told me. "And it's the best Malaga I've ever tasted. Wonderfully light, with a rare and pleasing sweetness." I had handed over a few coins carefully hoarded from my housekeeping money for emergencies and hurried home before I could be missed.

Jack said the Malaga was a fine idea, but insisted I should not disturb myself. "For once I shall wait upon you!"

"Thank you, kind sir," I said lightly, sketching a mock-curtsey from my seated position.

He left the room with a soft swish of his black gown. I pressed my cheek against a cushion and shut my eyes. The embroidery, Con's first childish effort with crewel yarn, was rough and thick; I knew from past experience that I'd have the imprint of a somewhat horse-like dog upon my skin. But the welcome sunlight glowed warm and hopeful behind my closed eyelids. *Can it possibly be that he is back, that my lover is back, after all this everlasting time? Everlasting wasted time, that's the sad truth of it, and yet I will gladly accept him.*

"The quintessential Malaga, I swear it." Jack stood beside me, two cups in his hands. "The consummate Malaga, the Malaga of my most fantastical dreams, and I — I am ravished! And what ravishment it is to be so ravishingly ravished!"

I took the cup he extended to me, wondering when I had last heard him talk in this funning and foolish way, when I had last heard him use this word ravished in playful conversation. Oh, it was such a long time ago. Such a very long time ago that the distant lostness of it wounded me afresh.

"My dearest Ann." His lips quirked suddenly in the old flirtatious way. "My hinny, my hin!"

My hinny, my hin? Impossible. It's sixteen years since we discovered this quaint Northcountry endearment, and surely ten have gone by since we last used it. But then, if I have truly regained him, what does lost time matter? And what can I not forgive if only he will say, in his old reckless wholehearted way, "For God's sake, woman, hold your tongue and let me love!"

"Jack," I said, waiting, waiting — and then I said, softer still, "Jack."

It was spring, too, when I first loved him. Spring on the Thames, with lute-players drifting in small boats during the misty lilac evenings and lovers singing "Sweet Robyne," "A Coye Joye," and "Flow My Tears." I lived at York House with my Aunt and Uncle Egerton. My uncle, who was Lord Keeper of England, fondly called me his Little Lady Hostess, my aunt being in poor health and unable to fulfill her social duties as wife to a highly placed man. At sixteen, I was old enough to feel the honor keenly, and young enough to find it all very good fun except when I wished to climb a tree, run away with gypsies, or become a sailor and fight the dastardly Spaniards.

That spring it happened that my Uncle Egerton invited his private secretary to quit his town lodgings and spend some months at York House. Now, it is true that I had met his secretary before, but I was younger then, just fourteen, and candied fruits suited my palate better than sweets of another nature. At sixteen, however, my palate had begun to change even as my hips had acquired a disconcerting curve, and my breasts jutted firmly against my square-boned bodices.

It was mid-afternoon when his secretary arrived. A member of the Queen's Privy Council unexpectedly arrived at the same time and both were made welcome by my uncle. I was in the back garden cutting spring flowers and a fine curling fern for the dinner table. My herb garden was mentally underway: rue here, lavender there, sage and thyme in the rose beds, and, over by the low brick wall, valerian for my aunt's sleeping draughts and hyssop for her health-giving purges. Upon the cook's apprising Uncle of my whereabouts, all three of them came out to greet me, Uncle discreetly miffed that I had not heard the carriage and come to welcome them properly. But all the courtesies were exchanged, and I must have played my part to Uncle's satisfaction because he smiled, then instructed me to amuse his secretary as he had several private matters to discuss with the member of the Queen's Privy Council.

"It will be my duty and my pleasure, Uncle," I murmured, conscious of very little save the man before me.

And John Donne — for it was he, then more generally known as Libertine Jack, adventurer, wit, courtier, poet, and ladies' man — stared at me with such sudden, astonished ardency that there came a delicate singing in my ears although there were no musicians boating on the Thames at that moment. I held a green willow basket in one hand, my favorite flower-cutting knife in the other, and promptly dropped them both upon the grass. Jack, released of his duties by my uncle's portly side, came close to me, his voice hushed, as if we stood together in St. Pauls for the New Testament Lesson, not in a back garden rather too near the Thames' stink of muddy sewage. He took my hand in both of his and said, "Your hand is lovely, but how I long for More."

Confusion and lust dizzied me. This newborn lust was so abject and dire that I scarcely heard Jack's pun on my last name. (A predictable one, in any case, and one that I'd heard before in these pun-loving times.) He gazed at me still more intently, and, when I did not simper coyly, he said with a sincerity I could not doubt, "I perceive, Mistress Ann, that the days of Libertine Jack are not only numbered, but abruptly come to an end. And yet" (he said this with wonderment) "only this morning did I, upon waking, damn the unruly sun, being of a strong desire to arise again."

I smiled obtusely, dazzled by such verbal effusions, inwardly calling myself a gormless cretin for my tongue-tied state, and he suddenly, and charmingly, blushed.

"Oh God, Ann, sweet Ann, my regrettable habits of speech

will die slowly," he said. "Forgive me, for our souls have already mixed, and when we die, we must lie together."

Sonnets to one's eyebrows were once and forever exposed in all their tedious artifice, and I pitied the woman who'd been loved by a lesser poet. I managed to overcome my cretinous state enough to tell him so, and then we picked flowers together. We picked narcissi. I listened to Jack speak of himself, of his ambitions to be a truly great courtier, of the vast scope of his unrecognized political talents, and felt the heart in my breast dissolve and flow toward him, rampant and wild as a moorish stream. And although Jack was recounting court intrigues and legal matters that he'd handled with tactful efficiency, I knew with a strange surity that he felt as I did, that his heart overflowed even as his tongue discoursed upon matters of the exchequer and the Queen's banishment of Lord Watelely-Burton. (Perhaps it was Burton-Watelely? Barton-Whitby? Someone else altogether?) When we kissed, as at last we did, every delicious colour in the darkening garden seemed to glitter behind my closed eyelids. Particularly the bright butter-gold of the enormous bunch of narcissi in the willow basket at my feet.

"You have rescued me from the Egypt of my Lusts and delivered me into the Promised Land," he told me with an almost reverent gratitude. "You are my very own Moses!"

His gratitude baffled and very nearly annoyed me, for I was just discovering an Egypt of my own, and would not have thanked anyone for rescuing me from it before I knew everything this exotic place had to offer. Certainly I had no wish to become anyone's Moses at the very moment that I learned to revel in my female nature. "Perhaps you will think me irreligious," I told him, "but I find old white-bearded zealots very dreary."

"Naturally, and so do I," Jack said hastily. "There are dozens of them in my family. Tiresome bores, all of them, and impolitic beyond belief — especially the Catholic martyrs! I simply meant that you, my dear Ann, have guided me to the Promised Land of Monogamous Love!"

"Oh, I see," I said, the garden regaining its glitter.

And he went on to explain that he'd considered variety to be the sweetest part of love, and that he had never loved any woman for one whole day together. His amorous affairs were always complicated, and often desperately entangled. Once he had actually taken to the high seas in the manner of Sir Francis Drake simply to escape them. "I have a talent, it seems, for making my lovers angry," he told me. "Why this is so I don't understand, but on my last evening before setting sail, one former lover tried to poison me, and yet another broke a bottle of claret over my head. Never say you were not forewarned, for I am warning you this very moment." (A pause, a puzzled crinkling of that fine brow, and then a devastating smile that made nonsense of his own advice.) "Take heed, Mistress Ann More. Take heed of loving me!"

As his poem "The Prohibition" was currently popular and much quoted, I recognized the line — but I did not, of course, take heed. What woman does, especially a young woman of sixteen? I loved him immediately and immoderately, irrevocably and unequivocally. He repaid me with singlehearted devotion, and once I'd observed how all those elegant court females with fake moles strategically placed upon their palpitating bosoms tried to seduce him, lying in wait when he went to his rooms, I was both awed and humbled by the compliment. The astonishing grace of the man, the thin triangular beauty of his face above a pristine ruff, his wit, his finely-muscled legs displayed to such delectable advantage in tight hose... In short, I succumbed to my own personal Egypt within a week. And as Jack had a remarkable talent for lovemaking, I quickly learned bliss. In fact, I learned it so well on that very first night that my involuntary screams brought several loyal servants to my rescue. Jack was forced to leap naked into the wardrobe while I, flushed and in considerable disarray, panted out improbable lies about having seen a rodent in the priest-hole. (All the more improbable given we were prudent devotees of the Queen's Religion and had no need of that recent invention for the concealment of outlawed Popish clergy.)

Soon we married, although in secrecy because my uncle disapproved. But I had no regrets, until I found my ardent and lighthearted Libertine Jack replaced by — Another.

"Ann, my dear," said my husband as he placed his empty wine cup upon the mantelpiece.

"Yes, hinny my hin," I replied, daring to be playful after a few sips of Malaga.

Jack's smile seemed to reward me as he again picked up the Netherlandish candlestick and, cradling it carefully in his hands, studied it as if he'd never seen it before. The candlestick was made of the new semi-translucent porcelain, its white base strangely and wonderfully painted with thin-whiskered Chinamen seated crosslegged among tame nightingales, flowers, and plump rabbits. Jack had sent it to me after the stillbirth some years ago while he was in Europe pandering to Sir Robert Drury in vain hope of political preferment. I had written him, begging him to come home, for I'd been gravely ill and remained weak for many months. When the parcel arrived instead of Jack himself, I had abandoned my usual resolute good cheer. In fact, I'd burst into tears and threatened to smash the candlestick against the wall. Little Constance, however, had protested, "Oh no, Mother, please! Such a pretty glaze, and those blowsy blue flowers are peonies!" And I had looked into my daughter's eyes, those grey eyes too wise and too tired for an eleven-year-old, and I had relented, ashamed of my outburst. Why should Little Con, burdened with a sickly mother and a half-dozen younger siblings, be robbed of her peonies because of my spleen? It was one small injustice within my control. I had placed the candlestick in Little Con's outstretched hands, and the joy that transfigured her grave little face had been all the reward I desired.

"I've long believed us divinely blessed in our daughter Con," Jack said now, the full sleeves of his fine black wool robe spreading like an enormous fan as he placed the candlestick back on the mantel. "Do you not agree, my dear Ann?"

This sudden confirmation that we still shared a single thought warmed me as the spring afternoon, in spite of its mildness, had not. It seemed the flame burned clear even now. Greatly reduced, perhaps, but clear, clean. Surely the rest (*oh wildness remembered, bright with leaping delight — and yes, joy's bonfire!*) would follow. For once I was not tempted to make gentle sport of him for lapsing into Pompous Pulpit Voice in the middle of a conversation. "Indeed, yes," I said fervently. "From her birth Con has been a blessing beyond anything."

A blessing even before her birth, I thought, remembering the day we first knew for certain about Constance. That day had shimmered with joyous meaning, and all our recent trials — Jack's brief imprisonment for marrying an under-age girl without her family's consent, my lost dowry, his lost political career, our banishment to the country — had faded away like the mists of a perfect midsummer day. What did it matter if we were in disgrace, poor, dependent on the good will of friends and my distant cousins? We had conceived something utterly original. Something just as original and improbable as if Jack had got with child that mandrake root he wrote the poem about, or actually heard those mermaids singing, or even caught that falling star. We had lain therefore amid the tender spring grass and the wild violets, suddenly convinced our banishment to Pyrford was nothing short of ecstacy. "You yourself, dearest Ann, are the veriest swelling bank of violets," he'd said, placing his hand upon my belly. "And although it is in our souls that our love has grown, it is your body which bears witness — like a book." And all at once, mutually overwhelmed, we'd wept upon each other, our tears warming cheeks chilled by the brash April breezes, his crisp ruff crushed against my shoulder...

"How I do miss spring in the country," I said, feeling relaxed, expansive, in the marvelous, if temporary, silence of my sitting room. "All the wild violets."

Jack glanced at me, then smiled. "What a talent you have for the inconsequential!" he said fondly. "But about our Con — she is her mother's glass, fortunate girl!"

I began to divine, at last, the truly impressive extent of his good humour. Jack was not given to quoting other poets, especially not Will Shakspeare, whose long narrative poem about Venus and Adonis he considered vulgar, ill-formed, and honored far beyond its desserts.

"My love!" I said, so moved, so delighted, that my heart turned toward him as it had not in many years. "Jack," I said, waiting, waiting — and then I said again, softly, "Jack!"

It was after the birth of our Constance that Master Melancholia emerged from my Libertine Jack like Athena from Zeus's forehead, a fully mature personage to be reckoned with. I had seen glimpses of Master Melancholia before, had experienced a certain unease, but now I feared he had come to stay. I do not deny that there were reasons for his melancholy. Our financial position was grim, and I was pregnant again within three months of Con's birth. This last, I suppose, was not surprising: Jack was a social man robbed of all customary social intercourse, a vigorous and intelligent man without a job to occupy him, a lusty man in possession of a wife he desired. Sexual congress did seem the only way to pass the long dark country nights. I struggled to be my old high-spirited self, but I was exhausted from both wet-nursing and nausea. All in all I was poor company most of the time, and Jack began to write piteous letters to his friends back in London describing our home as a veritable hospital as well as a dungeon, and saying that his heart had turned to clay.

I felt I had no right to take offense at the feelings expressed in these letters, for I knew I should not have read his private correspondence. Besides, I knew he felt guilty anxiety — even terror — about my continual pregnancies, five of which never came to term. My first pregnancy was the only one about which we experienced an untainted joy. After Constance, my all-too-regular Announcements became, for both of us, scenes reminiscent of those distressing Annunciation paintings in which the Virgin flinches in horror from the implacable angel, and even the lilies shrivel and the cherubs turn ashen. "My dear Ann," he would say miserably, his head in his long elegant hands. "Forgive me for bringing more suffering upon you." I would protest with false good cheer that there was nothing to forgive, that I was sure all would be well this time, but he would skulk off to his library like a hunting dog in disgrace for having flushed a covey too soon. And there he would write more letters, letters I continued to read in secret, hoping for some small suggestion that his clay-like heart was returning to a normal state. I would read by candlelight in his drafty library, sheltering the wavering candle flame with my hand while being determined not to shelter myself against knowledge, however unhappy. I needed to understand what a heart of clay really was, what it felt like to possess one. And God, oh dear, dear God, I so needed some idea of what this ongoing condition would mean to our lives, our marriage! But I gleaned little of use, certainly nothing I could interpret as consolation. "The walls are too thin, or perhaps the children are just unusually obstreperous," he wrote one friend of some years' standing. "Whatever the reason, I seem to live in the midst of a perpetual commotion." And this to the Countess of Bedford, who was old, doting, and doted upon by him in return: "Oh my dearest friend, it is altogether impossible to overstate my misery."

But it was not until we moved to Mitcham Place, yet another decaying and lonely country house donated for our use, that I realized how desperate his melancholy had become. I went into his library one afternoon in search of him. I had fortified myself with a large cup of claret, for I was not looking forward to delivering myself of another of my Announcements, but the claret had been unnecessary. He was not there. I hurried over to the window and saw him walking toward the woods, a book in hand. Suddenly dizzy and disheartened — claret sometimes sickened me when I was with child, and I should have known better — I sank into his great leather chair, rested my head upon my arms, and breathed deeply for long minutes. When at last I felt stronger, I lifted my head and rummaged among his papers. Who was he complaining to now? Sir Francis Wooley? Lady Magdalene Herbert? Not — please not — that toadying old coquette, the Countess of Bedford! And I discovered no letters, just the preface of an essay entitled *Biathanatos*, announcing his intent to write a defense of self-homicide. He confessed to having often felt the "sickly inclination" to take his own life, and that he did not believe it necessarily a sin. He wrote that he, when afflicted, found a certain comfort in knowing that he had the keys to his own prison in his own hand. He wrote that his own sword had often seemed a blessed remedy, and that one could argue that the holy Christian martyrs were actually self-homicides. And then I could not see what else he had written, for my vision darkened and the claret roiled about in my belly until I was drenched in a cold quick-silver sweat. I was forced to run for the chamber pot where I gave up not only the claret but, at long last, a certain stubborn sanguinity of nature.

When Master Melancholia — for this was how I'd thought of him for some years already — returned from the woods all wind-ruffled and smiling, I was in my sitting room darning a bedsheet. I found myself unable to speak to him, although I did manage my practiced "I-am-devoted-to-the-lifting-of-your-gloom" smile for a very brief moment. Then I returned to my darning (so discouraging, trying to darn threadbare linen) and waited to see what he had to say.

"Ann, my dear," he cried jubilantly, throwing himself down on a chair. "I have discovered just the right passage from Tertullian to support my argument in an essay I am writing!"

"Mmm," I said, darning on, taking care not to prick my finger like some frail fairy-land heroine enduring predictable miseries. "What excellent news."

I knew he expected me to beg him to tell me all about it. He usually did read me his work, and I knew most of his poems by heart. (Not that I meant to; the words took up lodging in my mind with a strange inevitability, as if they were fated to be arranged in this particular way. Rare proof, I realized with a certain dispassion, of the genuinely great poet.)

"I feel an extraordinary sense of accomplishment," he went on. "Even triumph — and that despite the fact that I can never publish this new piece. People would find it too shocking."

His sidelong glance told me that he meant to pique my interest, but I refused to be piqued. Why should I have to listen to my husband wax eloquent on such a subject as self-homicide? How could I not feel betrayed that I, that the children — that even the green world of spring, for that matter! — were not enough to attach him to this life? How was I to pass my days fearing his every absence, counting the kitchen knives and my stores of herbals? Worse, how was I to pass my nights? How was I to both sleep and be vigilant? And how, oh how, was I to be vigilant when I was suddenly angry enough to plunge a knife in him myself? Take heed. Oh, take heed indeed!

"Your favorite dinner tonight," I told him with all the calm indifference I could summon, and then I did, after all, prick my finger. I pricked it so badly that I had to suck the blood away lest I stain the frayed white linen. "Fresh capons with rosemary and leeks."

He said never mind his dinner, for the muse was with him, and he headed for his library with a downright jaunty step.

I did briefly wonder what Tertullian had to say on the subject of self-homicide, and then decided, decided absolutely and firmly, that I would read no more of Master Melancholia's *Biathanatos*. Nor would I listen to any more of his poetry recitations, for recently he'd begun to write poems I could not like. Pandering poems for old women with money, like that tiresome Countess of Bedford whose autumnal beauty he admired. Fulsome eulogies for young women he'd never met but whose grieving fathers paid handsome commissions. Or else religious bits and pieces (and these most upsetting of all) about drowning in Christ's own blood, about being fire, priest, sacrifice, and altar all at once, about… But no. Upon these bits and pieces I could not think.

It was during those days that I began to practice a terrible deception. I pretended that the love-making that resulted in all those pregnancies was something he did to me instead of with me. I lay quietly, my eyes closed against his exquisitely-haggard face in the throes of passion. I no longer sat, stood, wrestled myself a-top, a-bottom, or sideways with this man whom I loved to distraction. Instead, while he panted and groaned and his seed spilled against the carefully-tremorless walls of my womanly parts, I wondered if I should remove the most toxic herbs from my stillroom altogether. And at Mitcham, instead of listening to Jack read from his work, I began to read books for myself. Books borrowed from his library. They were philosophical works, most of them, but philosophers being notoriously opinionated about absolutely anything, I was as likely to find beekeeping hints, recipes for attar of roses, and suggestions for the management of servants, as I was something profound about First Causes or Ethical Principles.

I also worked in my garden, and it was about that time that I found myself planting vast quantities of *narcissus poeticus*. God pity the wife of a melancholy and embittered poet, I thought, especially a wife too well-mannered to indulge in fits of temper and further limited by an inferior education. Bandying words was out of the question, unless I wished to lose… but bandying flowers? Well, there was a certain grim pleasure in growing flowers whose name went completely unnoticed by one's famously metaphor-mad husband. Besides, I'd read that *narcissus poeticus* could be distilled into a drug with a pleasantly narcotic effect. I planned to try my hand at pharmacopeia, but I never actually did it; somehow the simple hard work of planting these flowers had effectively numbed something dangerous within me. And so I planted on — and on and on — until the blooms spilled extravagantly from the back garden to the roadside, the adjoining cow pasture, and even deep into the forest. Visitors often exclaimed at their profuse vibrancy, how they seemed to spread like ivy. One clergyman, however, joked that they were like unto the wicked, who flourished even as the green bay tree, and one day we should find they'd driven us out of our home altogether. And one female neighbor, with a wistful roll of her dewy brown eyes in my husband's direction, had supposed that the celebrated Mr. Donne wrote exquisite love poems about my radiant beauty amid the narcissi in the springtime.

"Mercy no, Amelia," I said merrily. "The celebrated Mr. Donne now prefers to write in praise of the dead. It's all decay and 'fraile mortalitie' to him, you know!"

"Oh yes, I've heard about his marvelous poems for poor little Elizabeth Drury." She sighed, pushing out her high pale breasts as yet undeformed by continual suckling. "So tragic and yet so beautiful."

"Indeed," I said. "Well, my narcissi are for myself, not for the inspiration of others. I like a bit of brightness and colour."

Master Melancholia smiled bleakly and agreed. "How Ann does love yellow. She tends toward despondency, you know. The narcissi and I, we do our best to raise her low spirits. And, of course," (a brief, uplifted pause) "we also rely upon God."

Amelia hastily agreed, but I rather wished he'd omitted the plural and simply spoken for himself. God functioned in my life only as a kind of occasional nostrum for my worst anxieties. I had begun to fear, however, that God functioned in my husband's life as his newest deliverer from his latest Egypt. And this Egypt, having metamorphosed from a strange land of indiscriminate lust to an even stranger land of melancholy which held me at a distance, terrified me. In my more sympathetic moments I thought I understood the need, the anger, the desperation, in my Master Melancholia; surely even a woman could imagine the pain of vaulting ambition which o'erleaped itself. (Oh dear, Will Shakspeare again. I mustn't, I really mustn't. However eminent — and Jack is that — quoting another poet is salt in the stinging wound of his poet's bitterness.) For the fact was, my own marriage-long ambition to be my husband's Deliverer from all his Egypts had been oh-so-gradually revealed to me as a grand fantasy. In truth, I was quite the reverse of his Deliverer. I was that very Egypt he needed deliverance from! An Egypt with an alternately slack or swollen belly, leaking nipples, and a repulsive habit of puking into the nearest chamber pot four months out of every twelve or thirteen.

Shortly after our move to the town house on Drury Lane, I discovered my twelfth pregnancy. I informed my chamber pot, with whom I was once again on exceptionally intimate terms, that I should go mad. Utterly mad. And then, even though on my knees and faint with retching, I had to laugh. I'd been reading my husband's volume of Aristotle's biological writings, and Aristotle opined that women should be kept in a pregnant state to prevent madness. He argued that pregnancy was the only sure way to ground a woman's womb, to keep her womb (and hence her emotions, for he appeared to conflate the two) from drifting up to her brain and making her excitable and irrational. Well, God knows I felt entirely incapable of making a calm, rational Announcement for the twelfth time in fifteen years, and so I postponed the telling until I felt more equal to it — or perhaps just more equable. At the end of my fourth month, however, I knew I could postpone it no longer. It was nothing less than a miracle that dearest Con had failed to detect my condition; usually she was so quick — but then, the girl had romance on her mind. (So sweet they were, Con and Michael, and so certain no one had noticed. As if I, or anyone else in Drury Lane, could help it! He, being her own tender age of fifteen and obviously inexperienced, was content to bring her untidy bunches of wilted violets and gillyflowers, gaze at her raptly, and perform boyish acts of daring beneath her window.)

"Ann, my dear, could you possibly bring yourself to listen to me?" my husband asked. "I must tell you something of importance, and this is a rare opportunity I've taken pains to arrange."

Alas, I'd fallen into one of my distractions again. So unwise. Jack sounded peevish, and with reason. Lately these distractions came upon me almost like spasms or fits, and there was no gainsaying them. Perhaps Aristotle was right, and the womb really did wander. Perhaps my own particular womb had actually wandered all the way up to my brain in spite of my pregnant condition. And if it had done so, if it had rebelled against its state of perpetual groundedness, who could blame it? Not I! How was one to endure yet another birthing struggle, the loneliness of pain, the despair of extreme exhaustion? How was one to bear all the very reasonable fears of tearing, of bleeding, of contracting childbed fever? Some wombs, usually worn out wombs like mine, killed you by wandering right out of your body altogether and refusing to be put back in again. And some wombs, as I had reason to know, stubbornly refused to part with a dead child no matter how many concoctions of marigold flower and hyssop you drank and how many guilty tears you wept, wondering if your unborn child died because it knew it wasn't welcome... Enough, enough. Attend to what he is saying, Ann. He was in such good spirits, and now your inattention has offended him. You have foolishly spoiled a rare moment...but what is this? A beaming smile?

"Our most merciful and loving God has provided most wonderfully for us," Jack said. "Such a marvelous blessing, such evidence of His providential care, both for us as well as our dear Constance."

Wonderful? Marvelous? I gazed at him, baffled by this formal paean of gratitude to God when my husband was more in the Jacob-like habit of wrestling with Him, imploring Him to cooperate with his, Jack's, wishes. And then, if God did not cooperate after all his argumentation, collapsing like David the Psalmist into bitter wretchedness, his soul in the dust and his sense of general persecution so strong that the entire world was peopled with his enemies! What could possibly have happened to so transform the cast of his mind, and what could our sweet little Con have to do with it? I stared, amazed, for all the grooves and shadows of fifteen years' discontent had smoothed and lightened as if by magic — or by the possessive caress of a Divine Hand.

"Our Con has caught the discerning eye of Lord Everly," Jack announced. "And he is so besotted that her lack of dowry makes no difference to him. In fact, he's offered to make a large settlement on her, educate the boys, and pay all our outstanding debts!" He raised his eyes reverently to the ceiling. "I shall never doubt Him again."

I stared at my husband, stupified. Lord Everly? Fifty-three-year-old Lord Everly, who picked incessantly at his decayed teeth with a filthy sliver of bone and whose rank paunchy sweat could not be sweetened by all the lavender fields in Norfolk? Why, Lord Everly's first wife was so demoralized by his lecherous habits that she ran off to France with their bailiff, never to return. His pretty little second wife, upon being told she had the consumptive habit and was unlikely to last the winter, had said, "Ah well, the other side of sorrow is joy. My life will be short, but then so will be my marriage." And his third wife — oh, the very thought of innocent Con, who blushed so sweetly over young Michael's pitiful posies, married off to such a man! A man older than her own father, and charmless save for the charms of his purse. Dizzied by anger as I had never been by nausea, I dropped my face upon my knees and clutched fistfuls of skirt to my ears. *Don't listen, just breathe. Breathe in the comfort of this old skirt. How soft it is, how worn and faded from many washings — many years of washings, really, for didn't Con used to clutch this self-same skirt back when she was just learning to walk? Back when the linen was still stiff, the yellow-green nettle dye as bold and vibrant as my spirit?*

"Why, Ann, do you dislike His providence?"

His gentle note of uncomprehending concern penetrated the bunched linen at my ears.

"Surely, Ann, we must joyfully submit, having courted God and received such a sign of His favour?"

I lifted my face then, and stared at him. Courted indeed. The flirting courtier was his nature, had always been his nature. I had not objected when the courtier was also the lover and courted me, but the courtier now courted both God and Mammon, and my lover had departed. I found I had no wish to speak to my old lover's ghost.

"It is the answer to our prayers," he added.

Our prayers? I thought of the nights, the many many nights in recent years, when I could not sleep because of the earnest, prayerful mumblings and groanings coming from his library. Groanings deep-drawn, squeezing up through his trembling, shuddering diaphragm. Groanings oddly familiar, oddly not, and which threatened our marriage as even his Melancholy had failed to do. (Thin walls on Drury Lane. Thin walls at Mitcham. Such thin walls everywhere.) In the grip of an excruciatingly cold clarity, and mad with much heart, I glared at my old lover's ghost standing there mantled in clergy black. "Your prayers, per-haps," I said. "Your fervent, fawning, amorous prayers — but not mine. Not mine for myself, and never mine for Con."

"My dearest wife!" he said in perturbation. "You cannot have considered…"

"Husband," I interrupted. "Do not pretend that I am your dearest wife, your "beloved Rachel," when my position has be-come that of Leah, second-best bride and prime breeder. I have become — oh, do pardon my abuse of Holy Writ — merely an ever-present cunt in time of trouble."

"Ann!" His slim writer's fist rattled the pewter and porcelain upon the mantelpiece with surprising force. "Ann, I insist…"

"My daughter, however, is no cunt to be sold to an aging lib-ertine, and you shall not call it God's doing when it is Lord Ever-ly's lechery and your greed." I looked into his exquisitely-pained face very straitly. "Your prayers may have been answered, but what of Con's?" *And oh, what of mine? God, God, cure me of this loving madness and restore me to myself.*

Righteous anger gave me the strength to stand, maternal af-fection gave me the crude hard words, but I knew to my shame that the deepest source of my outburst was something far less worthy. For night after night I had heard my husband's prayers, and heard them only too well. I had realized that, despite our married state, he had abandoned me to join that august company of Beatific Bachelors (including his beloved Dante and Aquinas) who believed that God and His Creation passionately attracted and romanced one another. Such a beautiful theology! Such an intimate, seductive struggle! And how my husband's prayers were hateful proof of it. I had lain in bed living and reliving those prayers in each racked, jealous bone of my miserable body: *Batter my heart, three-personed God… Divorce me, untie or break that knot again, take me to You, imprison me, for I, except You enthrall me, never shall be free. Nor chaste, except You ravish me.*

Rain. Soft warm August rain, not (thank the gods) the rain of late November, all hard-slanted, cold and furious. This is rain as it should be: bearable.

"Con, my dear," I say. "Take the children next door to the Scullys' and amuse them as best you can."

Con protests, insisting that no one can rub my back the way she can, but I will not allow her to stay. Then she wants to tuck a lavender-stuffed pillow beneath my head, and this I do allow. "Very soothing, my love," I tell her. "But Old Jane is here now, so you must take the children. And take this penny too, for sweets."

"Mother, I am not a child to be dismissed with sweets," she says. "Let Julia mind them. Or Peg. You know you need me."

"No, dear," I tell her. "I need Old Jane."

Con's soft upper lip trembles. "Why her?" she whispers. "I don't like her. I wish you'd asked Mistress Taylor instead."

Taking refuge in anger, I tell Con I need obedience from my daughter, not backtalk. Con's grey eyes darken with hurt and she turns away. I do not watch her leave. Instead, I watch Old Jane scrabble about inside the dirty fireplace. There hasn't been a fire lit since early May, but I haven't cleaned it or ordered anyone else to either, and the room smells acridly of cold ashes. I suppose I am a slut of a housekeeper. I suppose I should be ashamed. But Old Jane is having a splendid time kicking up ashy clouds that burst over floor, bed, and coverlet in a fine grey rain.

"Oooh, Mistress Ann," she crows joyfully. "It's a right filthy mess in here wants mucking out!"

And muck it out she will, for, old or not, she's a tiny vigorous woman from the north country who works as a chimney sweep when she's not midwifing. Old Jane lives in one tiny room with a great number of half-wild cats with rheumy eyes and mange. She smells of the cheap gin they sell outside Newgate Prison, she boasts that she hasn't washed her hair since the Queen died more than a dozen years ago, and her scraggly fingernails must contain half the soot of London. I find her repulsive, and certainly she has never been in my home before today. But she will manage to deliver the child when the moment arrives, and I am confident that the outcome, given her reputation, given the dreadful tales I've been told by the good mothers of Drury Lane, will be as I have chosen.

He will kneel beside me (I shall be tidied up by then, my hair combed out upon the pillow) and I expect that I shall have all his heart again, for I will no longer be an exhausted, jealous wife and mother, but the innocent victim of "frail mortalitie." Perhaps he will even write a poem in my honour. A poem that will give me place at last among those wealthy old women of faith he loves so much (damn that Countess of Bedford for playing Mary to my Martha) or the beautiful dead young girls whose fathers pay for eulogies to their virginity. My very own little hard-earned scrap of immortality — and even then, I will lay you any odds you like that "my" poem will be more about himself and his God than me!

Sickened by the depth of my own bitterness, I sit up arrow-straight in the bed. "Jane," I say. "I need air."

Her back to me as she wields her smutty broom, Old Jane does not respond. So I sit there for a moment, trying to fix him in my mind as he truly is, unmediated by rancour. If I am just, I know that melancholy has always been part of his nature. In repose, the lips that framed Libertine Jack's witty words always had a slight downward twist. The laughter in his eyes always warred with sadness, and his high forehead betokened the gravity and religious passion natural in a devout family with more than the usual number of missionaries and martyrs. And I also acknowledge, if I am just, that he has aged even more than I. He is forty-five to my thirty-three, but the reddened pouches beneath his eyes and the loose skin under his chin make him look more my father than my husband. The truth is — and how I have resisted it because it should not be so! — Jack is an old man.

"Jane," I say, more loudly this time. "Jane, I need air. Would you open the window?"

"Oh, Mistress," she replies, turning around and frowning as she wipes her hands upon her soot-streaked skirt. "It'll rain in, it will, and rain is that unwholesome for a birthing!"

"Never mind." I heave myself out of bed and draw my old blue shawl around my shoulders. "I'll do it myself. I'm between them anyway."

Leaning my head outside, I feel the rain mist my face and savor whatever unwholesomeness lurks there. I smell the sweat of late summer roses blooming madly along the wall, and listen to the creak of the old rowan tree. Young Michael is across the street, loitering with romantical intent but striving for nonchalance. Obviously he did not see Con leave the house with the younger children. I consider calling down to him. "Michael, my lad," I will say, "Con is at Mistress Scully's. Take her away and seduce her — no, seduce each other — for Lord Everly not only picks his teeth with a filthy bone, but his ears and nose sprout thick white hairs." Michael will look bewildered, as well he might, for Lord Everly has been very ill with the gout for several months now, and thus the betrothal is not yet common knowledge. Even Con herself does not know about it, in fact, for Lord Everly may die. Not that his death would make any real difference to Con; her father would just find another Lord Everly. Her father, I fear, would sell her off to anyone with an ample purse — even some oafish boor of a bear-baiter!

No. That he would not do, not ever. But why, then, do I suddenly imagine a Lord Everly-turned-bear-baiting-lout with such terrible clarity? And why am I all at once so cold despite the August warmth and my wool shawl? Oh, my sweetest Con, my unequivocally welcomed first child, how can he, when he knows what is possible between a man and a woman? When he knows what we had between us before he became Master Melancholia and The Man of the Cloth? He would alter everything past, while I — even now, with my rags of heart that can love no more — would alter nothing. I inhale all the rainy air I can (why not, for who can say what really causes childbed fever?) and then I cry, "Michael, Michael!" But before he can look up, I slump against the window ledge gasping from the tug and grind low in my belly. Could any womb be more well and truly grounded at this moment than mine? If Aristotle is right, it is near impossible that I should be mad. More than likely I've never been so sane.

"Now, now, Mistress," says Old Jane as she takes my elbow and propels me toward the bed. "Come away."

"Help me do this," I plead, panting hard. "Please, you will do this for me, won't you?"

Old Jane smiles at me. There is true kindness in her gappy smile, and her sunken blue eyes hold nothing but the purest good will. "Aye, girl, you're coming on fast. Up, up now." She grunts pig-like as she lifts me onto the edge of the feather bed, but her filthy hands are all tenderness. "That's it, sweeting, that's it," she says as she presses me back among the pillows. Gripping my puffy ankles, she gently swings my legs up onto the bed. Then she parts them. "And now," she says, "It's time for a wee look."

SOUSAPHONE

HE WILL SPEAK TO THE LORD about it, he says, and let me know. In the meantime, I must be patient because the Lord moves in mysterious ways, His wonders to perform.

Yes Reverend, I say. Mr. Palmquist is called Reverend even though he is the music teacher at the Northwestern Congo Academy for Swedish-American Evangelical Missionary Children. A missionary is always called Reverend even if he just teaches or went to medical school or something else unspiritual — unless that missionary is a lady, of course, and then she is Miss or Mrs. If she is Miss, everyone feels a little sorry that even the Lord couldn't land her a man. If she is Mrs., then she is often called a Helpmeet, which makes me think of a helping of meat, any kind, Spam to water buffalo.

Reverend Palmquist walks away, his hands behind his back. He is singing a hymn fragment in his syncopated bass: *Dressed in His righteousness alone, faultless to stand before the Throne.*

I do not like this hymn. I didn't always feel this way. In evening devotions I used to tell Birgit, Well, it's a good thing it isn't my righteousness alone, or I would have to hide behind a tree. Then Birgit would pretend to be a little shocked, say oh-Ingrid-you-are so-bad, and we would both giggle until our dorm mother glared at us.

163

But now I don't like it. And I never feel dressed enough. Being twelve is a lot less fun than I thought it would be. I need that sousaphone.

Birgit asks how it went.

I tell her that Reverend Palmquist is quite sure that the Lord does not approve of girls playing the sousaphone, but he'll ask Him just to be sure. He'll get back to me as soon as the Lord gets back to him. Because the Lord moves in mysterious ways, it could end up taking a while.

What a lot of getting back to people over playing the sousaphone, she says. But then I don't suppose those American churches that donated the instruments to us ever thought a girl would want to play a sousaphone. I'd give up if I were you.

But I really want to play, I say. And soon. The Rapture could happen any day now.

Birgit agrees that the Rapture is a problem. While we all claim to look forward to the Imminent Rapture of the Believers, Birgit and I privately admit we'd really prefer the Lord didn't sweep His Believers up into Heaven any time soon. Birgit's reason is that she wants to get kissed first — kissed on the lips, no less — which isn't likely to happen for a few years yet. My reasons are a little more complicated.

And besides, I tell her, once rainy season hits we won't have marching band anymore.

She nods. We both know how impossible it is to march in Congo's sticky mud. But Ingrid, she says, I really don't get it. Sousaphones don't make pretty sounds, and you never get to play the melody. Why do you want to quit the French horn and make boring oom-pa-pa noises just when you're starting to sound really good?

I don't want to sound good, I tell her. I want to sound like a sousaphone, and I know I could do better than Dave.

Since Dave graduated last June, the band is doing without the sousaphone. His brother Paul was expected to take it up, but he chose the trumpet instead. Dave is in America now, at Trin-

ity Evangelical Bible College in Chicago. His latest letter is post-
ed up on the bulletin board in the dining room. He is studying
something called the Teleological Argument from Design in his
freshman biology class, which he says means that photosynthe-
sis proves the existence of God.

Honestly, Birgit, I sweep on, irritated. You're the one who
said Dave tripped over his own enormous feet every three minutes. You're the one who said a brain-dead baboon would keep
better time!

All right, all right, Birgit says soothingly. Maybe the Lord
will hurry up about getting back to Reverend Palmquist. Maybe
He'll even say yes. And maybe rainy season will tarry. I mean,
the Lord is always tarrying. Tarrying seems to be popular.

Certainly we all know the Lord has tarried about the Rapture. He is doing this because He is merciful and wants to give
more people one final chance to get saved. Besides, he needs to
organize all those Signs and Wonders. One of the newest Signs is
that back in America the Anti-Christ has arrived. He may be the
American Vice-President but he is also a Pro-Union Communist,
Reverend Palmquist says. His name is Hubert Humphrey.

There are three good things: the Lord hasn't said no yet, the
rains haven't started — though they have to soon, as it's so dry
that everyone's gardens are beginning to wither and the cracks
in the ground are big enough to bury a rat in — and Mom has
sent me one of Dad's shirts that he doesn't like. She says she can't
figure out why I want to wear a shirt with shoulder seams that'll
hit my elbows and a hem that'll hit my knees, and she warns that
it is polyester, and polyester doesn't breathe, which is why Dad
won't wear it in the first place. The rest of the letter is her usual
brisk stuff about the banana cake she made for mission prayer
meeting, her Bible studies with Congolese ladies, and the dead
tarantula she found inside a brand new box of Omo detergent.

I write back that we've had no rain for six weeks and there
isn't enough water in the school cistern to baptize a kitten. I wish
I spent most of the year where they do, five hundred miles south

on the banks of the Congo River. Plenty of water there. But I don't say so because wanting things God doesn't want you to have is a sin. And I am already starting to feel really guilty that I prayed for a delayed rainy season.

Everybody's crops from manioc to peanut to corn have completely shrivelled up. The mission doctor worries there could be a cholera epidemic because water is scarce and people are getting careless about where they find it. The hot north wind is blowing so much dust down from the Sahara that the sun is blurred, blunted. We wear dust on our clothes, our skin, our hair. Breathing means breathing in dust. Even so, we have marching band practice in the soccer field every morning at nine. Dad's polyester shirt feels like a plastic shower curtain, and dust settles on my French horn like a punishment. Reverend Palmquist says we do fine with the Sousa pieces but our performance of "I Must Needs Go Home By The Way of the Cross" lacks inspiration. And our "Joyful, Joyful, We Adore Thee" would give Beethoven amoebic dysentery. Since when, he would like to know, is four-four time so difficult for a marching band worth the name?

Reverend Palmquist has begun to pray for rain before every meal. He reminds God about the eighteenth chapter of the First Book of Kings, which tells the story of Elijah and the cloud the size of a man's hand that turned into a great rain storm. He reminds God that righteous Congolese are suffering crop failure as well as the unrighteous. He reminds God of the promised Rapture and suggests moving up the date.

At night Birgit and I sleep on top of the covers with wet washcloths on our foreheads.

The Rapture would be fine with me after all, Birgit says. Just imagine how nasty getting kissed would be in heat like this. Disgusting.

Birgit's only concerns about the Rapture have to do with timing. Her particular dread is that it might happen while she is in the outhouse. Imagine, she says, floating up to Heaven with a piece of toilet paper dangling from your bottom.

I wonder why it is she never questions she'll be Raptured. Last vacation I awoke from an afternoon nap to find the house empty. I wandered uneasily from room to room in the silent house — was it possible? could it be? — and suddenly remembered the eleventh chapter of the Book of Revelation about post-Rapture water being transformed into blood. I opened the door of our little kerosene fridge to find a clear plastic pitcher that should have contained boiled drinking water filled to the brim with a bright red fluid. Horror slid my legs right out from under me. I sat on the floor through the darkening afternoon until at last my parents walked in and my mother said, "Figured if you were sleeping you must need it so we went on our walk without you. Did you see the surprise? Aunt Alice, of course. She mailed us five packets, and I know cherry Kool-Aid is your favorite." She never asked what I was doing on the kitchen floor and I never said.

Wednesday morning Reverend Palmquist welcomes us to marching band with a big grin and big news. He's just had a message from one of President Mobutu's officials in Gemena, the regional capitol. This official says that President Mobutu will be visiting his home village of Gbadolité on Saturday. Since Gbadolité is only a two hour drive from our school, President Mobutu is requesting that our school band play for the occasion of his arrival. We all cheer; President Mobutu is anti-Communist. He is also a Christian even if he is Catholic, which is second-rate Christianity at best but still better than animism. We all wonder if we will get a chance to shake his hand.

This is a tremendous honor, says Reverend Palmquist. We must live up to his expectations. President Mobutu is a Believer in the Free World. And pray for strength; it's going to be hot — if the Lord tarries.

After band practice Reverend Palmquist takes me aside and says that the Lord answers prayer in His own time, not ours. He doesn't believe he's been truly answered yet, he tells me. However, he also believes the Lord would have nothing against me playing the sousaphone on Saturday for Congo's fine, new Christian president. We'll be playing, he says, for the greater glory of God.

Shivers of joy run down my back and arms. I'm small but stronger than most people realize. I can already feel the vast instrument surrounding me as I march steadily on through the dry season heat, kicking up red dust with my worn Bata sneakers and oom-pa-pa-ing for the greater glory.

Between now and Saturday you'd better practice hard, Reverend Palmquist says. Wind instruments aren't all alike. You'll find the embouchure very different from the French horn, and of course the instrument is heavy, but all you have to do is play a few pieces. I'm relying on you. We absolutely cannot perform for the President of Congo without a sousaphone.

For the next three days I practice. Temporarily excused from two of my morning classes, I march back and forth across the soccer field encircled by the shiny majestic weight of the sousaphone. The other hymns aren't awfully exciting, but our third one, the Bantu National Anthem (with Christian words in Lingala, of course, sung by our marching choir), allows me a wonderfully loud POM-pom-pom-POMMM before the chorus, which starts with "*Yesu Klisto, awa na Congo*" and gets boring in a hurry. Afterwards my lips tremble from the effort. Reverend Palmquist is right; the embouchure is demanding in a different way. I lift the sousaphone over my head and set it down deliberately, unhurriedly, so that people will not realize how near I am to the end of my strength.

On Saturday morning the sky is clear. Not the teeniest hand-shaped cloud. Reverend Palmquist says this is an answer to prayer, but I can't help thinking this is just how dry season is this year. Even the papaya trees have quit producing papayas, which I consider a great blessing as papayas are generally our breakfast fruit and I would rather eat an uncooked python steak than the bruised, overripe specimens that always turn up in our boarding school dining room.

All twenty-five of us band members pile into two trucks together with our instruments, Mr. Palmquist supervising. Our drivers are two missionaries who hope for an opportunity to speak privately to President Mobutu about becoming a Protestant Believer instead of a Catholic one. Joyce Dangerson, who is in ninth grade, says what an opportunity the Lord has given us, allowing us to play before President Mobutu, and she has brought her Diary of Precious Days with Our Lord to record all her impressions. Joyce is always saying things like "I hope you'll become a real Christian someday, Ingrid, as I do worry about your Eternal Home," and I think it might not be a bad idea if the Lord chooses to take Joyce to her Eternal Home. The Lord took Beth March from *Little Women*, and I was happy because sweet, boring Beth was as limp as a dishrag. I say this to Birgit and she says oh come on, poor Beth had consumption and died beautifully — but personally I don't think that would make up for being dead.

At three p.m. we have been waiting for four hours. The first hour we all stood in formation in the late-morning sun, instruments in hand — except for my sousaphone, which lay on an elephant grass mat on the ground beside me. The past three hours we've clustered in the skimpy shade of the trucks and a few dusty Nandi flame trees with long, withered pods. An officer of the Congolese National Army arrived by motorcycle around one p.m. to tell us that the President would arrive very soon. His motorcade had been slowed by the massive outpouring of goodwill, the officer said, and President Mobutu was overwhelmed by the love of his grateful people as he approached his ancestral home.

Another officer arrived on another motorcycle an hour later He told us that the President would be arriving shortly, and reminded us that we were honored to be present for the occasion of this great moment of his long-awaited arrival at the home of his forebears. Our patience, he said, would very soon be rewarded, and the President might even incline his head to all of us in appreciation of our services. He is the father of us all, the officer added, his voice thick with emotion, and we are his beloved children who celebrate without ceasing our imminent reunion with him.

As I sit on a dry patch of semi-shaded grass I begin to think President Mobutu's arrival is a bit Rapture-like in its ongoing imminence. I don't mention this to Birgit. She is sweating hard, having just played an energetic game of hopscotch with the first clarinet (Debbie) and the third flute (Darlene).

Birgit says she could sure use a Coca-Cola or a Fanta Orange. She hopes the next motorcycle messenger will have a sidecar filled with cases of soda. Distracted by this vision of rich-people soft drinks, we fail to notice that the wind is picking up and the temperature dropping until we discover goosebumps on our forearms.

Heavens to Betsy, I say, which is the nearest thing to swearing we're permitted.

We compare our arms, their puckery flesh and raised blonde hairs. We haven't had goosebumps since we had that three-day downpour almost four months ago and got completely soaked from a roof leak, which our dormparents said would we please not mention to our parents in letters home because they'd only get distracted from the Lord's Work.

A cloud like a man's hand hovers above a distant palm tree. Then, within minutes, there's a whole great huge village of cloud-hands.

When President Mobutu arrives at last, in a car with a silvery Venn diagram thing on the front of the hood, we are still shaking rainwater off ourselves like dogs. Birgit, I say, I don't care if he's the President and loves the Lord and hates Communism; I'm only playing because it's our Christian duty. Birgit is shaking her flute like it's a giant thermometer, trying to get the water out of it. She says even if we're wet and tired it is the opportunity of a lifetime, that not many people get to perform for great political heroes, and I really ought to appreciate and take advantage of God-given opportunites. In the Parable of the Talents Jesus

Himself says so.

I am envious. Birgit has a gift with Jesus' parables and how they relate to ordinary life.

President Mobutu emerges from his car but we can't see much of him because of all the bodyguards. He is escorted to a wooden platform some distance away, and ceremonial greetings and military salutes seem to go on and on. Then a dozen Congolese women in grass skirts sing and dance and shake painted gourd rattles. At last an official approaches Reverend Palmquist, and several minutes later we are sloshing slowly through the red mud toward President Mobutu's platform. We march in place at a respectful distance, facing the President and his entourage. The President wears a khaki uniform with gold medals and ribbons and sits very straight in a large chair, his arms draped along the armrests. He looks like a statue in a book. To the vigorous beat of Reverend Palmquist's Congolese mahogany baton, I blat and blare every ounce of sound and energy I have into that sousaphone. How wonderful it is to be surrounded by this vast metal apparatus. How protected I feel. Were anyone now to say that my tight cotton teeshirt had caused him to sin in the Lord's eyes, I'd blast him with every last bit of air I could squeeze out of my ribcage into my sousaphone. Were anyone now to say he'd never have pushed me up against the outhouse wall and touched me *there* if I had not driven him to unwilling and unChristian lust — well, I'd charge him like an elephant and he'd turn around and run for his sorry life. Everyone — yes, everyone, every single solitary boy in the Northwest Congo Academy for Swedish-American Evangelical Missionary Children, and maybe even Reverend Palmquist himself — would scatter in fear. Of me. And when my embouchure gave out I'd just scream into the sousaphone instead.

After Reverend Palmquist tells us we did a fine job, thank the Lord, and we'd better pack up our instruments and head back before it gets full dark, we all slog through the sticky red mud to the trucks. Our two missionary drivers are disappointed they didn't have the opportunity to bear spiritual witness to President Mobutu, but pleased with their exchanges with two of his aides. They consider the day well spent because spiritual seeds were sown that could bear fruit — if the Lord tarries. Mr. Palmquist helps me lift the sousaphone into the wooden crate lined with old sheets and a moth-eaten grey blanket. His sunburned hands arrange the fabric around the sousaphone with care. He tells me I did better than he expected, and then he says: But the Lord finally decided, and He said no.

I nod. I am unsurprised about his Lord, who has seemed increasingly unpredictable and maybe even a little flirtatious in His tarrying, withholding ways. As Reverend Palmquist urges the others into the trucks, I place the wooden lid on the sousaphone crate. Then I sit down on top of the crate and inhale the rain-cleansed air. A few early stars float above the Nandi flame trees. My almost dry polyester shirt bells out in the warm light wind like a balloon, or maybe a parachute, and for a moment I feel on the verge of being swept up high, then higher still, and away. This, I realize, is the most Raptured I ever expect to be, ever want to be. And I settle myself solidly upon the sousaphone crate for the long, bumpy ride back to school.

THE DELUGE

PIERO HAD EXPECTED IT for all his young life. So when disaster finally struck, when the great greeny-brown wall of water that was both the Sieve and the Arno Rivers crashed into the Trinita Bridge, Piero experienced great fear but no great surprise. Hadn't Grandmother Giulia prepared him for exactly this calamity? And hadn't she done so with a tireless, even passionate, dedication? What he had not expected was the possibility that he might survive it. As equipped for Death and the Last Judgment as anyone could be at fourteen years old, Piero was profoundly jolted by the fact that Death had passed him by. For here he stood in relative safety on a stumpy fragment of one of the bridge supports while the wreckage of the bridge's many small shops swirled below him, and the pale limbs of the less fortunate Florentines flailed and vanished in the brown foam.

He thought of Uccello, of course. He had seen Uccello's Universal Deluge in the cloisters of Santa Maria Novella at least once a week as far back as he could remember — Grandmother loved ritual, and so ritual they must have, with Mass only the beginning — and he knew every tiny detail of the frescoes by heart. They would walk slowly, slowly, studying each individual scene as if beholding it for the very first time. "Just look at that poor man on the raft fighting off the bear with a club! I expect he's trying to protect that child as well as himself, but I think there is little hope for them. And look at this poor oak tree — dear Mother of God! Lightning has split it right in half." Even now Piero could picture the people clawing frantically at the rough sides of the ark, their battered hands and faces streaming blood. He could hear their last despairing thoughts like cries: *Oh merciful God, save me, help me, preserve my life and I swear that all I am and have is yours.* Drowning multitudes clogged the waters, wild animals attacked some of the still-living victims with huge yellow teeth, and the inexplicable presence of centaurs somehow compounded the terror. Strangely, the frescoes felt more vibrant to Piero than the reality, perhaps in part because Piero had always thought he'd be that pale drowned boy whose eyes were pecked out by a voracious crow. Grandmother claimed that Piero bore a strong resemblance to the drowned boy; even their chins were identical, she'd say, her smile wide, satisfied. But Piero saw no crows here today — no arks or bears or centaurs either — and his sense of confusion increased. He was not going to be the drowned boy after all, it seemed. And so the question was this: who would he be instead?

And there was another question: his grandmother's whereabouts. About her actual fate, however, Piero was horribly certain.

The pressure of the floodwaters caused the bridge support to tremble beneath his cold, naked feet. Fearing his small island of stone and mortar must collapse at any moment, Piero stood very still while great vast tracts of time passed as inexorably as the floods roared, the heavens thundered, and screaming horses, dogs, and humans streamed past in a violent parade.

Piero's body discovered a whole new kind of coldness, his brown linen tunic plastered wetly to his torso and legs. How fiercely he'd resented this garment, a cast-off from an old, large-bellied neighbor. Only yesterday he'd complained about it yet again, and Grandmother Giulia had assured him he'd eventually grow into it since his large wristbones told her that he would be tall, like his grandfather before him, God have mercy on his soul.

"And God have mercy on Florence too," she had added. "Although He shouldn't. Even this endless rain is not punishment enough for Florence's sins — godlessness, greed, wanton lechery and lewdness. Florence deserves to be visited with the Universal Deluge." And only this morning she had said, tsking as she looked out the narrow window at the ceaseless downpour, "I feel like Noah's wife — but never mind! Let us savor the day, wet as it is. God made it, which is reason enough. And I think — yes, I do really think — we can afford a little sausage for our dinner tonight, and a beaker of good wine." Then she had kissed the top of his head with a brisk and noisy smack, which she had to know he hated, and propelled him out the door in the direction of the stalls and shops that crowded the Trinita Bridge.

"What are you crying for?"

The voice came from behind him, and because he disliked the voice at once, Piero did not immediately turn around. But when he did turn, moving his head with difficulty — how had he failed to notice that his head was stiff and sore; he must have been hit by debris — he saw a girl, a very thin bedraggled girl about his own age, standing at the opposite end of the ragged stone platform. Piero doubted the distance between her and himself was more than the length of a man.

"I said, what are you crying for?"

Only now did he realize that the great gulping sounds he had accepted as some kind of natural accompaniment to the situation were coming from his own throat. And that his throat burned rawly. He couldn't deny the sobbing sounds but he could, and he would, deny this rude girl something.

"My parents," he said pathetically. "My parents have drowned." As he spoke he was filled with both satisfaction and wonder at his own lies, for his mother had died of a fever four years ago, and it was now five years since his father had been killed by falling masonry during the Grand Duke's remodelling of the Palazzo Vecchio.

The girl gave no indication that she had heard him; instead, she gathered the stained fabric of her skirt in her hand and began to wring the water out of it with sudden white-knuckled vigor. When the skirt was as dry as she could make it, the girl sat down and drew her knees up beneath her chin and encircled them with thin arms. "You should sit down," she told him in that voice as bony and sharp-edged as her elbows. "Before you fall in."

Piero resented her tone but knew that she was right. He sat down, his back to the girl, and stared through the roiling mist and rain at the faint outline of the hills. Although he did not allow his gaze to drop down to the floodwaters, he could not shut out the dull thud of objects large and small bumping up against their fragile refuge. Nor could he shut out the image of his grandmother pitching forward into the churning river, the loaf of bread she'd just purchased still in her hand.

"It seems as if it's been dark for hours already," he said. "Are you asleep?"

"No," she said. "Are you?"

"Don't be so stupid."

"If the question is stupid, why shouldn't I give a stupid answer?"

"But it's not stupid," he said patiently. "It's nighttime. People sleep then."

"Of course they do." Her voice was scathing. "But if you fall asleep you might roll right down into the water, and I'd guess it's a goodly distance. "

He knew that, and this knowedge had kept sleep at bay even though his exhaustion was so deep that he yearned to sleep despite the coldness of his body, the pain in his head, the pain in his heart. Perhaps this extreme tiredness was to be expected; according to Uccello's frescoes, even Noah, great flood-hero that he was, had grown tired. There was a scene of Noah sleeping soundly after drinking a great deal of wine, but the relationship between his drunken sleep and the flood had never been entirely clear to Piero. The only thing that was clear was that Savonarola, whose oracular voice his grandmother had heard and so ardently believed over sixty years ago, had spoken God's truth: *And behold I, even I, do bring a flood of waters upon the earth.*

All at once Piero remembered that God — Grandmother's God, Savonarola's God — must still be taken into account, pacified, obeyed. He could not afford to alienate this God of Judgment; he had seen what this God could do. If he, Piero, wished to live, then he must be kind, generous, and good.

"If you want to sleep, I'll watch so you don't fall," Piero said.

"How do I know I can trust you?" she asked in a resentful little voice, a voice filled with thorns.

"You don't know," he said honestly, "but you can."

He crawled from his end of the platform to hers, groping his way in the waterlogged darkness, moving with a terrible slowness across the rough surface. He felt first her small cold foot, (at which she yelped), then took her grudging hand. Her presence relieved him almost to tears once again — but only almost. They arranged themselves on the wet, uneven masonry with a tacit understanding that they didn't have to like each other in order to help each other survive.

"Boy, boy! Wake up!"

The girl was shaking his shoulder with no consideration for his bruises, and Piero felt like giving her a thorough shaking in return. He had let her sleep for most of the night; couldn't she have allowed him one more hour?

"Look," she cried. "They have seen us!"

Blinking irritably, Piero stared first at the girl, then at the little crowd gathered on the river bank. When both he and the girl waved, the crowd waved back, shouting greetings, admonitions, and thanks to the Virgin. One man threw a brightly feathered hat into the sodden air while the woman beside him wept loudly, convulsively. Piero and the girl stared at one another, taken aback by the suddenness of all this attention.

A man pushed through the crowd to the water's edge. Even from a distance Piero could see that he was someone of importance from the severe elegance of his black cloak.

"We can't rescue you until the floodwaters go down," the man shouted. "But take heart. We will arrange to get food and wine to you. And dry clothing."

All at once Piero was painfully aware of his empty belly. Grandmother's sausage dinner had never come to pass; he hadn't eaten for almost twenty-four hours. Another need made itself felt as well. When the crowd on the river bank had dispersed he would turn his back to the girl and piss into the Arno.

"Thank you, *signore*," the girl shouted in reply. "Thank you very much!"

Until now Piero had thought the girl plain, her face as angular and graceless as her voice. Now, though, the girl glowed with a radiance that was strangely beautifying. Piero did not believe the mere thought of food could effect such a transformation, but he determined not to betray any curiosity. She was already too self-important, too officious and superior. "Puffed up in her own conceit," Grandmother would have said with an audible sniff. "Children in these decadent days lack humility as well as manners." No, Piero had no intention of indulging her in any way. He would, however, have to suffer the river bank audience after all; the need to piss, once acknowledged, would not be denied. Turning away from the girl, away from the river bank crowd, he fumbled with his clothing, clumsy in his hurry. As he watched his own water disappear down into the waters of the Arno his whole body shuddered with relief.

"I pissed on a painting once," the girl announced. "I meant to. I enjoyed it."

Piero's urine dried up mid-stream but he kept his back to her and said nothing.

"It was the middle of the night," she went on with a kind of loquacious vivacity. "The painting was so new that it wasn't quite dry, but they'd put it in the chapel anyway, to honor some feast day. It was another Blessed Virgin and Child, and the *Spedale* has far too many already. They hadn't decided exactly where it was to be hung so they put it on an easel temporarily. I took it down, pissed on it, then put it back up again."

So she was a foundling, an orphan. Piero should have realized; he had seen the white dresses of young females of the *Spedale degli Innocenti* often enough. He'd never seen them soaked with river water before, though. And he certainly hadn't seen them bunched above some girl's spindly knees while she squatted in a darkened chapel over a painting…but this was not something he wanted to picture, not at all. Only think what Grandmother Giulia would have said about such sacrilege!

Asking the girl why she had pissed on a holy painting was out of the question, but asking her why the orphanage had too many Blessed Virgin and Child paintings was not. So Piero asked.

" Because it is all a lie," she told him belligerently. "The *Spedale* is full of people with no mothers. Does no one think we might grow tired of paintings of mothers everywhere, even if they are Blessed Virgins?"

Piero was too shocked to speak. What kind of girl said she was tired of the Blessed Virgin? Savonarola would have had her burned along with the other material evidence of Florence's sin. Savonarola would have believed this statement alone was sin enough to call down upon Florence the new Universal Deluge he'd predicted back in 1494, the Deluge that would destroy every single living creature. Piero hoped God hadn't heard her — and it was possible, surely, with so many more people praying to Him than usual. God must feel downright distracted… After a moment Piero said, "I've heard that some of the *innocenti* do have mothers. It's just that their mothers don't want them."

It was not until she turned her damp narrow back to him that he realized he had said a cruel thing.

Because the sky was sunless, with faint and ominous streaks of yellowish-green here and there, time was difficult to gauge. Perhaps it was mid-morning, perhaps mid-afternoon, and it worried Piero that he couldn't tell which. It also worried him that the floodwaters were not yet receding, for who knew how much this small platform could withstand? He paced the width of it, which was slightly more than the length of his own body.

The girl watched the bank eagerly, even greedily, and superiority swelled his narrow ribcage beneath the soggy brown linen. He would not betray his own hunger and thirst to a poor orphan nobody wanted. Especially when it seemed foolish to hope that those people really could get any food to them. Not that the distance to the riverbank was great; perhaps five men — very tall men, like his dead father — lying end to end.

Something bumped up hard against their stone refuge. Piero felt the shock of impact all through his body down to his smallest, most well-protected bones. He braced himself for the platform's collapse. When collapse did not happen, when the fast-moving waters did not close over his head, he peered downstream. It must have been that large chest — at least he assumed it was a chest although only a small portion of it bobbed above the swollen floodwaters. They had a wooden chest at home that his father had made for his mother upon their marriage; Grandmother Giulia used it to store valuables like clothing, spices, money. Should anything that large hit them again, Piero held out no hope for either his own survival or that of his tiny island of masonry. The platform, immeasurably weakened by no longer being part of a larger balanced whole, was vulnerable. The Trinita Bridge was like a toppled giant in a tale for little children; all that remained of this giant, however, was one severed leg — and did a severed leg have any real reason to keep on standing upright?

Because his fanciful thoughts did not cheer him, Piero welcomed an authoritative shout from the shore: "Listen, children, you must catch this rope."

The next several hours were all the distraction he could have hoped for. After many misses, accompanied by *fortissimi* groans from a throng of spectators that grew larger every moment, Piero finally caught one end of the rope. The black-cloaked man who held the other end on the bank explained that they must now reel in about half of the rope, then throw their end back across the water. "And you must hold on very tightly to the rope's midsection while you do so," he instructed loudly. "'We're going to make a pulley."

The girl hung onto the rope's midsection as instructed while Piero painstakingly formed the rope's end into a coil, which he threw back to the man on the bank. The onlookers cheered, more than one expressing thanks to the Virgin for Piero's exceptionally strong right arm. Then both children clung to the rope — and how very much more than a rope or incipient pulley it now seemed. It was a means to warmth, to sustenance, to survival. They watched with anxious attention as the black-cloaked man slid one end of the rope through the basket handle and knotted the two rope ends securely together. Piero, still flushed with pride over his rope-throwing success, explained the pulley concept to the girl.

"It's a careful, hand-over-hand process — for that man on shore as well as for us," he told her. "Working together, we slowly move the basket forward until it reaches us."

The girl gave him a look that said his explanations were completely unnecessary and just what she expected from so self-important a boy. "If God wills it," she sniffed.

— As indeed He seemed to, after several near mishaps. By this time the children were trembling both with hungry anticipation and the effort to move the basket along slowly, smoothly. "Strange how much harder it is to deliberately not hurry," the girl had observed once, and Piero had grunted in reply. Otherwise they'd preserved their silence, their small reserves of energy dedicated to the task at hand.

Now the basket rested securely upon the uneven stonework between them — like the Ark upon Mount Ararat, Piero thought, but did not say — and he gazed upon its contents with greedy awe. Because the basket itself was near to weightless, being made of some variety of balsa wood, their benefactor had managed to include a bottle of wine along with the bread, ham, sausage, and dry clothing. The ham was redolent of rosemary and the bread made of the finest, whitest flour Piero had ever seen, but it was the beautifully marbled sausage that took Piero's breath away.

"Wild boar," he said. "Just look at that rich dark color. Have you ever in your life seen anything so magnificent?"

"Never," the girl said, but Piero noted that her eyes, large and hollow with desire, were not fixed upon the sausage. Instead, they followed the movements of the man in the grand black cloak, who was giving orders of some kind to several hovering men. And she was radiating a happiness that had nothing to do with food, a circumstance Piero found puzzling when they had been without food for more than twenty-four hours and now had before them surely the finest meal of their lives. He broke off a piece of the bread, followed it with a bite of sausage that tasted both wild and elegantly spiced, and drank a deep draught of the wine. His mouth ran so pleasurably with juices that he feared he might choke on his own spittle.

"That's the Strozzi palace over there," the girl said. "At least I think it is. So of course he must be a member of the Strozzi family."

Piero could not imagine why this should interest him. He took another mouthful of wine and held it, savoring the faint tang of ripe plums.

"Very probably he is also my father," she said. "In fact, I'm certain of it. Why else would he go to such trouble to help us?"

Piero was taken aback. How on earth was he, their benefactor, supposed to know who she was anyway? Piero considered telling her a few things that he himself was certain of, both from his own ponderings of Uccello's Universal Deluge and his grandmother's trenchant observations during the city-wide outbreak of fever that killed his mother: that some people consider disaster an excuse to behave viciously, like the bandits who robbed the homes of fever victims too ill to defend themselves. That other people actually thrive on rising to the challenges disaster presents, like their ailing and elderly apothecary neighbor who worked twenty hours a day while the outbreak lasted and fairly glowed with health and good spirits. That the wealthy and the noble are frequently generous in a crisis just because they can afford to be, but otherwise keep their distance — like that contessa who had meat and produce from her country estates delivered to every fever-stricken household in her part of the city, but put her own ill servants out on the street. And sometimes, as Piero well knew, generosity is a bribe or a salving of conscience; the last time Piero had tasted truly fine wine was when he was nine and the Grand Duke Cosimo, his father's employer, sent his mother several bottles of wine after his father was killed in the accident. But Piero didn't have a chance to tell the girl anything, not even about Uccello's man on the raft trying to protect the little child from the bear, because she was now telling him that she was one of those unorphaned children at the *Spedale*, that as an infant she had been anonymously deposited in the little basin or *presepe* on the front portico.

"It was completely dark, of course, the utter dead of night," she went on in a dramatic way that he found annoying. "So no one actually saw who brought me. But it must have been someone important and wealthy because around my neck there was a little gold medal on a red silk ribbon, and in my left fist a small ivory carving of a ram's head."

Piero stared at her, a piece of salty ham halfway to his lips.

"It's beautifully carved, that little ram's head," she went on. "Sister Catherine keeps it locked away, but once — just once — she showed it to me."

Piero wondered what kind of girl didn't recognize the significance of the carving. The kind of girl, he supposed, who did not live with a devout grandmother who continually discoursed on sin and the inevitability of judgment. And yet it seemed so obvious. A ram represented sexual lust; a baby with a ram's head in her fist would therefore have to be the product of lust. When he thought about it, a carved ram's head was an unkind legacy for a child. He didn't know a great deal about lust, but he suspected that it was a poor substitute for love — and that he did know something about. His father and mother had loved each other.

"Have some bread and ham," he said with rough pity.

Across the darkly churning Arno, Piero could see the faint here-and-there glow of candles and lanterns. Families were eating their evening meal just as they had before the Deluge. He could almost hear the laughter, the squabbles, the admonitions to eat, to sit still, to not kick one's sister. How he and his grandmother used to roll their eyes and grimace at the noisy meals that went on in the household upstairs: the father shouting one order after another, the mother scolding, the son complaining, the daughters giggling, the baby babbling. How carefully he and his grandmother had supported one another in the belief that they were fortunate in their mealtime calm and order. After all, who could wish for confusion and chaos? And who could honestly wish for the miniscule servings that are the lot of large families with many mouths to feed? Piero never ever considered saying what he really did wish for every single day of his life: his mother, his father, and the palpable third presence that was the love they had created between them. Death may have put an end to their happiness, but it had no power over Piero's vivid memory. How he longed for them, longed to feel again his old secure place in their happiness — but silently! Otherwise Grandmother Giulia would have done her finest Savonarola imitation, preaching doom until she was hoarse, and then they'd have had to go to Santa Maria Novella to pray forgiveness for his ingratitude in wanting more than God was willing to give. After that, of course, they'd have made their usual slow tour of the cloister walls awash in the first great Deluge and gazed upon the horrible image of the crow pecking out the eyes of the dead boy... It occurred to Piero that his grandmother's piety had been in vain. Judgment had been visited upon her even though she did not commit those sins she most despised, the sins of greed, of disbelief, of wantonness and lechery. Perhaps it was impossible to obey God enough; perhaps God simply enjoyed judging more than forgiving. But then why had he, Piero, been spared? Why had Florence, so steeped in sin of every kind, suffered a mere Deluge rather than the second Universal Deluge? Why had he ever believed in Grandmother's God in the first place?

Piero curled on his side, away from the dim glow of lanternlight. He had never drunk so much wine before, and he both liked and disliked the giddy hollowness in his head. As for this sudden embarrassing desire to weep, surely there was no good reason for it. Grandmother Giulia was so irritating that he wouldn't miss her; oh no! He was all at once very certain he'd never liked her. No, he hadn't liked her even the smallest little bit. He was in fact very happy that he wouldn't have to mind her anymore, wouldn't have to listen to her grim warnings and stern diatribes, wouldn't have to wear enormous linen shirts that the old man down the street no longer wanted. Death by drowning was a poor reward for her many years of religious devotion, he supposed — but oh, what a relief. Yes, that's what it was: a relief. And yet now, all at once, he missed his parents with an even greater urgency than usual. This should not be. Certainly this should not reduce him to tears. Piero had missed his father for five years already, more than a third of his life, and his mother for four.

He lay listening to the ceaseless rush of water, and sadness flowed so deeply through his flesh and bones that all at once it seemed it would be so easy, so natural, to just roll over a little more, and then a little more yet, until he was a part of the swiftly-moving flood. So tempting was it that he moved just enough to suspend one leg over the side. It hung there heavily, as if waiting to be sucked in and swept along. The crow could have his eyes after all, Piero didn't mind. The crow was welcome to anything it wanted of him, and so was the snake, the centaur, the man wielding the club...

"Boy, wake up, wake up!"

The girl's frenzied voice startled Piero into an upright position before he had time to consider the advantages of feigned sleep. Belatedly, he rubbed his eyes in a bewildered fashion, his knuckles coming away so wet that he was grateful for the darkness. He lay back down again, his head dizzy and thick. Would the girl believe him muddled by sleep? He could hope so.

"You stupid drunken fool," she cried. "You nearly fell in."

"Did I?" Piero allowed his voice to fill with astonishment.

"And you mustn't," she went on. "Not when the Strozzis have gone to such trouble for us. "

Piero suddenly disliked her as much as he disliked pious Grandmother Giulia.

"Your dress is filthy," he said. "You've got streaks of mud all down the back."

He watched with mean satisfaction as she craned her head around, trying to see her back in a darkness alleviated only by a moon partially blotted out by clouds. Served her right, this vain silly girl who believed herself a Strozzi. And why shouldn't he have drunk that wine? He was thirsty, probably as thirsty as he'd ever been in his life, and anyway, Noah got drunk and slept after the flood. What was so wrong about that?

After a moment's futile effort, the girl gave up trying to see the back of her dress. She sat there silently, hands in her lap. Then she said: "I am sorry about your parents."

Startled, Piero peered into her deeply shadowed face. He'd completely forgotten about yesterday's lie.

"I didn't lose anyone, you see," she went on. "So none of this matters to me the way it does to you. I'm sorry if I have been rude or unkind."

The moment to admit to the lie was long past. "Thank you," Piero said.

"If your house got swept away and you need a place to live," the girl continued, "I'm going to be in a position to help, once we're rescued. I'll just tell the Strozzis they need to take in both of us. If they're ready to take me in, they probably won't mind another one."

Piero opened his mouth and then shut it again with such a loud pop that she giggled. Her giggle was surprisingly appealing — the kind of giggle you expected from a very fat and happy baby, not a rude, thin foundling. Certainly not a foundling with absurd ideas about having gained a father just because some well-dressed man either didn't like seeing children go hungry or was exhilarated into action by a context of urgency and disaster. Or both, perhaps.

"Thank you," he said again. "Now, if you don't mind, I'm going back to sleep."

It was the penetrating chill that awakened him. He should have put on that clean dry tunic before, but somehow he hadn't liked to; it had seemed too grand for him, the fine linen dyed a showy and expensive shade of royal blue instead of one of the cheaper yellows and browns. Now he pulled it on top of his own brown tunic, and in a moment began to feel warmer.

Judging by its rush and roar, the Arno was still perilously high, but Piero hoped that by morning it would be navigable once again. The weather had cleared enough that the stars were out, and what a display! Great shining tracts of them spread thick as butter across a soft dark sky. The lack of lantern-glow on either side of the river suggested that it was late and all of flood-weary Florence was sleeping.

"I'd like some more of that ham," the girl said. "Would you?"

After agreeing to save a bit of the bread for morning, they finished the meat and most of the wine. Then the girl ordered him to turn his back while she removed her waterstained *Spedale* dress and pulled on the wine-colored gown provided by their benefactor on shore.

"I can't see anything," Piero protested, annoyed. He stretched out full length and gazed upward. "And I don't want to. I'm looking at the stars."

A sniff suggested that she was offended, but after a moment she wrapped the *Spedale* dress shawl-like around her shoulders and lay down beside him.

"That cluster of stars over there to the left — yes, there — looks sort of like a boat," she remarked.

Remembering the bold and convincing lines of Uccello's rough ark, Piero said in a disgusted tone, "No, it doesn't. It looks like a basket. A silly little shapeless basket too."

She shrugged, her shoulders momentarily pressing against Piero's as she pointed out a cat with a long tail, then the draped head and shoulders of what she insisted was the Holy and Blessed Mother and not merely a woman who was perhaps shy, her gaze turned downward. Piero thought all this far too much to read into the outline suggested by a few stars, and he was more than a little surprised that she spoke of this night-sky Blessed Mother without bile or venom. Piero observed an armored horse with a plume, then a dragon-like creature with great, clawed feet. Pleasantly aware of being warmer and drier than last night, Piero felt a sudden rush of gratitude to the girl for the life he had come so close to parting with this afternoon. While she was talking some rapt nonsense about the Blessed Mother's bejeweled crown, he stretched out his hand toward hers. He meant only to touch the soft back of her hand for the briefest instant, hoping she would understand what he could not say: *It was a momentary thing, if you are wondering, an impulse only; I am indebted to you, for I am one of those who keep on living; I am one of those who keep on clinging to the side of the ark no matter what, and this is a valuable thing to know.* To his shock he found that his hand had closed not upon hers, which earlier had hugged her improvised shawl to her torso, but upon one tiny cloth-covered breast. A paralysis seemed to afflict his entire body, leaving his hand immoveable as stone; he could no sooner have removed it from her breast than he could have singlehandedly removed the Duomo from Florence and carried it up to the hilltop of Fiesole. His hand just lay there, helplessly aware of the tight little nipple pressing up between the second and third fingers. After a moment Piero's strength returned, and he was tempted almost beyond bearing to roll the nipple between his fingers, maybe gently squeeze it. Through a heavy bee-like buzzing in his head, Piero heard her quick intake of breath, her faint hiss of exhalation. He waited for her to scream at him, perhaps slap his face, but she merely curled her fingers over his hand and pressed it down upon the fabric so that he could feel the small hard bones of her narrow ribcage as well as the slight, almost imperceptible rise of flesh. Such soft flesh it was, such surprisingly warm, soft, live and lovely flesh. A sudden mortifying sob shook him. When she made no comment, simply continued to lie in silence beside him, Piero could have wept with gratitude. In a moment he was on the verge of sleep, her breast still in his possession.

A small sunshot trail of fog floated above the water. The hills were clearly visible, the sky a gentle, innocuous blue. The wispy clouds were pale, ethereal; Piero knew that such clouds would never swell and darken into rain-bulging monstrosities. The girl sat back on her narrow haunches, her arms stretched up behind her head as she struggled to tidy her dark, tangled hair. Her face had lost the pinched defensiveness of two days ago, and her brown eyes held an almost feverish glow.

"I cannot meet my family looking like this," she cried. "In the Name of God and the Blessed Holy Mother, please help me!"

Why she had decided to believe in so many things all at once baffled Piero. A wealthy and welcoming family was only part of it. No longer did the Blessed Mother of God seem in any way tiresome to her; rather, the girl now seemed convinced that the Blessed Mother had taken a special interest in her and begged God to spare her life so that she might be united with her supposed family. "Who really knows," she had said to Piero as she carefully divided the last of the bread for their morning meal. "Perhaps God brought about the whole Deluge just for this purpose alone!" Piero had stared at her, his ears suddenly ringing with desperate cries, with final pleas and fervent prayers, all cruelly unanswered. He could have sworn he heard Grandmother Giulia's voice among them promising even more devotion and duty should God extend a merciful hand to save her. Piero had snatched his share of the bread and stuffed it in his mouth so he wouldn't have to reply.

Piero watched as the boat drew near, then nearer still, the prow plunging up and down in the surging waters of the Arno like a half-broken horse trying to rid itself of its rider. The rowers worked the oars with unsmiling concentration, fighting the pull of the current with grim might. Their black-cloaked rescuer, however, smiled distantly from the center of the boat. He was standing despite the roughness of the floodwaters, his chest outthrust and one hand resting upon his sword hip with threatening elegance. Noting that he looked exactly like one of Florence's many statues of great men, Piero decided the pose was deliberate. The man was flaunting his own heroism, savoring to the fullest this crowd of approving onlookers who admired his exceptional good will, organization, and courage. After all, how many of them were willing to dare the Arno until the floodwaters had retreated completely and the Arno was its placid self again? How many of them would trouble to save two children of no particular significance? As their rescuer drew close to their stone sanctuary, that formal smile told Piero exactly what would happen once they all reached the shore: Piero and the girl would be generously permitted to keep their new clothing, most likely they'd also be given another excellent meal — and that would be the end of it. Then the two of them would part company as well. He would find out what remained of his home, his neighborhood, and then he would work at becoming someone who tried to think for himself. She would assist the nuns with putting the *Spedale* to rights. If she was lucky, the nuns might agree to store the wine-colored gown for her until she was older; if she was unlucky, if the *Spedale* was badly damaged with furnishings ruined and provisions spoiled, they might sell it for food and other necessities.

"Another moment and he'll be here," the girl cried, a world of impatience in her voice.

Two days ago, perhaps even just yesterday, Piero would have felt superior to the girl; what kind of silly female invented so unlikely a fantasy for herself anyway? She claimed to have lost no one in the flood, but now Piero understood that in a few short minutes this claim would be proven untrue. When their rescuer hurried off to perform other civic-minded acts — likely not aiding in such homely tasks as mud-removal and grave-digging, but searching for other stranded victims in improbable places that might give him another chance to display to a cheering crowd — she would lose a sustaining dream, a dream of family. Her unguarded radiance saddened him. All at once he felt much older than the girl and infinitely more prepared to move forward into his reprieved life.

"Here," he said. "Let me." And while she knelt there on the rough stonework, leaning forward in her eagerness, he combed his fingers gently through the long curling strands of hair. How soft her hair was, despite the knots and tangles. And how remarkable to find no lice, not even the tiniest of nits clinging to her scalp. His grandmother, who had inspected his head for lice on a daily basis, would have been favorably impressed. His grandmother, who enjoyed concocting malodorous herbal remedies that burned like the fires of Hell, would also have been disappointed that her skills were not needed.

And he would miss his grandmother, Piero realized. But he would not miss her god.

Marabou

A STANLEY POCKET JOURNAL? He couldn't have. Not after her open, if affectionate, scorn. "Oh what bliss, what joy!" Gretchen had jeered when he first showed her the Cavendish catalog ad. "For the bargain price of $39.95 we, too, can pretend we're glamorous, murderous, plundering, Victorian explorers." Now here it was, in all its tiny, tan, top-stitched-leather glory, and Gretchen was tempted to spill a bit of her orange Fanta on it.

"I knew it would drive you nuts." Sam tucked the journal in the inside pocket of his cotton vest and leaned back in his chair. "So I hid it 'til we got here."

Sam's love of expensive writing implements usually amused her, which was a good thing since their apartment was littered with Mont Blanc and Waterman pens, exotic paper handcrafted from Irish linen, Japanese rice, even recycled teak from Bangladesh. He had a gold-embossed Italian leather Post-It dispenser, a Canadian deerskin pencil holder shaped like a teepee, and — elegantly resting upon a silver tray on the upper left hand corner of his desk — a Waterford whiskey decanter with two matching shot glasses. A few things had been given to him by fans of his novels, but the majority Sam had ordered from chic and extortionate specialty catalogs.

"This journal's a lot more practical than you'd think," he said, grinning at her. "It's exactly the right size for this pocket. Listen, Gretch, are you going to finish those chips or just admire them?"

Gretchen grinned back as she pushed her plate of chips toward him. Of course the Stanley Pocket Journal was the right size. Cavendish specifically designed it for the kind of person who'd buy a safari vest cut on traditional lines with traditionally-proportioned pockets. And it wasn't as if Sam had no journals or notebooks that wouldn't have done the job perfectly well. He had sixteen of them at last count, a few plain little spirals but most much fancier; Georgia O'Keeffe poppies adorned the cover of one, Navaho art another, the Celtic Cross of Killamery yet another — and so on. He'd buy a few more on this trip, although the poor quality of Ugandan paper would annoy him no end. He'd buy local pens and pencils too, just for the experience of it, and then complain loudly if the pens leaked or the pencils wouldn't sharpen to a fine point. Gretchen relished what she thought of as his lovable writerly wierdnesses.

"Time to get on the road," Gretchen said, draining the last of her orange Fanta. "I don't want to drive back in the dark. It's like begging to die."

"Really? Why is that?"

Sam's habit of curiosity seemed undaunted by jet lag, which Gretchen found impressive and yet unsurprising. Sam liked — no, needed — to understand things, people, places, situations. This need made him gregarious, a quality that endeared him to his readers and partially explained the success of his book tours.

"Too many vehicles don't have headlights, for one thing," she told him. "Also, too many drivers decide to stop in the middle of the road for no apparent reason. And too many cows and goats have no sense of self preservation…"

"Okay, I get the picture. Lead on, MacDuff." He smiled. "You're the boss."

Although Gretchen wasn't at all sure this was true, it was

certainly their rhetoric on this vacation. For the next two weeks Gretchen, Ugandan-born and raised, was responsible for every major decision. And since she hadn't been here in decades and remembered only a handful of words in Lugandan, Gretchen was not comfortable with her Experienced-Africa-Traveller role. What if Sam decided she was an incompetent idiot? Or worse yet, a fraud? She fought the impulse to make a fresh disclaimer every few minutes, sometimes every few seconds, but there really was no denying that they were on turf that was more hers than his. And this being a first in their two years together, Gretchen couldn't help but take some pleasure in it. (Not that the Kampala Sheraton felt like her turf. The lobby, with its grand piano and elaborate bar-cum-restaurant, was only just rescued from luxurious anonymity by an African crafts shop that sold everything from Kenyan elephant-hair bracelets to Ugandan beadwork to antique Congolese fertility statues. The Sheraton was a reluctant concession to Sam, who had what he called "the immune system from hell" and worried about germs.)

Gretchen paid the bill. It seemed a bit steep for one Nile beer, a Fanta, a couple of samosas, and an order of fish and chips, but that's what you got for eating at the Speke Hotel. Atmosphere did not come cheaply, and there weren't many places that had the Ye Olde Out-of-Africa glamour she still pleasurably, albeit guiltily, associated with pre-1972 Uganda. In all of Kampala, only the Speke Hotel seemed unchanged from her girlhood; the dining room had the same dark woodwork and wide-windowed breezes, the lobby had the same cool elegance that was both stark and shabby, and she'd have sworn that the long whitewashed verandah had the same number of tables and chairs in exactly the same places back in 1966 when her parents brought her here in honor of her eighth birthday. She remembered the thrill of that first of six wonderful birthday lunches at the Speke. How delightedly she'd agonized over her order: Orange Fanta or Coke? Meat or vegetable samosas? Chips with vinegar — so terribly sophisticated! — or familiar, comfortable catsup?

"Lordy, this place is crowded," Gretchen said as she and Sam headed up the hill to the Sheraton parking lot. "This public garden thing with all these fancy paths is new. Well, new to me, I mean. And it used to be quiet up here, except for a few marabou storks flapping around." She paused, reconsidered. "I take that back. They didn't really flap much. Just skulked around like gloomy adolescents."

Sam didn't appear to have heard her. He was avidly watching all the little knots of people who circled the paths, stopping now and then to pose before the tidy palms, or the oleanders, or the great awkward stub of a baobab tree. Because Gretchen was pleased with her comparison (living with a writer had made her more word-conscious than she used to be) she repeated herself, adding, "They really do look amazingly like adolescents, I think. All slouch-necked and sullen and scruffy, with messy eating habits."

"Hmmm," he said absently, and then, "How much do you want to bet those guys over there are Mormons? White shirts and black trousers, short hair, polished shoes — the whole works."

Gretchen followed his gaze to a park bench occupied by two young men eating sandwiches and reading magazines. They looked straight out of a 1950s yearbook photograph of the school debate team, their monochromatic clothing worn without the confidence that might have lent style. Gretchen found them refreshingly different from the other white people wandering around in khaki safari outfits with Ray Bans perched à la Jackie O on top of their heads. Sam now turned to give the safari people that disdainful look he reserved for Tourists-with-a-capital-T, the kind who attended Native American powwows wearing war-paint, or who went to Ireland "just to kiss the Blarney Stone and buy hokey shamrock jewelry." Then he looked back at the Mormons and reached inside his vest for his notebook. Gretchen grabbed his hand. "Don't be so obvious," she pleaded in a whisper. "Wait 'til we get in the Land Rover, and then you can take all the notes you like."

"I wasn't going to be obvious." He stared at her with hurt astonishment. "Give me a little credit."

Gretchen nodded, withdrew her hand, and after a moment Sam moved away to study the intricacies of the severely-barbered bougainvillea at close range. She stood still on the path, watching his pale thick fingers move curiously, carefully, across the magenta leaves and tiny bracts. Her sudden impulse to protect the supposed Mormons baffled her, for Sam was not unkind. His prose was much admired for its sensitivity, in fact, and this had played a large role in her initial, somewhat-awed attraction to him. Other attributes hadn't hurt, of course: his wide shoulders and rangy build, his spontaneous friendliness and sudden enthusiasms, especially his thick straight mane of prematurely-white hair so suitable for an ILL, or Illustrious Literary Lion, as she sometimes teasingly called him. (Odd how his hair still captivated her, reminding her of the gothic-novel heroes with whom she'd whiled away whole long days in junior high... *Remember the National Assembly, Gretchen child? It was dissolved three weeks ago. But since your nose was buried in some trashy paperback, I guess you could hardly be expected to notice that you're now living in an absolute dictatorship. And no, Naomi my love, I am NOT being hard on her! I just think a little reality could be healthy, all things considered.*)

A touch on her arm made her gasp and take a quick step backwards.

"Sorry. I didn't mean to startle you." One of the young men stood beside her, smiling apologetically. His accent was British, but more North Country-Working-Class than Plum-in-the-Mouth-Oxbridge-Posh, which was the kind of distinction she'd learned to make growing up in a former British colony. His eyes were frank, blue, and bright. "I'm Andrew and this is my friend Colin. We'd like to have a word."

"What about?" Gretchen asked.

"Your quality of life, actually." The young man drew a deep breath and his eyes darkened with apology. "We hate to intrude. We're just simple missionaries..."

Gretchen stared. She'd known missionaries with Yale medical degrees and no degrees at all, non-creedal missionaries and missionaries who subscribed to every one of the original, early-twentieth-century Fundamentals, missionaries who liked to go skinny-dipping, missionaries who collected old Bibles, cigarette lighters, and Barbie dolls. She'd even known a missionary who played the Ugandan thumb piano, the *kalimba*, like a pro, and regularly voted absentee-ballot for his widowed, white-gauze-capped Mennonite mother to be the next American President. But she'd never met a simple missionary. Not ever.

"Can we help you?" Sam was back, his arm across her shoulders, his tone proprietary. He clearly thought she was being propositioned, and this tickled her vanity. The combined ages of the two young men probably didn't equal her own.

"Actually, they want to help me," she told Sam. "Turns out they are missionaries after all."

"Well, I'll be — darned!" Sam's lips quirked and his brows scooted up almost to his hairline. "You just can't get away from them, can you?"

"Apparently not," she replied.

"Yes, she can," the young man said so softly, so evenly, that Gretchen almost missed the hurt in his voice. Almost — but not quite. So he was one of those missionaries, the kind who had to battle his own personality in order to witness, or evangelize, or share, or whatever they called it these days. Gretchen always felt sorry for the shy, retiring ones; even as a small child she'd been acutely aware that her mother would rather face a cobra with a dull machete than ask someone nosy questions about the state of his or her soul. And so she looked at the young man's reddening face, took his hand and shook it.

"Thank you, Andrew," she said. "I appreciate it. Really."

"You're very welcome," he replied with equal sincerity, and then a glint of humor. "Really."

As they started up the hill again, Sam said, "You're too much," he said. And then, his hand sliding up to caress the back of her neck, "I'm glad you let me come with you."

As if the trip had been her idea. As if she would have come on her own. As if she had the power to deny him access to Uganda according to her whim. Gretchen realized how tensed up she'd been when she felt the sudden warm softening of the cords in her neck. She smiled at him gratefully, her own uncertainties lessening. "But you better behave," she said. "Or I'll send you home."

He threw his head back and laughed delightedly, his white mane rippling in the noonday sun.

Because she had almost forgotten the shimmering green stillness of mid-afternoon, the thick ripe smell of standing water and rotting undergrowth, Gretchen drove slowly with the windows down. Her breathing slowed as well, and she felt her exhalations rise into the air like her childhood soap bubbles from a plastic hoop. Little acacia-shaded markets crowded the roadsides so closely that she could smell the heaped produce, especially the clusters of bananas, which she recognized as the small sweet *ndizi* and not the starchy *matoke* used for cooking. Gretchen was tempted to stop and buy some, but decided to resist temptation until she was free to enjoy them properly, fully, without the distraction of driving. She'd waited a long time to eat a real Ugandan banana. She could wait a little longer.

"Watch it, Gretch!" Sam's voice sounded like someone was slowly severing his windpipe. "My God, that was close! What do you suppose they have against staying in their own lanes here?"

"Drivers don't always stay in their own lanes in the States either," Gretchen said as she watched the overloaded Toyota swerve madly out of sight through her rear view mirror. "And as for Ireland last month…"

"All right, point taken." Sam said agreeably, then leaned back and closed his eyes, his white-stubbled jaw slack. Gretchen sympathized. She, too, was sliding into that early-afternoon slump when she could've gone to bed and slept for hours. Oddly enough, she was almost glad to be driving under these jet-lagged circumstances. It meant she was too tired to be nervous about driving on the left, about being swallowed whole by potholes, about hitting frail old gentlemen on rickety Raleigh bicycles with squawking chickens tied to the passenger seat. After all she'd heard and read, Gretchen had expected to find the old Jinja road in worse condition than this — but then, the Jinja road was important. If the Ugandan government didn't keep it in decent repair and something went wrong at Owen Falls Dam, the repercussions would be serious. Most of Uganda and a good part of Kenya relied on the dam for their electricity.

"I used to know this fifty-mile stretch like the back of my hand," she said, suddenly expansive and fond. "What a blast we had, Sarah Jantzen and I."

They'd all had a blast, really. The Clausen/Jantzen friendship had been that rare thing: a friendship with something in it for each family member. Gretchen's doctor father had openly savored his friendship with Dick Jantzen. "God bless the man for appreciating a good joke and a good smoke," he'd say. "And the relief of knowing another white guy who doesn't tote a gun around!" Gretchen's mother and Doris Jantzen had bonded immediately over the humiliations of being "conchie daughters" during the Second World War, and later "conchie wives." They enjoyed long comfortable gossips about everything from lentil soup recipes to the young Mennonite teacher in Fort Portal who had not only discarded her starched gauze cap but cut and permed her hair as well. And Sarah and Gretchen would play hopscotch in the dirt, dare each other to cut off their braids, and plan and re-plan their double wedding to gun-toting game rangers from Murchison Falls or Queen Elizabeth National Park.

After they'd had their usual argument about wedding location — Sarah wanted to get married in Kampala's Namirembe Cathedral while Gretchen wanted a steamboat wedding on Lake Victoria — they'd bicycle to the market for Fanta sodas, little packets of McVitie's Digestive biscuits, and tangerines. Then they'd head across town to the golf course, making a brief detour down Bridge Street to collect Amrita Ramanujan from her family's shell-pink, many-balconied mansion. The three of them often argued about the best places to watch the golfers, but always agreed that no matter the vantage point, Mr. Lowry from Barclays Bank was the best one to watch. Dressed in his blue-

and-green plaid plus fours, green knee socks, and blue roadster cap with pompom, Mr. Lowry provided the most visual entertainment value by far. What was more, Mr. Lowry drank spirits from a fancy silver pocket flask, swore mightily when he landed a ball in a water-filled hippo footprint, and ranted to his golfing partners about his head teller, Rajee, who was a Bloody Stupid Colored of the Bloody Hindu Persuasion. Whenever he went off on one of his tirades about Rajee, Amrita would call him a Bloody Stupid White of the Bloody Christian Persuasion under her breath, and all three of them would laugh until their bladders forced them to find relief behind the moonflower bushes. Then, exhausted, they'd walk down the steep hill to the water. They'd crawl out onto the crumbly chunk of concrete that they'd dubbed The Keep, dribble their fingers in the whitewater surging around their tiny-but-well-moated castle, and feel night settle dankly on the river like a gigantic tarpaulin. Amrita would have to go home before the darkness was absolute, or Mr. and Mrs. Ramanujan would send her old *amah*, or maybe her handsome, cricket-playing cousin Ajit, down the hill after her. Sarah and Gretchen would stay at The Keep a little longer, congratulating themselves on having easygoing parents who didn't worry. At last, chilled and clammy, they'd push their bikes up the hill to Cliff Road, then leap on and race all the way home, shrieking and pressing their bell levers.

"The three of us wanted to go to Emmanuel College together," Gretchen said now. "It's beyond me how we thought we'd convince Amrita's parents that an American Mennonite education was okay for a Hindu girl, but we were going to try. And then things got crazy, and it was all — all moot." Gretchen glanced sideways, suddenly self-conscious. After all, she'd told Sam nothing about Amrita before today — absolutely nothing — and little more than nothing about Sarah. Then she realized that Sam's head was bouncing lightly against the back of the passenger seat. His mouth hung open so wide that she could see his chapped lower lip and the metallic gleam of his molar fillings.

At this moment he didn't look much like the Illustrious Literary Lion who had wooed her with silk-ribbon-tied scrolls of love poetry written just for her. Although she wanted to laugh, she contented herself with smiling. The book tour in Ireland had exhausted as well as gratified him, and she knew that he hadn't really looked forward to getting on another plane and living out of a suitcase for two more weeks. Especially living out of a suitcase on a continent that had never held any interest for him — at least, not until he met her. Gretchen's heart caught with love and guilt; she had to remind herself that this trip was really his idea.

Gretchen didn't see the marabou stork until she was almost upon it. She gaped at the enormous, bristly-headed bird standing motionless in the road, his baleful eyes staring right into hers — and then she braked. Braked bone-jarringly, even though she was sure it was too late. The Land Rover shuddered to a stop, and Gretchen was aware of many things all at once: the safety belt pressing hard against her ribcage, her hands trembling wetly on the wheel, the sun shimmering on the Land Rover's green hood, Sam's angry voice shouting what the hell, Gretch!

"I'm sorry," she said feebly. "But it's a bird. A marabou stork."

Sam leaned his head back for a moment, then took a deep breath. "You all right?" he asked.

"Yes, I guess so. But I don't suppose the bird is."

"We'll have to take a look," he said, undoing his seat belt. "Come on."

Gretchen climbed out on shaky legs. By the time she'd slammed the door and walked around to the front of the vehicle, Sam was already squatting on his haunches beside the felled marabou stork. The stork lay in the rainy-season mud, its great ragged wings feebly flapping while Sam's hands probed with brisk skill.

"What do you think?" she asked anxiously.

"I'm not sure," Sam said. "I can't find any obvious injury."

Three Ugandans had by now clustered around, and Sam turned to them. "Okay, any opinions? Any advice?" he asked.

"Have we killed it?"

The two women looked blankly apologetic — Gretchen supposed they spoke no English — but the man, who was old, bearded, and thin to the point of emaciation, poked the bird's breast with his walking stick and said, "These marabou, they're a national nuisance and very hard to kill. You wait and see. In a minute it will be fine."

"This is one really massive bird," Sam observed. "I bet it's almost five feet tall. What do you suppose its wingspan is? And do you have any idea why it's making that noise?"

The old man began to tell Sam all about marabou storks, how they rattled their bills when they were agitated, how they often had a seven foot wingspan, how they ate carrion like vultures, which was why people didn't eat them. He was clearly enjoying himself, basking in Sam's interest and attention, and when Sam told him that he had written a novel about an Irish birdwatcher, the old man grabbed Sam's hand and shook it, exclaiming again and again that he'd never met a real author and this was a great day for him, a very great day. "When I was in secondary school I dreamed of writing," he said. "And I have a cousin who once heard Ngugi wa Thiong'o read at Makerere University. But that was many years ago — and of course my cousin never actually met him."

Gretchen repressed a smile. Wherever Sam happened to be — a bookstore in Dublin, a party in New York, a road in Uganda — he found himself a writer-loving audience. And if he exerted himself even for just a minute or two, that audience was starry-eyed, enslaved.

The stork flapped its wings a little harder and Gretchen said, "I think it's trying to get up."

All of them watched carefully as the marabou stork thrashed and struggled to a standing position. It tottered around with a fierce glare, its bill grinding and crunching as if subduing live prey, and then it stalked off into the bush, leaving an evil carrion stink in its wake.

"Well, thank goodness for that," Gretchen said, drawing a

deep breath of relief. Marabou storks might be the lowest of the low, scavenging and multiplying all over Uganda in a downright Hitchcockian manner, but she had never wanted to kill one.

"I told you how it would be," the old man said with evident satisfaction. "A marabou always survives."

After an elaborate exchange of good wishes and farewells, he went on his way. The two silent women nodded politely, then crossed the road to a little produce stall that Gretchen hadn't noticed before. They sat down on two low stools and began to fan themselves with magazines. Gretchen supposed they must be the proprietors and wondered with a flicker of greed whether they had any finger bananas in stock.

"I was really worried we'd have to take the stork with us," Sam said as they climbed back into the Land Rover. "And I wasn't looking forward to playing Florence Nightingale. My God, what a filthy bird."

"Nursemaid to a stork? You?" Gretchen eyed Sam with bemused tenderness as he washed his hands with a British Airways towelette. He wasn't usually so sentimental, having accepted the "nature red in tooth and claw" business long ago on that family farm he rarely mentioned. She supposed it must be The Exotic Factor kicking in again; she had always known that Sam was attracted to her — in part, at least — because he found her background strange and exciting. More exciting than his own Illinois-farm background, a heritage distinctly lacking in marabou storks, a heritage that he never ever wrote about. Fictionally, Sam preferred to concentrate on other, more distant aspects of his ancestry: his mother's great-grandmother, who had been one-quarter-Sioux, and his father's great-grandfather who had come over from Ireland during the worst of the famine years. These were, in fact, the only relatives ever included in his book jacket biography, where his ancestry was described as Sioux-Irish. Sam once said he worked the Sioux connection so hard because it allowed him to check one of those invaluable non-white categories on grant application forms. Gretchen had feared he wasn't joking.

"Listen, Gretch, can we stay here another minute?" Sam asked as he reached into his vest pocket. "I want to jot a few things down, and I can't do it while you're driving."

Deciding this might be her chance to eat that first tiny finger banana, Gretchen said of course she didn't mind. She left him hunched over his Stanley Pocket Journal and headed for the produce stall across the road. The two women smiled as she approached, and Gretchen smiled back, delighted to see several compact bunches of *ndizi* on the little wooden table. After selecting a bunch with skin the color of zinfandel blush wine, Gretchen negotiated her purchase with more smiles and upheld shillings. Some things hadn't changed much after all, she realized; English might be the official language of Uganda, but once out of the big city, you were hard-pressed to find villagers who spoke it. Especially women.

Under the skimpy shade of a nearby acacia, Gretchen broke a banana from the bunch, peeled back the skin, and discovered that sweet, succulent memory had not betrayed her. She ate the banana as slowly, as solemnly, as she had once eaten communion bread. Her eyes closed, but she still sensed the warm frenzy of green behind her, the shimmer of reddish mud before her, the bright, steeping sun upon her face. And suddenly she felt a strange and joyful slippage within, a displacement of her adult self. She seemed to stand once again beside the Mpanga River in Fort Portal, her home until the age of seven, the water flowing cheerfully past her bare feet. Congo's Ruwenzori Mountains filled the western horizon with their distant blueness, and she deliberately savored the whole of her short life as well as the flawless, rose-tinted banana she'd purchased in the market square. Purchased from her favorite fruit seller, Regina Bwamba, whose arched eye brows gave her an expression of permanent alarm, and who jokingly threatened her with the dream-haunting monster *Ekibobo* because she was so thin. ("That *Ekibobo*, he comes and GETS children who don't eat enough, you know. Here, little one, buy just a few more bananas!") Yes, she had consciously, very consciously, loved her home in the heart of the old Toro Kingdom. Loved, too, the lavish green of the tea estates surrounding Fort Portal, and the twenty different kinds of bananas one could bring on picnics to the old Toro Palace ruins. Nearly everything had seemed lovable to her then: the slow wheezy clacking of the train heading up to the Kenyan coast, the black iron-lace balconies on the big houses on Kyebambe Road, the hot curries washed down with fresh passionfruit juice and cardamom-scented chai at Toro King Tandoori… Hadn't she taken Sarah and Amrita there once, when they visited Fort Portal for the weekend? Yes — yes, she had. She was sure of it. Just before President Obote abolished all the Kingdoms in 1966 and Mr. Patel had to rename his restaurant, choosing the safe, predictable Taj Mahal. Poor Mr. Patel had slapped up a still-wet sign in a matter of hours, terrified that the authorities might consider him a trouble-making tribalist even though his parents came from Bombay. She wondered what had happened to him, to his tiny wife with the fondness for shocking-pink saris, to his mother who predicted it would all get so much much worse…

"I've made my notes." Sam was beside her, giving her arm an affectionate squeeze. "Thanks for waiting."

"Oh! Oh, fine. No problem," Gretchen replied, momentarily disoriented. *How is it possible, this sudden estrangement from my adult self? I must resist this wierd slippage backward. It's nostalgia of the very worst kind, the neo-colonial kind. And it's all so completely indefensible anyway, my idyllic early childhood in this country that so many still associate with Idi Amin and tragedy.*

"A good source of potassium, you know," Sam said as he reached over and snapped off a banana from the bunch in her hand. He ate it quickly, tossed the peel into the vine-ridden fringe of forest, and said, "Not bad. Not bad at all. I'm going to eat lots of these while we're here. With that nice thick skin, they're unlikely to have germs."

Gretchen walked back to the Land Rover and wrenched the door open with a savage jerk more suited to the rusty-hinged 1956 Ford her father had driven years ago. As she climbed into the driver's seat she thought she caught a whiff of the lingering rancid stink of marabou.

The town of Jinja reminded Gretchen of Mrs. Beranek, who lived down the hall in their Brooklyn apartment building and whose bone structure hinted at a former beauty even while she slopped around in a ragged housecoat and dirty slippers. The basic outline of the town was familiar enough, but the old colonial mansions were decayed and overcrowded, the stores in need of fresh paint. And the burned-out tank on the otherwise empty lot where the Jantzens' house used to be bore stark witness to Uganda's years of trouble. Gretchen slowed to watch the half-dozen small children crawling over the blackened tank, vying for an apparently coveted place in the turret. They treated the massive weapon like a playground jungle gym, and she listened to their spilling, squealing laughter with a twist of shock.

"Now that's an original concept in children's toys," Sam remarked. "I should make a note of it."

Gretchen drove on without telling Sam that this particular tank-turned-toy had replaced Sarah's home. She was afraid of sounding too melodramatic, too attention-seeking, especially since Sam's sympathies were unlikely to be engaged by one lost missionary home when there were dispossessed Native Americans and potential bombings in northern Ireland to worry about. And why should his sympathies be engaged anyway? Several years ago Gretchen had heard a Ugandan refugee musician sing an upbeat song insisting that "homeless is not my name," and she had huddled in her uncomfortable concert-hall seat, diminished, cold with mortification at her own habit of self-pity. How little sympathy she and Sarah (wherever Sarah was) really deserved… Besides, Sam would write it down.

"Main Street," Gretchen said as she signalled, then turned right. "And over there — yes, kittycorner — is the mosque."

"When you visited here, where did your family go to church?" Sam asked.

"A tiny mud-brick church near the railway station," she told him, then smiled. "It didn't have a door, so all the goats and chickens treated it like a hotel during the week. On Sundays, Sarah's father and the church elders had to go sweep out all the droppings before…"

Sam interrupted her. "I sure hope that old guy was right about the marabou," he said. "He might have had internal injuries after all. He might have gone off into the bush to die."

The marabou? How does the marabou come into this? And why is it a "he" all of a sudden?

"Then again, I do really think he was going to be fine," Sam went on. "I thought I knew a fair amount about birds, but he was a new experience. Literally an ugly customer — but what strength, what resilience!"

You're always and forever begging me for stories, so why aren't you listening? "Don't hold out on me, sweetie," you say. "Here, have a glass of wine and put your feet up and tell me something incredibly exotic." And so I do, wannabe writer that I secretly am in my heart of hearts. I produce a colorful anecdote, a strange and vivid moment that isn't about Sarah, isn't about Amrita, isn't about anything that truly matters. And if that doesn't make me feel like some bargain-basement Scheherazade with a talent to amuse instead of a real live person.

"I wonder where we could have taken him if he'd needed medical care," Sam said. "Does Jinja have such a thing as a vet? And what about the SPCA — or is it the RSPCA in a former British colony?" He paused consideringly. "I suppose it's possible they've got their own chapter of the Royal Society for the Protection of Birds."

Am I annoyed? Yes, I think I must be annoyed, just a little. So this church, Sam, it didn't have any shutters or screens either. And this one rainy Sunday there was such a terrific east wind that the rain blew inside, drenching everyone. Although Sarah and I were nearly fourteen and constantly struggling for a jaded dignity in public, we laughed hysterically, hugging each other with goose-pimpled arms. The congregation was in an uproar, but Dick Jantzen, who 'd been called upon by the Ugandan pastor to close the service with prayer, just prayed resolutely on. Afterwards, though, Dick said, "The rest of you were pretty darn lucky to be sitting down. That wind nearly knocked me off my feet.

Would have given whole new meaning to the phrase 'prostrate before the Throne of Grace,' don't you think?" And then Dick laughed boisterously, his mouth open so wide that I could see his tonsils quivering like bright pink flames at the back of his throat.

My father didn't laugh. "I wonder if it was some kind of omen," he said. "Really, I do. The Ugandan elements trying to drown us."

Suddenly I went even colder in my rain-drenched Sunday dress, but my mother said, "Oh, honestly, darling, how childish! I suppose you'll have Ekibobo monster dreams next!"

"Believe me, Naomi, I already am," he told her soberly. "Dreaming about monsters seems only too appropriate these days."

There was silence, save for the residual drip-dripping of the rain, and then Doris Jantzen said, "Oh, never mind all that now. Everyone has to go change into dry things. And you, Sarah Jane, on the double, before you catch your death in that skimpy dress — which, by the way, I see you've re-hemmed indecently short unless your legs grew about five inches last night!"

And Sarah and I scurried down the hall to her room, only to discover that we'd forgotten to close the shutters before leaving for church, and rain had pooled on the floor, soaked the bedclothes through to the mattress, even doused the dresses hanging behind the batik curtain which served as a closet door. We stamped and splashed in the standing water like two toddlers, then dropped onto the wet bed half-sobbing with laughter. If Amrita had been with us right then, our moment of utter silliness and release would have been perfect.

"Hey Gretch, are you in there?" Sam's voice had a petulant edge. "I asked if Jinja had such a thing as a vet. Or the RSPCA or whatever."

"Try the yellow pages," Gretchen said irritably. And then, repenting, "In my day there was at least one excellent vet. There was also a man people often consulted about animals. He lived on Bridge Street at Firefinch House."

"Firefinch. Isn't that the pink mansion you told me about?" Sam asked. "The one where the bird-lover lived?"

She had told Sam that much, knowing he'd enjoy hearing about Mr. Ramanujan's fondness for birds. Especially Mr. Ramanujan's fascination with the little Red-billed Firefinches that roamed his property, feeding in gorgeous rose-pink clusters that dazzled the eye. "Yes," she said now, wanting to make amends by giving him more of the exotic details he delighted in. "Mr. Ramanujan drank his tea on the front porch every morning just so he could watch them. He wanted African Firefinches too. They're an amazing deep red color, and sing with this bell-like trill. But they don't like living around people, not like the Red-billed ones, so he was out of luck."

"Pity." Sam took out his Stanley Pocket Journal, then put it back again. "This damn road. I wish I hadn't eaten that banana."

Although inclined to defend it, Gretchen had to admit that Nile Avenue had deteriorated sadly. The tall trees lining it retained their stateliness, but the avenue itself was just a gravel track crusted here and there with old grey bits of tarmac.

"The Bridge Street turnoff is just ahead." Gretchen hesitated, then said slowly, "We could stop at Firefinch House if you like. It's not much out of our way, and you never know. The finches might still be there."

"Good idea," Sam said. "I've been thinking about that sequel to the birdwatcher novel. Maybe I'll give it an African setting instead of an Irish one. Complete with bird safari to Firefinch House, of course."

Gretchen thought back to her first conversation with Sam. It was at a Barnes & Noble reading shortly after the publication of *Bluebird's Eye*, and she was almost too stunned by his attention to breathe. He'd told her that he wrote the book for the sheer fun of dipping into his huge store of esoteric bird facts. "What's the point of learning things if you can't make use of them?" he'd said. "I like exhaling it all back into the world in some new form." She had been charmed.

"Bridge Street," she said briefly. "You better brace yourself. It looks bad."

It was bad. Except for the rock-filled potholes, it was one long slippery trail of thick red mud. As Gretchen swerved to avoid a particularly large pothole, she imagined Mr. Ramanu-jan's horror. His much-cherished and meticulously polished VW Bug wouldn't last a mile on Bridge Street now.

"Some of these places must be abandoned," Sam said. "Look at that huge old pile on the left, the crumbly one with all the orange bougainvillea and no roof. It's a shame."

Gretchen did not reply. Having returned to Uganda at last — to Jinja, even — she couldn't not visit Firefinch House, but dread clogged her throat and tightened her chest. What if it, too, was abandoned, roofless, overgrown? She drove past the landmark mango tree and turned down a long acacia-shaded lane.

Like every other expat at this impromptu airport reunion, Sarah seemed full to bursting with news. Bad news, I guessed, since that was the only kind available. She was also very pale, the Jantzens having kept her housebound in Jinja for nearly three weeks. I supposed, if I thought about it, that I was pale too; I'd been stuck indoors myself. Until this morning, when my father appeared in my bedroom doorway and said, "Put your book away and pack one bag, Gretchen honey. Favorite possessions only."

"About a month ago her Uncle Vijay was attacked on the tea farm," *Sarah told me in a whisper. "He got a terrible head wound as well as a broken arm. But the police wouldn't investigate, of course."*

Of course. I waited; I could see that there was more to come.

"Then, just a few days after that, her cousin Ajit went out to a pub near Makerere University. He went with another Indian poli. sci. major and that cute Acholi guy who was into archaeology…"

"The one studying all that Middle Stone Age stuff around Chobe?" I asked. "Amrita wrote that she had this huge crush on him."

"Yes."

"I thought he sounded very nice." I did not mention the other things I'd thought: that it was mean of her to quit writing altogether after that besotted last letter, and that falling in love was a rotten excuse for neglecting friends. For abandoning friends.

"And the three of them haven't been seen or heard of since. By anyone, anywhere."

I fiddled with the leather drawstring on my Kikuyu bag from Nai-

robi. The endless static from the airport intercom made me want to scream. There were dozens of people standing around with nothing to do but wait, so why didn't somebody try to fix it? Was an intercom really that hard to repair? Maybe I should volunteer. "I didn't know," I said. "I hadn't heard."

"The rest of the family left the day after The Big A announced the expulsion of all Asians. They'd given up looking for Ajit and the others by then anyway. Especially since the police weren't helping this time either."

"Did you get to see her?" I asked.

"No."

"She didn't even try to say goodbye?"

"I don't think so, but I don't know. They took what they could carry and left in the middle of the night for Entebbe." Sarah's mouth crumpled. "We heard they flew to Bombay even though they had relatives in England and The States. Seems Mr. Ramanujan said since the West had supported The Big A's government, there was no way he'd be a refugee there and get treated like some charity case they thought they were being extra nice to. And who could blame him?"

My father had said that Britain recognized the Big A's new government with positively indecent haste because Mr. Heath was so mad at former President Obote for criticizing the British government's attitude about arms sales to South Africa. "Every GOOD reason in the world to be mad at Obote, the oppressive bastard, and Mr. Jackass Heath has to go and pick THAT one!" he'd fumed, and for once my mother did not say, "Language, honey, language." And so I said to Sarah — said belligerently —"Well, I sure don't blame him, so don't look at me."

"Of course I didn't mean you."

"I mean, how could I blame him when I didn't even know? No one tells me anything."

Sarah's eyebrows winged up like frightened birds. "Well, I'm sorry. But my parents said they'd tell your parents, and then your parents could tell you."

"So why'd you tell me then?" I asked.

"I don't know."

I took a deep dank breath of Entebbe air and let it out very slowly.

Then I shifted my weight from one foot to the other. "This line isn't moving," I said. "And I'm thirsty enough to drink the water out of the faucet in the Ladies."

"A couple of diplomat brats already bought up all the Cokes and Fantas anyway," Sarah said, her eyebrows dipping down again. "They must have huge allowances, those over-privileged pigs. If this line ever does move, we'll be lucky to get tonic water."

"Oh shit. I hate tonic water."

"My deah Gretchen." Sarah put on the Oxbridge-Posh accent she'd learned at the Jinja Academy. "How too, too dreadfully Anglo-Saxon of you!"

"Oh well," I said airily. " At least I'm not a Bloody Stupid Colored of the Bloody Hindu Persuasion."

And giggles burst out of my mouth. Burst out forcibly, like projectile vomit.

"That is not funny," Sarah said in a tight cold little voice. "That is so horribly not funny that I can't believe you said it."

And then Sarah slapped my face hard and left the drinks line, stepping carefully around the great piles of luggage topped with sleeping children. For a moment I thought I really might be sick, as sick as I'd been with malaria last summer. But I wasn't. I watched Sarah rejoin her parents, then walked over to one of the plate glass windows facing the runway and stared at the line-up of jets and transports. Except for the hot bright patch on my cheekbone, my body felt cold as our concrete Keep, immovable and uncaring, while intercom static and currents of conversation swirled and eddied around me:

"…and after she heard, the old lady walked right out into the lake in her best silk sari."

"The toilets are full up and won't flush. I just hope to God I can wait til I'm on that plane."

"Richard says the forest just off the Kampala-Jinja Road stinks for miles from all the bodies they've dumped in there. He drove our cook to the forest to look for a missing relative, and they couldn't stand it more than a few minutes."

The Jantzens left on the next plane. Sarah, like Amrita, did not say goodbye. I watched Sarah's African waxprint dress, the one with the

embroidered sash that bordered on the flashy for a ninth grade Men-
nonite girl, disappear inside the low, curving door. Then I bought a
tonic water I couldn't drink, and watched the airport ceiling fans spin
ever more slowly until at last they quit spinning altogether. Although a
lot of people complained about the heat, I didn't mind; I was cold. Our
plane left around five. The late afternoon sun ignited a rose-colored fire
on the surface of Lake Victoria, and that fire stretched as far as I could
see.

The house glistened with pale yellow paint, the lawn was
well-kept, and the gravel drive lined with trimmed shrubbery.
Orange bougainvillea softened the square outlines of the fresh-
ly-whitewashed cookhouse, and the oleanders blooming beside
the doorway looked like giant purple popsicles. For a moment
Gretchen was too stupefied to speak. Was it possible that the Ra-
manujans were among that small percentage of Asians willing to
forgive betrayal and return? She reached for the door handle, astonished by her upwelling of delight, of joy. In this moment she
could believe in anything, hope for everything — and then she
saw the sign by the front door: "Bridge Street Christian Guest-
house."

"No firefinches that I can see," Sam said, but he reached for
his Stanley Pocket Journal anyway.

Gretchen parked as close to the Memorial as she could, put
the Park Service receipt stamped "Paid" on the dashboard, and
got out of the Land Rover. She waited for Sam to collect his camera gear, and then they walked downhill to the stone-and-con-
crete marker smudged with red dirt. Several laughing African
nuns, arms entwined, were having their picture taken beneath
a royal palm. A sunburned man with a Cubs baseball cap worn
back to front and a video camera at the ready was reading the
words on the marker aloud: "'This spot marks the place from
where the Nile starts its long journey...'"

"Let's go down to the water," she said. "That's the real Source
of the Nile, not the marker."

"I'd still like a good look at it though," Sam said. "And maybe a picture. You go ahead. I'll join you."

Gretchen walked down the green slope of Coronation Park wishing she hadn't remembered her nasty adolescent bout with malaria. Her stomach had the horrible fragility that had always plagued her under stress: her first months in America, exam time in college, and especially — oh exquisite misery! — those first weeks after meeting Sam. "I've decided being in love is like an all-day morning sickness," she'd told a teaching colleague at the time. And now it was back full force, that old queasiness, dizzying her, afflicting her with a strange conviction that something of tremendous import was about to happen. Something that might enrich her if only she could summon the wit to recognize it and the stamina to endure it.

As she neared the water, Gretchen saw that The Keep, that worn and familiar lump of concrete, was still there after all. It rose greyly out of the fast-moving river, distinctly separate from the walled square where half a dozen tourists clustered. And she realized for the first time that The Keep must once have had a purpose apart from its function as private sanctuary for three little girls. The base of a bridge that failed, she guessed now. Or a bridge simply abandoned unfinished, perhaps scarcely even begun. She managed to clamber upon it, turned her back on the people in the walled square, and stared blurrily up-current at the spreading blue-white pallor of Lake Victoria.

The Nile flowed around The Keep like a great smooth sheet of old-fashioned milk glass. Flowed north, flowed quietly but tenaciously up the continent toward the Mediterranean. And long moments passed as Gretchen hugged her knees like a child, the journeying water a warm, opalescent taste on her tongue.

When at last she went looking for him, she found Sam leaning against the trunk of a royal palm talking to the man with the video camera. This was no surprise, for Sam fell into conversation the way another person might fall in love: passionately, noisily, and uninhibitedly. Gretchen wondered what he was giving voice to this time. Was it his Irish agenda again, maybe the more surreal aspects of the Queen's visit? Or a discussion about the Pueblo ceremonial dances, how most of them had gotten so touristy that any religious and cultural integrity was lost? She advanced quietly upon the two men's khakiied backs, preparing to be engaged even as Sam's listener undoubtedly already was.

"…all a bit too much, frankly, for a fourteen year old. Kampala was chaos. In the weeks before we left I remember lying awake at night listening to gunfire and people screaming in the streets."

"Were you ever shot at?" Sam's listener asked avidly.

"No, but I knew I could be. My parents kept me indoors, but that didn't ensure safety. One night a bullet came through our kitchen window and shattered the light fixture. God, how I hated windows after that. I'd read by candlelight on my bedroom floor and wish I lived somewhere else. Anywhere else."

Gretchen withdrew her outstretched hand and rammed it in the pocket of her jeans. She stared at the back of Sam's head, stared as she knew she must: fixedly, even sternly, as if to make up for not having seen him properly before. He seemed to take on a sudden ungainliness, balancing uneasily on one long leg while he leaned against the royal palm's smooth trunk. His Illustrious Literary Lion mane had greyed with the fading light of late afternoon, and all his wordsmithing glamour had faded with it. She supposed she should be angry. She knew she should be angry. What earthly right did he have to borrow — no, steal — her experience, her history? How dare he lay claim to her own private fears and then expose them to a stranger? Yes, she was angry now, her throat constricted, hands trembling, face burning — but where were the words? What words would possibly suffice? And all at once she remembered a British neighbor she hadn't thought of in years, Old Hand Harold, as everyone had called him, and a mad desire to laugh seized her. Old Hand Harold had regularly updated the Clausen household on the state of his wife's volatile temper. "Her Ladyship's in high dudgeon today," Old Hand Harold would say ruefully. "Very very high dudgeon. Think I'll drive into town and stay at the Club, what?" When she asked her parents about this "high dudgeon," her mother had said it meant Old Hand Harold's wife was a little out of sorts and her father had said, "Balderdash! Means words have completely failed her and she's howling like a rabid dog and throwing all his favorite hunting trophies at him." Gretchen supposed that when this sudden idiotic urge to laugh went away, a very very high dudgeon would remain. But she couldn't think about it right now; her most immediate need was distance, physical distance, between herself and Sam. She backed away and began to climb the hill.

When she reached Cliff Road, Gretchen paused. She told herself to go back down to the Memorial and find Sam. She told herself it was the adult thing to do, talking things through. But she knew that she simply couldn't bear to listen to Sam do any more talking — at least not at this moment, and certainly not here in this place. She caught a bicycle taxi to the *matatu* park in the town center. Since the next *matatu* for Kampala was leaving immediately, she scrambled off the bicycle passenger seat and into the taxi van with no time to spare for second thoughts. And for the next two hours she didn't think at all, simply allowed her body to be bounced and jounced for fifty kilometers in a spring-less, airless van built to hold ten people but crammed with twice that number and a baby goat in a wicker basket.

It was well after seven when the van lumbered into the heart of the city. The enormous *matatu* park was dark, save for the ghostly fleet of empty white vans and the two street lamps that guttered unsteadily, like dying candle stubs. Aware that it wasn't the best place for a woman alone, Gretchen quickly headed north on Burton Street where there were still a few enterprising people trying to do business on street corners and in small, poorly-lit shops. Gretchen purchased a tattered paperback edition of *Tintin and the Cigars of the Pharoahs* and a bottle of the local gin at Hobart's Bookmart and More. Something enjoyable to read, a little *waragi* to drink (*why not finally satisfy an old adolescent curiosity?*) and she might manage to get through the night.

"Listen, lady-miss, you want to buy some flowers?"

Gretchen stared down at the boy thrusting a plastic bucket of flowers at her knees. She couldn't tell what kind they were — something with a glisteny pallor that lightened the shadows. "Okay," she said, shrugging as she parted with more shillings and accepted a soggy armload. It was only when she turned onto the comparatively well-lit Pilkington Street that she bothered to take a good look at her purchase. Realizing that she'd bought moonflowers, she laughed so hard that sheer weakness made her collapse onto the concrete ledge near the Aeroflot office.

Oh, how she adored Jubilee Park! And oh, how luminous the gibbous moon above the lovely, lovely Sheraton! (*Was there such a thing as a gibbous sun? If there wasn't, there should be. I must investigate.*) And oh, oh how coolly clean the night air on her overheated skin, how romantic the long fanlike shadows of the traveller palm, how adorable that plump stump of a baobab tree. Her Tintin book and great dripping bouquet lay beside her on the bench, and the sticky-sweet moonflower scent tickled her nose and made her want to giggle.

Gretchen poured more *waragi* into the glass she'd borrowed from the Speke Hotel bar and took another sip. It was terrible. So extraordinarily terrible that when she swallowed, fire seared the back of her nose and eyeballs. Well, she'd been warned. "You want to be careful with that stuff," the waiter had told her. "It gives you a whole new pain even while it cures your old one." Gretchen had asked him what made him think she had a pain, and he'd shrugged. "Everyone has a pain. You don't think Ugandans drink so much *waragi* because they like the taste, do you? Here, take some club soda to mix it with." Gretchen had to admit that the soda really did help.

Somebody somewhere was singing Sardou's "Afrique adieu." The singer was straining out one embarrassingly-dated line after another about the beautiful blue waters of Lake Tanganyika and women with golden breasts temptingly near his fingers. The piano accompaniment — she suspected the singer of abusing the grand piano in the Sheraton foyer — was equally bad. Gretchen swallowed another mouthful of *waragi*. "*Peuples fous qui dansent*," she sang, amused and revolted to find she remembered some of the lyrics from a cassette tape she'd owned in her teens and kept a secret from her parents. And then, after another quick swig, "*...mourir de joie.*"

"Still happy about your quality of life then, are you?"

The young Mormon missionary's silhouette emerged from behind the bougainvillea. His impossibly long shadow floated across the short grass toward her, then slid over her sandaled toes and up her jean-clad legs. Although he stopped several feet away from her, Gretchen was disconcerted.

"Well, if it isn't Andrew, the Fisher of Men," she said. "Of course I'm happy. Happy, happy, happy. Pretty much dying of it, in fact. Didn't you hear?"

"Where's your husband?"

"At the Source of the Nile," she said. "Or maybe, since he's got his own set of car keys, on the road. And Sam's not my husband. He's not my anything."

"Do you mind if I sit down?"

"Not at all." Gretchen moved her moonflower bouquet from the bench to her lap, then picked up one large bloom and held it out. "Want one?"

"No thanks." He sat down beside her. "They're a bad omen."

"I know. I bought them from a little kid who figured I wouldn't realize," she said.

"What are you going to do with them?"

She reflected, then said, "Have them delivered to Sam's room in the Sheraton. I've checked into the Speke."

He looked very young and deeply shocked in the moonlight. "But they're a bad omen particularly indoors."

"Yes. Where's your friend?"

"Back at our place e-mailing his girlfriend back in England."

"Where do you live?"

"Kololo Hill, near the intersection of Prince Charles Drive and Malcolm X Avenue."

Gretchen splashed more *waragi* into her glass with a giggly snort, and he sighed.

"I can't help my address. But listen, you really ought to eat something. *Waragi* rots your insides. And besides, the *Ekibobo* will get you if you don't eat."

"I'm too old for the *Ekibobo* to get me," she replied, then peered at him. "And how do you know?"

"I grew up in Kenya but my nanny was a Ugandan refugee. Not Asian though. Langi."

Now she homed in on the truth she'd sensed all along. "And your parents?"

"Missionaries."

"Mormon?"

"No. British Baptist."

"What's your costume in aid of then?"

"I'm Mormon now."

"Oh yes. And just a simple missionary." She paused. "So tell me honestly, do Mormon missionaries really have to dress like that?"

"The rules are a bit looser now, but male missionaries still have to dress conservatively. And woe betide the female missionary who gets caught wearing a black bra."

She snickered and *waragi* went stinging up her nose. "So why do you do that whole 1950s look then?"

"It's more up front, more honest. People know who you are."

"True." She arched a brow — or at least she thought she did. The *waragi* seemed to have a facially freezing effect. East African Botox. "And it's more embarrassing for your parents, I suppose."

"Oh, I got that kind of meanness out of my system in high school."

Gretchen could well imagine how. The teenaged missionary boys she'd known used to hang out at some of the wilder clubs on the outskirts of Kampala. When chance presented, the same boys had made forays into the Nairobi nightlife as well and bragged about it to the more cloistered teenaged girls. Sarah and Gretchen had been both intimidated and envious. "Bet you got drunk at the Green Bar and got in fights on River Road," she said. "And then I bet you tried good old hippie haven Lamu. Tell me, do they still have nude beach parties?"

"I don't know. I spent six months in Lamu after I graduated from the Rift Valley Academy, but I don't remember much of it. A Mormon missionary found me sleeping in a sewer."

"Good God," Gretchen said, startled out of her flippancy. Lamu's open sewage system was one of the technological wonders of the Middle Ages, but unfortunately it hadn't been improved since then. "No wonder you like all that starchy Mormon cleanliness."

"Too right." Andrew laughed. "It's been two years and I'm not tired of it yet. But I'm definitely tired of no alcohol. May I?"

Gretchen poured more *waragi* in her glass and handed it to him. She watched him drink, observing the frail bob of his Adam's apple as he swallowed and then laughed gaspingly. She admired the sweet thinness of his throat and neck above his narrow, perfectly-knotted tie; it was so very unlike Sam's football neck, which was all thickened and marshmallow-soft and criss-crossed with lines. She wondered if Sam was even now driving the Land Rover to Kampala in the darkness. Sam was an anxious driver under the best conditions, but she felt little sympathy.

He's welcome to appropriate The Exotic Factor for himself, she thought, and I will happily give over playing Scheherazade and let him do it instead. But then he's got to do his own damn driving. His own begging-to-die night driving among vehicles travelling at high speeds without headlights. Maybe he will crash; maybe he will die; maybe — oh, this is awful — I won't even mind. And who knows? Maybe I'll lay claim to all his unused notebooks and try to summon the courage to start writing myself.

"I am not," she announced mournfully to Andrew and the gibbous moon, "a nice person. Even though I have labored at niceness for years."

"Have you? Why?"

"I don't know," she said. But she did. For as far back as she could remember, she had known she needed to make up for lots of things: for being American instead of Asian, Ugandan, or any other group arbitrarily labeled Opposition. For being hunger-free, polio-free, TB-free — and now, these days — HIV-free, AIDS-free. For having saddened and bewildered her aging parents, who insisted on terming her job "teaching ministry" in order to hide its utterly secular nature from their missionary friends, and who brooded over her unmarried state even as they referred to Sam as her "husband." But at last she knew the right answer, the real answer: she needed to do penance for having enjoyed, even exploited, that same Exotic Factor she had lately come to resent. The truth was, she loved being considered a woman of immediate interest. She loved having stories to tell that other people wanted to hear. Hers was a history to dine out upon simply because she could oh-so-casually say, "I remember the day Amin took power. Lots of people celebrated because the Obote dictatorship was finally over. My dad grilled Nile perch and my mother made a mango pie and we watched people dance and sing in the streets." Because she could say, "I went with my father to a fancy function honoring medical missionaries, and we both shook hands with Amin. His palm was very fleshy, his thumb was all swollen and oozy from a bad hangnail, and he reeked of Faberge's Brut cologne — which in retrospect seems horribly appropriate." Because she could say, "When I was a small child in western Uganda, we had a night sentry to protect us from encroaching wildlife. This sentry, Robert, taught me how to throw his homemade spear."

No, it was not so much the nostalgia of an idyllic early childhood she felt guilty about after all. Even her adolescent callousness was probably forgivable. What induced self-disgust was her larger betrayal, her cobbling together of an adult personality of interest upon the great scarred back of Ugandan history. She had cultivated The Exotic Factor — and cultivated, too, a coy reticence so as to avoid realizing how much she savored it. The Exotic Factor had helped to win her several intelligent men who were both charmed and charming; Sam was simply the most recent of them, and the only one impressed enough — vulnerable enough, perhaps? — to claim it as his own.

"I just remembered something," she said, turning to face Andrew. "Sinbad the Sailor came from Lamu, didn't he?"

"So legend has it, but I don't remember if Scherazade herself actually said so," he replied. "This *waragi* is vile. Can I have some more?"

Gretchen refilled the glass and handed it to him. He took several large mouthfuls, gasped, then said, "What do you do back in the States?"

"I teach English." She took the glass from him and drained it. "Volunteer at a soup kitchen. Trail Sam around the literary party circuit wearing African malachite earrings and trying to sound knowledgeable about Museveni's expansionist agenda for Uganda." She grimaced. "And the fact is, I don't really understand a thing about African Great Lakes politics."

"Does anybody? I'd let go of that particular guilt," he said. "Hey, just a minute! That man with his back to us in the Sheraton parking lot — isn't that your Sam?"

Gretchen peered up the hill. It was indeed Sam. She recognized his longlegged stride and the backlit nimbus of his hair, but the forward slump of his shoulders was less familiar. She found that she was relieved he'd made it back — found, too, that she was relieved by her relief.

"He looks knackered," Andrew said.

"I expect he is," she replied. "Sam doesn't like to drive, not even in the States, and this was our first full day in Uganda."

Andrew looked thoughtful. "Poor bastard," he said. "Whatever the guy did, remember verse twenty-two of the Epistle of Jude and spare him the moonflowers, won't you? Somehow I don't think he needs a bad omen tonight."

Gretchen watched Sam grow smaller and dimmer until at last he dwindled away in the darkness. She did vaguely remember verse twenty-two; one of her father's favorite texts, it had to do with compassion or forgiveness or something. But how did you forgive someone for displaying those qualities you most despised in yourself? And if you did genuinely forgive that someone's posturing and scavenging neediness, didn't you also have to have a little compassion for yourself? Maybe tomorrow it would all come clear.

"What an awfully Biblical missionary you are, Andrew," she said, patting his arm affectionately. "And now I'd better turn in. I'm pretty smashed."

"So am I. What of it?" He took her by the hand and pulled her to her feet. "Let's go dancing at the Half-London. I'll teach you the Kasai Fuck Dance."

"The *kwasa-kwasa*?" Gretchen was muzzily aware of the eager clasp of his fingers. Aware, too, that the *waragi* had failed to create any false passion between them — maybe because she was old enough to be his mother, maybe because their histories made them siblings. Incest either way. Besides, she'd heard that the *kwasa-kwasa* required exceptionally strong knees. "I'm not that smashed," she told him dryly. "And I don't intend to be."

"Oh, I do! Come on. Mormon absti… absti… — whatever — is pretty damn dull."

"Dear me," she said, grinning. "Is one of us getting converted after all?"

He smiled with great sweetness and said, "Like bloody hell."

Although it was only ten o'clock, Gretchen lay in bed drinking tea and reading *Tintin and the Cigars of the Pharoahs* just as she'd told Andrew she would. These tame plans had wounded his ego. "You'd really rather snoop around Egyptian tombs with old Tintin and the Captain than go dancing with me?" he'd asked reproachfully. She'd given him a peck on the cheek and said, "Yes, Andrew, I'd really rather." After a last disgruntled protest, he'd gone in search of a taxi.

Tintin was just as she remembered. The same silly tuft of hair above round black eyes, the same bony knees below the baggy khaki shorts, the same gigantic question marks littering the pages in evidence of his ongoing perplexities. Gretchen followed Tintin's adventures without curiosity; she knew all the predictable twists and turns of plot and dialogue, recalled each one of Tintin's many narrow escapes from the murderous and greedy grave-robbers. Every Tintin book they could get their hands on they'd learned by heart, but they'd particularly loved this one since it was set in Africa. She could see them yet — the three of them — huddled together on The Keep, reading aloud in a state of pre-teenage, pre-betrayal grace and harmony. She could see even the smallest details: the tiny new hairs on their skinny legs, the sun-roughened split ends wisping out from their long tight braids, the filaments of tangerine rind beneath their fingernails as their hands lingered on the open pages. She could smell both the dried salt on their scabby knees and the fresh salt rimming their upper lips. She could hear them breathing in unison, and almost — almost! — taste their sympathetic affection.

The last two pages were missing, but Gretchen realized with surprised pleasure that it didn't matter. She knew them from memory. Gretchen switched off the lamp, closed her eyes, and reenacted the final pages in her mind while the night moths thumped against the window screen like synchronized heartbeats.

DISLOCATION

OUR FEET ARE COLD in spite of wool socks half an inch thick. We walk quickly, my sister and I, and every now and then our eyes tear up with an especially sharp gust of wind. To distract ourselves we look to each side of the woodland path, searching for evidence of spring. We expect this evidence to be white, purple, and yellow, for we've been told about the snowdrop, the crocus. There is nothing to see but an occasional faint suggestion of green poking through a wilderness of semi-frozen mud. Our disappointment is much less bitter than the wind; we don't expect much of timorous, ground-hugging flowers anyway. Our floral ideals are tall, bold, and firmly in place: bird of paradise, red cannas, bougainvillea, and hibiscus, both single and double.

"No leaves on the trees yet either," my sister says, her tone treading a fine line between disapproval and pity.

In Congo a leafless tree is usually a sick tree — except in dry season, when both the teak and kapok trees lose their leaves. At this moment Illinois looks like a wasteland of sick trees. After a glance at my wristwatch I say we're pulling it a little close. "We've still got at least a mile to go. Maybe we ought to run."

And so we do, but with a clumsiness we didn't have a year ago. Our backpacks slow us down, as do the extra pounds that have fleshed out our breasts, hips, thighs. If the church ladies back in northwest Congo could see us now, they would pinch our cheeks admiringly and say how wonderful it was to have plenty of *mafuta*, fat, and how beautiful we have become. Our *mafuta* does not please us. Although we are still not accustomed to TV and steadfastly ignore the one in our college dorm lounge, pictures of Farrah Fawcett and the other Charlie's Angels are everywhere. We cannot avoid the knowledge that both of us currently weigh more than American beauty standards consider acceptable. But food is solace. Food is also not scarce, which it sometimes could be at our missionary boarding school in Congo. And what variety: my first breakfast in the cafeteria I couldn't choose among all the dry cereals so I ate a bowl of each.

We huff. We puff. Gasping, we slow to a walk, crossing highways and railroad tracks as we near the suburb of Deerfield. Woods give way to large residences with multiple garages and just the occasional free-standing tree. Now we're on sidewalk, and hurrying is easier. We've passed the Presbyterian Church, a Deerfield landmark; hurrah, we're almost there — and just in time too! The bus is already parked across the street by the drugstore. We rush across the street against the light, conscious of having narrowly avoided disaster. What if we'd missed it?

We stow our packs at our feet. Our cold feet.

"Think anyone would notice if I took my shoes off and rubbed my toes?" my sister murmurs. "They're ice cubes."

I say that I think not; I also say that people who spend their lives in such a climate ought to be given a special dispensation to cope as best they can, and if that means subjecting others to their bare feet now and then, so what? My sister responds with her rare soft giggle.

The bus surges slowly down the slush-filled street, past square brown and grey office buildings for realtors and dentists, past the little strip mall with the Safeway, past the new two-story enclosed mall in cruciform shape with a large department store at each of the four ends. Deerfield merges almost imperceptibly with Highland Park and the bus stops for a red light near Sunset Foods, where teenaged baggers are filling the trunks of chauffeured cars with sack after sack of groceries.

"Lots of *Wa-benzs* today," my sister observes.

"*Wa-benzs*" is Congolese shorthand for "People of the Mercedes Benz." In Congo the *Wa-benzs* are mostly other Congolese who are in good odor with President Mobutu and enjoy showing off their affluence.· In the suburbs of Chicago, however, we have noticed that the *Wa-benzs* are always white. Black or white, we do not approve of the *Wa-benzs*. Our parents are missionaries who drive a battered pickup, and we know all about the rich, the eye of a needle, and the Kingdom of Heaven. Until last fall we have always lived without hot water on tap, without round-the-clock electricity, and we've frequently done without eggs, butter, or fresh meat. We have often gone "out back" to a latrine with a sun-silvered wooden door and an ever-expanding family of lizards. We have rarely been robbed because we have so little of portable value. We cannot but wonder why it is that our parents' denominational Bible college has been established in what appears to be the heart of *Wa-benzs* country. As we can't think of anyone to ask, we keep our wonderment to ourselves.

The bus rumbles onto the access ramp of the highway with a rasping shift into higher gear, and I watch the driver's uniformed back with a mixture of admiration and anxiety. How can anyone bear to drive a large machine at such speeds? And yet others drive much faster; even VW Bugs pass us by. In northwest Congo we sometimes drove all day and never encountered another vehicle — but when we did, we dropped our speed from 30 to 10 miles an hour, agreeing via friendly hand signals which side of the road we would occupy. Nothing seems friendly about driving relations here; the rare hand signal is not a good-humored one. A pressure builds behind my breastbone, and I inhale and exhale with self-conscious effort. I am relieved to see a sign for O'Hare Airport.

"Eight miles yet," my sister observes. "But we're making good time, I think."

I nod affirmatively, willing myself to be patient with those eight miles. My feet have thawed out, the thawing process accelerated by the warm vibration of the bus floor. I tip my head back against the seat and glance across the aisle. A young woman sits with her coat folded upon her lap. She is wearing "casual clothes," as the American magazines call them, but there is nothing casual about them except that they are not a dress. She is wearing that complicated series of pastel layers that seems to be necessary in the late nineteen-seventies: a pink-and-blue sweater over a blue shirt over a pink turtleneck with a blue enamel butterfly stick pin. Beneath the pale blue hem of her trousers I catch a glimpse of pink-and-blue argyle sock, and she wears little blue butterfly earrings that exactly match the stick pin. I close my eyes, weary of all these complexities. Sleep tempts me as it always does after any exposure to the cold, but I don't dare fall asleep now. We are too close.

"Now it's just four miles."

I nod again, anticipation replacing lethargy. In a few minutes the bus is exiting the freeway and making a series of sharp turns that pitch us left, right, then left again. Grey concrete looms, one fragment of wall lit by a red flare to warn people away from the site of a minor accident where two taxi drivers are yelling at one another. The bus makes several slush-splashing stops, people disembarking in orderly haste, and our driver clambers out to oversee the removal of suitcases from the luggage compartment. It seems to me that this process takes a great deal of time. Time I worry we can't afford. *Kitisa motema*, I tell myself.

"*Kitisa motema*," my sister says. "Calm down. There's plenty of time."

In Lingala the phrase literally means "to bring down or lower your heart or internal organs." I used to assume I understood this, but now I sometimes wonder where on earth I am supposed to be bringing my heart down from. I don't take the verbal shorthand of colloquialism for granted anymore, not since that first day in the cafeteria line when I stood beside a boy wearing an "Archie Bunker for President" pin and asked if Mr. Bunker was a Democrat or a Republican.

Our stop at last. We sling on our backpacks and rush off the bus. In a moment we are through the sliding doors and hurrying past the cluster of telephone booths on the left. We pause briefly at the glassed-in area where you can peer down at the travelers snailing along through customs on the floor below. Several women dressed in Air France blue are chatting with one of the customs officers. Unmistakably European from their chic French rolls down to their sleek pumps, these women fill me with an emotion I find reassuring for its sheer familiarity over many years: envy. Theirs is an elegance that has dazzled me since early childhood, when our family would sometimes collect incoming missionaries on Sabena and Air Afrique flights. There we would be — sunburned and dowdy, yes, but rich in Things of the Spirit, as our mother would hasten to point out. And there they would be — these exquisite examples of Things of the Flesh, almost arrogantly at ease, laughing as their polished heels clicked on the grimy tiles of the airport floor and their cigarette smoke floated languidly in the still Central African air.

"Come on," my sister says. "We'd better get moving."

The escalator puts us down within a few feet of the International Arrivals rope barrier, and we take up our position just out of the line of traffic. Other people mill about, some noisily, some quietly. One of the quiet ones is a tall slender man in a trench coat who paces back and forth with a palpable impatience.

"Desperately in love," I say in an undertone. "Too reserved to make a public display of it, but red roses back in the car."

"Tiny dark-haired French wife just returned from visiting her family in — where?"

"Um, Marseilles. Where they have a little stone and stucco vacation home down the street from her parents. Two apricot trees and oodles of lavender in the front yard. And of course a back yard for the children."

"The girl takes after her mother, everyone says so, and the boy wants to be a soccer star when he grows up. Like Pélé."

We go on to imagine the romance of their first meeting (probably on a yacht), their honeymoon (a charming cottage on the Brittany coast), and the ongoing perfection of their lives. They belong to each other. They also belong in their world, which is a large one. Equally at home in America and France, they ride that expensive jet stream which is somehow always at their back. They vacation in the Caribbean and in Scandinavia (they have an aunt in Stockholm). Sometimes they go to Glamorous Africa, as we call it: Casablanca, Capetown, Mombasa. Places we've never been.

First there is a slow trickle of passengers from the Air France flight, then a torrent. People embrace, laugh, wave, talk madly in both French and English. One girl is wearing another current fashion favorite, a floral-print Gunne Sax dress encrusted with lace, satin ribbon, and pearl buttons. A young man with wind-burned cheeks carries a pair of skis as easily as many men carry a briefcase. An exhausted-looking older couple are met by what appears to be several generations of their family, and they hug and tumble all over each other like a litter of kittens. At last the Frenchwoman we've been waiting for emerges — yes, petite; yes, beautifully soignée down to her suede boots — and walks into the outstretched arms of Pacing Trench Coat Man. However, they do not kiss, nor do they smile. We cannot hear their quiet exchange of words, but it is clear that their relationship is far from perfect. They are uncomfortable; perhaps that discomfort is just with each other, but perhaps it extends to the larger world. Perhaps he was pacing not with a yearning impatience for her but from anxiety, from a wholly separate and unbearable strain.

"Something sad has happened."

"Maybe there is a divorce. Or maybe somebody is ill. Or dead."

"Yes. Let's not guess."

We do not admit aloud that this flaw in the life of this couple is somehow consoling; we know very well what the Bible has to say about rejoicing in the misfortunes of others. But we also suspect that the Bible advises against this because it is such a perfectly natural way to feel.

The arrival of British Airways Flight 2407 is announced by a female voice on the intercom. We raise our eyebrows meaningfully at each other, remembering the good old days before New Caledonian merged with BOAC. Well, to be honest, we don't remember those days; we've been told about them by a British Baptist missionary neighbor in Congo, a neighbor who does not like change of any sort and who, like us, has never gotten used to President Mobutu renaming Congo "Zaire" and says it won't last. In fact, she probably wishes it was still called the Belgian Congo, although she's not unwise enough to say so.

"BOAC," I say. "Better On A Camel."

"Sabena," she returns. "Such A Bad Experience, Never Again."

"Speaking of which, maybe we'd better head over to Departures."

"Do we have time to pick up some coffee on the way?"

"Definitely."

Because there are no two seats together, we decide we are free to establish ourselves on the floor. We've always preferred floors to chairs anyway. Often in dry season we've preferred floors to beds; the relieving chill of a poured concrete floor is much more conducive to sleep than a heat-retaining mattress, however soft. We select a spot with an unimpeded view of the runway. The thin grey carpet smells of old shoes and rancid pizza with just the faintest overlay of Love's Baby Soft cologne. We dig around in our backpacks for the peanut butter sandwiches we made in the cafeteria at lunchtime and the chocolate doughnuts we filched from the breakfast bar. We have also brought apples, but they are just for show; we both know we won't eat them. We prefer the memory of mangos to the actuality of apples.

At last the moment we've been waiting for: Sabena Flight 1403 to Brussels is boarding. We watch avidly as travelers present passports and boarding passes for inspection, then disappear through the gate. At the final boarding call the Dewaele family is paged, and moments later a man and a woman carrying a small child rush up to the gate apologizing profusely in gutteral Flemish French. They are hustled through with a disapproving sniff, and the gate is closed.

As the plane pulls away from the terminal, I note that the jet engines are located at the back instead of on the wings. It must be a Caravelle then, not a Boeing. The plane joins the short lineup of other planes waiting for clearance to take off. In a few minutes it reaches the head of the line, and in just a few more it is in the air, heading east. Although we do not say so, we each know what the other is thinking: that this very plane could arrive in Brussels tomorrow morning, refuel, collect a fresh crew, and be in the air again before noon. And as Sabena's flights are the most direct available from Europe to Congo, this very plane could be landing upon the heat-softened tarmac of the Kinshasa airport by late tomorrow evening.

"Tomorrow," I say to my sister. "What've you got going on tomorrow?"

"*Lobi*? A test in music history."

Lobi is Lingala for tomorrow. It is also Lingala for yesterday. Only the context will tell you which it is, but one thing is certain: it never means today. Not ever.

"What about you?" my sister asks as she pulls a sweater from her backpack and tucks it over her knees and around her legs. (O'Hare is drafty.)

"A quiz in biology. Plus I have to read this enormous chunk of Isaiah for Hebrew Prophets."

Here we are, stuck with today instead of yesterday — but at least we are not alone. At least we belong to each other, even if we don't belong here.

We take out our textbooks and class notes, ready now to study until the nine o'clock bus.

Note regarding "Doing Good"

For my own sotry-telling purposes, I have placed a bus boycott similar to the famous Johannesburg boycott of 1957 in the year 1960, shortly after the Sharpeville Massacre.